BEYOND

WHAT SEPARATES US

BEYOND

WHAT SEPARATES US

R. A. MORRIS

IGUANA

Copyright © 2020 R. A. Morris
Published by Iguana Books
720 Bathurst Street, Suite 303
Toronto, ON M5S 2R4

Publisher: Meghan Behse
Editor: Paula Chiarcos
Front cover design: Ruth Dwight, designplayground.ca

ISBN 978-1-77180-412-7 (paperback)
ISBN 978-1-77180-413-4 (epub)
ISBN 978-1-77180-414-1 (Kindle)

This is an original print edition of *Beyond What Separates Us*.

Table of Contents

To my good friend Melissa

Prologue

The grey, brightly lit room is full and stifling, with only a couple creaky ceiling fans providing any circulation. Everyone is wearing the same green-and-brown uniforms. But that's where the similarities end. There are young and old, men and women, and all the ethnicities of the world. Everyone has come to hear the latest progress report.

The woman speaking on the stage at the front of the room is tall with an athletic build. She has olive-coloured skin with dark-chestnut hair pulled tightly back. She stands upright with her chin held high, gazing across the assembled members of the movement.

"Greed, ignorance, selfishness, there are many words to describe our downfall. The belief that we were somehow special, unique, above the laws of nature. The warning signs were there. Yet, we continued on blindly, believing the very economic and political systems that created the problem would somehow solve them. Sheer arrogance."

To everyone in the room, the woman speaking is known as the boss. She is very animated. Emphasizing each syllable and pausing for dramatic effect. She throws her hands up in the air for the *sheer arrogance* part. She's been preaching like that for at least fifteen minutes and is likely to go on a lot longer. The more veteran members of the movement have heard this speech before. They respect the boss, even if she is fond of her own voice.

On the stage with the boss are a mix of the other Elects. There's one new face. Sitting in a comfortable chair at the end of the podium is a strong and proud-looking black woman, dressed in an assortment of blues, yellows and reds. She stands out from the other Elects in their dark greens or browns. She is very old, with a slight hunch, which she tries to hide. Her face is wrinkly and her eyes milky. She is listening intently as well, nodding frequently.

The boss stops her speech to direct attention to the old woman. "Please welcome Katherine, from Kenya."

The room erupts in applause while a couple of the Elects help Katherine to the podium. She walks with a cane but stands proudly at the podium, surveying the crowd, smiling. She clears her throat and begins.

One
Budapest

It was hard not to think about that day. The images and sounds replayed in my subconscious, haunting me for months after. The square crowded with thousands of unwashed and malnourished workers. The speeches that led to everyone's anger boiling over.

The carts of food were the gravest mistake. We had no way to control the crowds. Once the shooting started, the screaming stampede drove me from Anna's side. Without Anna, I was a shell of a man. She was my heart and purpose.

Before that day, I truly believed that all people could be categorized into four distinct types. After that day and my slow awakening to do something, I realized perhaps I'd been wrong about the four types. Each type had their own characteristics and responded to adversity differently. As things slowly went to shit in the world, my theory on the four types solidified.

The first type of people were the Fatalists. People would have called them submissive or pushovers. They spent their days striving to please others. Insecurities ate away at them. Most suffered from extreme anxiety. They were paranoid, fearful, passive, shy, and meek. When things got really bad, most of them couldn't handle it. They were the first to go.

Suicides were common among the Fatalists. They just couldn't cut it in a world without stability and comforts. It was easier to give up. Before things got bad, these were the people who had never really been challenged in their lives. Things were given to them, and people pitied them for their apparent modesty and passiveness. They had no place in the new world. They were easy pickings for one of the other types — the Depraved.

The second type of people were the Depraved. These were the selfish, sadistic, cruel and deranged. They have always existed, taking pleasure from the misery of others. History's dictators fit nicely in this category. In functioning societies, laws were put in place to control these people. Some fell through the cracks to become the most violent of criminals. Others found different outlets for their depravity. Bullying, fighting, abusing — they hid their own insecurities to prey on others. When things got bad, these people thrived. They preyed on the Fatalists and had good sport until there weren't very many Fatalists left. They desired no structure, no order, no authority. Their world was one of chaos.

The third type of people were the Reconciled. I used to think they were similar to the Fatalists, but the Fatalists gave up. The Reconciled accepted their fate and lived with it. They weren't necessarily passive or fearful, just indifferent, complacent. They never really stood out from the crowd. They blended in, neither weak nor strong. They were the neutral players. They could get along with all the other types. When things got bad, they grinned and bore it. Neither selfish, nor selfless, they just survived. These were the most abundant people. The ones who stayed in a job they neither hated nor loved but did because it kept them in relative comfort. They were creatures of routine, unwilling or reluctant to fight for change and easy to persuade and control.

The final type had always been the least common. They were the Valiant. The selfless heroes humanity had always revered. Children grew up pretending to be them. We created cartoons, comics and fictions about their deeds. We gave them powers and moral codes. They were uncompromising, fearless, ambitious and brave — the people who sacrifice themselves to save others. The ones who gave no thought to their own well-being. The problem was, they've always been too few. Because of their sacrificial and selfless nature, when things got tough, they tended to not be around too long. The Valiant were the dreamers and idealists. They believed in the common good. These were the people we should have put in power. Unfortunately, they never desired power or glory. The Fatalists wished they could be them. The Reconciled wanted to help and serve them. And the Deranged, they wanted to destroy them, like the comic book villains that our heroes battled day in and day out. I thought there must still be some out there, hiding and waiting for the right time to make the world a better place. At least, I hoped.

If I had to categorize myself, I guess I would be among the Reconciled. I dreamed of being one of the Valiant and had plenty of opportunities over the years to try, but I was too selfish for their ranks. I didn't want to see others harmed; I wanted the world to be a better place, but would I stick my neck out for someone else in mortal danger? For so long, I didn't think so. On the day that still haunts me, I had a chance to prove my devotion, my strength and courage. Yet, I did nothing. I ran away and hid, leaving braver people behind.

Two
Bangalore

"Aashi, hurry, gather your things. We have to go," Jahi said, running into our little shared hut, jamming our goods into canvas bags. Randhir followed close behind, sweating and shaking.

"But, why?" I asked.

"Aashi! Hurry, it's not safe here anymore." Jahi yelled my name with an angry tone, indicating he didn't want any argument. I got up off the floor to help pack our minimal goods.

"Where is it safe?" Randhir said. "We move from building to building, always hiding. We should keep heading south."

"The roads aren't safe," Jahi explained. "We'll move to the old city centre. The buildings are crumbling, but few people go there."

I carried a single canvas bag loaded with some clothes and blankets while Jahi and Randhir each carried two bags that held jugs for water, our limited food and cooking gear. We left the wooden hut, with its dirt floor, and headed down a garbage-strewn alley toward the city centre. There were rows and rows of makeshift huts crammed together along this narrow alley. Young families were also fleeing every which way with children in tow.

"What about our gardens and hidden food stores?" I asked my cousins.

"I'll come back later to grab what I can," Jahi said. Jahi was in his early forties and really my father's cousin. The left side of his face was badly scarred from a fire during a riot before I was born. Randhir was in his early twenties, and the only remaining son of my mother's sister. The three of us were all that was left of our extended family. They were my protectors. I was their little sister, small for my age, but a replacement for the true sisters they had lost.

As we approached another dirt street with burnt-out concrete buildings, I could hear shouting. A mob of people had assembled in the street. There was a lot of yelling and pushing. We hurried off in the other direction. Things had been getting worse lately. Food was scarce, and clean water was even harder to find. I had a constant pain in my stomach. My ribs stuck out from my body. My skin was covered in a permanent layer of dirt and dried sweat. But Jahi and Randhir were strong. Jahi had always kept us safe.

After darting from alley to street, avoiding groups of people, we reached the ruined city centre in a couple of hours. Chunks of concrete littered the streets. Entire buildings had fallen over or had gaping holes in their sides. It was quiet and empty.

"Stay close and together. Be careful where you step. We'll need to find a stable building," Jahi said.

Eventually we found one, with three intact floors, on the corner of a narrow street. All the other buildings around it had fallen apart. There was a small group of trees across the narrow street.

"I'll go in to look around. You two, stay here and keep an eye out," Jahi said, as he slowly walked inside.

Randhir walked off to look around the area, but I stayed put and listened. There was no sound coming from anywhere.

"This is a good spot, lots of hiding places and routes in and out," Randhir said, coming back.

Jahi appeared at the main door of the building and waved us in. "The floors and walls seem stable. There are three stairwells, all intact. I couldn't find anything of use. The top floor will be safest."

We followed him up one set of stairs. The building was empty. No furniture and nothing on the walls. It looked as if no one had ever been here.

"It's been a long day. Let's rest here and we'll see what we can find tomorrow," Jahi said.

We emptied our bags, drinking the last of our water and eating the small amount of food we had left, some mushy fruit and wilted vegetables.

It had been a while since I'd slept on a concrete floor and it felt uncomfortable. I awoke to Randhir shaking me. "Up you get, lazy," he said.

"I'm going to go and get some of our hidden stores and see what I can take from our gardens," Jahi said, as he headed down the stairs. "You two, stay together and search around here for anything of value. Be careful."

It was another grey and hot day. Randhir and I started exploring at the small group of trees across from the building.

"Aashi, look, mangoes," Randhir said excitedly. He reached up to grab a couple. "And they're ripe!" He threw me one. I used my fingernails to peel back a bit of the skin and bit into its sweet, juicy flesh. We each ate a couple and left the others in the tree, excited to show Jahi when he returned.

We continued exploring along the narrow street, avoiding the buildings that had completely fallen over. We found a large, black barrel under some ruins that would work as a rain barrel and some clean sleeping mats in a building that was still partially intact. We were having good luck. We even found some spots hidden between ruins for some new gardens. I was starting to hope that we could make a home here.

It started to rain that afternoon, which was perfect, since we needed to refill our water. It was a cool and light rain, which Randhir and I used to clean our grimy bodies. Even with all the new things we'd found, other than the mango trees, we hadn't found any food. It got dark, and Jahi had still not returned. Randhir and I ate another mango each and returned to the top floor of the faded yellow building. Neither of us could sleep, thinking about Jahi.

"He'll come back, he always does," I said to Randhir. He just smiled at me.

The next morning, Jahi still hadn't returned.

"Should we go look for him?" I asked Randhir.

"He told us to stay here. Besides, I'd have no idea where to start."

"So, what do we do?"

"We keep searching for more supplies."

We each had another mango and headed in a different direction to search for things. The day was wasting away, and we found nothing of value until we came across a small store. Its shelves were bare, but Randhir managed to break into a back room, which still had plenty of canned goods.

Randhir shrugged. "They're all expired, but it's better than nothing." It wouldn't be the first time we were forced to eat questionable food.

There were vegetables, like corn, potatoes and peas, and soups, lentil and tomato. The few bags of rice had all been chewed through by mice or rats and were ruined. But with the canned food, there was enough to last us weeks. Randhir took most of the cans and was noticeably struggling to carry it all back. We buried some of the cans near our new home in case our place was discovered, then headed back up to the top floor. Jahi had still not returned. I was really worried now.

"Do you think he's okay, Randhir?" We were sitting on the floor eating another mango.

"Jahi. He's a survivor." Randhir had short, black hair and had always been strong. While the rest of our family fell ill or was killed, Randhir was always a caretaker.

"I miss them … I miss them all," I said.

Randhir moved to sit beside me, putting his long arm around my shoulder, pulling me to his.

"Me too. Me too. But we have each other still."

"Do you really think things are better down south?"

"There has to be somewhere better than here. Jahi will see that soon."

I lay down on one of the sleeping mats for an afternoon nap, picturing a vast jungle with crystal-clear pools of water. And Jahi, Randhir and I building a real home together. Randhir lay down as well, quickly falling asleep. Jahi still hadn't returned.

He had never been gone this long.

Three
Ontario

Monotonous.

Tedious.

Dull.

Few other words explained life in the city as accurately as these. And that's the way they wanted it to be. Who *they* were wasn't really clear to anyone. To be perfectly honest, no one really talked about *them*. Not because doing so was a punishable offence, but simply because it didn't matter.

It became so hard to separate the lies from truth, reality from fiction, that people occupied their time with other thoughts. In truth, it was the perfect system. No more war. No more poverty. No more political ideologies. A sheltered oasis in an otherwise chaotic world.

Every weekday, I woke up at 7:00 a.m., got showered, ate breakfast and got dressed. By 7:45 a.m., I was out the door to wait for the tram, about a five-minute walk from my housing complex.

My one joy was running. There was a river that served as the eastern border of the city and essentially marked the start of the no-go zone.

My own personal rebellion started when I decided to cross that river one Friday night. The sun had just set and what few lights there were on the paths were starting to come on. Very few people ever ventured as far east as the river. It wasn't far; it just meant descending steep paths into the valley. The trails at the top of the valley were crowded with other people, so I took a dirt trail down the hill to run alongside the river. I found a partially overgrown path and followed it for a while to a crumbling bridge where the river was narrower. There was a fence blocking access. Where the bank sloped down, I could see a tree had fallen over the fence. I must have been crazy, but I wanted to cross that river.

The no-go zones were strictly enforced. I wasn't sure what would happen if I was caught there, because I'd never known anyone who tried to go. My heart was racing, finally a little thrill in my dull life. I could still see the glimmer and silhouettes of buildings on the other side, where the old city extended, but it had been abandoned a few years after the war ended, when the zones we all lived in now were set up.

I used the fallen tree to climb over the tattered fence and walked back to the ruined bridge, which had fallen in many places, clogging the flow of the water. I had to jump from stone to stone to make it across, but I did it. I was in the no-go zone.

I crept quietly and scurried from tree to tree, not knowing what type of enforcement measures were actually in place. I could see lights back on the other side of the river, but on the east side, there was only darkness. I decided to tempt fate and climb up the hill to walk the streets, where no one had been for at least as long as I'd been alive.

It was slow-going, as I was intently listening for any sound or movement that would indicate I'd been caught, but the only sound was the wind in the trees and the occasional bird. Finally, I made it to the top of the hill and a street that ran parallel to the top of the valley. There were many side streets filled with buildings, the likes of which I'd never seen. There was the occasional tall structure here and there, but most were short houses, only one or two floors, all detached from each other, some caved in on themselves, with no uniformity of colour or design. Each had a little road beside it or in front. Some had these things made of metal on them. Then I remembered what they were even though I'd only heard stories. They were cars, used by previous generations to get from place to place.

I wanted to explore more, but I was getting more and more nervous the farther I went. Plus, it was really late and if I didn't get back in time to catch the last tram, I would have to walk all the way across my zone to get home, increasing the chances of running into a Civic Guardian who would ask me what I was doing out at that time.

There was no curfew in the zone, but people were suspicious, and I was a terrible liar. Once in high school, I'd gone to a party and walked home really late. I was stopped by a Civic Guardian who asked if I was lost and why I wasn't in bed. I told him I was heading to my place from a friend's house. The whole time I was shaking and could barely get any words out. He asked me what quadrant and transect I lived in, and I started to cry. I was seventeen. The Civic Guardian was so freaked out that he'd simply said, "Kid, grow up and run home." That was the first time I spoke to a Civic Guardian.

I was twenty-six when I snuck into the no-go zone. I didn't know what I'd do if a Civic Guardian caught me there. I'm sure long sessions of psychoanalysis would be in the future of a grown man who peed his pants. I could only hope that if I got caught again, the more pathetic I seemed, the greater the likelihood they'd just let me go.

That night I crossed the river, I was about to turn and run back home, when I saw a light at the end of one of the side streets. It looked almost like a fire, but controlled. Civic Guardians wouldn't make a fire. Still, I got so scared that I ran back to the river, barrel-rolling down the hill and almost falling into the water. I made it back to the other side, climbed up the hill to the lit paths and ran, as casually as I could, to the nearest tram station. I made it back home, my heart still racing, and stayed up half the night, expecting a knock at the door. When no knock came, I settled in with the biggest grin on my face.

Four
Colombia

No, don't take her ... I'll kill you if you hurt her ... Come back Alejandra, please. Where are you?

A face came out of the dark, smirking. It wasn't a friendly or kind face, but an evil one. Other times, people with no faces were holding me while she was hurt, and I couldn't do anything. Still, sometimes we were together and the sun was shining.

My dreams woke me up most nights.

One night, I had a very bad dream. I lay sweating and crying out for Alejandra, my sister. Senora Vasquez, the woman I lived with, quietly approached me, looking unsure of how to comfort me. We shared a small hut on the edge of a village called Paraiso, near a cool and clean stream. My room was small but private with a straw mat and wool blankets on a wood-plank floor. There was a three-drawer dresser in the corner.

I got up off the mat and grabbed Senora Vasquez for comfort. I was crying, pleading for the memories to stop. She led me to one of the two chairs in the common space between our rooms. The only other items we had were a table, a stove and some shelves with pots, dishes and glasses. Senora Vasquez put the kettle on the stove. "I'll make you some tea to help you sleep. Miguel, would you like to tell me more? Sometimes it makes a person feel better to share a story." Senora Vasquez sat in the other chair looking at me with her kind eyes. She had long, straight, grey hair, which she kept pulled back. She was a short woman with few wrinkles for someone her age.

That night, I told Senora Vasquez a happy story.

Alejandra and I were playing hide-and-seek with some other kids in the hills above the slum. I was at least seven; Alejandra a year older. We had chores to do but were having fun instead. Abuela would be mad when we got home.

I was climbing a rocky and steep portion of a cliff. Alejandra was hiding in a tree nearby. I wanted to get higher than Alejandra for a better view. She yelled for me to be careful. My hand slipped from one of the rocks and I fell from the cliff and cut my leg open. I was crying a lot, sitting on the ground, grasping the cut and rocking back and forth. It hurt so much. There was so much blood. Alejandra ran over, telling me it would be okay. She kneeled beside me, ripped a portion of her shirt off and tied it over my leg. She sat on the ground beside me, holding my bloody hand, pointing out across the city below. Alejandra told me to look at the mountains in the distance, the birds overhead, the fluffy white clouds. I started to calm down. Alejandra squeezed my hand tighter. "I did tell you to be careful," she said. Then she picked me up, but she couldn't carry me far. She got one of the older boys to come help, and he carried me back to our place. Alejandra cleaned my wound and bandaged it, telling our abuela not to worry. She kissed my forehead and hugged me. It was a happy memory.

"Thank you for sharing that story with me, Miguel," Senora Vasquez said.

I finished my tea. "I'm going to go back to bed. Good night, Senora Vasquez."

"Sweet dreams."

The next morning there was a package on the table with my name on it. "What's this?" I asked Senora Vasquez, who was preparing breakfast.

"A gift. You've been in Paraiso for four years now. Open it."

Inside the cloth package were two ink pens and a brown leather book with mountains drawn in gold across the bottom. The pages in the brown leather book were empty.

"Your writing has improved so much. I thought you could use a nice new journal."

I walked over to Senora Vasquez and hugged her. "Thank you."

I took my gift to the garden and started writing.

It has been four years since I left Bogotá. My seventeenth birthday must have been sometime in the last few weeks. In Paraiso we pay attention to the seasons, not the days. My abuela used to throw me a birthday party every year sometime after the start of the new year. Senora Vasquez celebrated the anniversary of me coming to Paraiso instead.

For four years, she has been my teacher and friend. She taught me to read and write. When I first arrived in Paraiso I would help gather food and tend the crops. Then I helped building shelters and repairing things. Now I help with the water.

The village is on the edge of a mountain stream with a small dam for electricity. The dam also moves water to a few narrow channels the villagers have dug to water crops. One of the channels leads to a cement pool where villagers get water for cooking, cleaning and drinking.

Life before Paraiso was hard. We never had enough to eat in the slums. My body always felt empty and weak. And even as small children, we had to hunt through the scrap piles for anything of value. Metal, pieces of wood, anything that could be burned. Or we went to the fields to collect food, which others would get most of.

Alejandra and I lived in our abuela's apartment on the top floor of a concrete block connected to a long row of other blocks. We had no windows, and the roof was made of tarps and sheet metal. We had no electricity or running water, only an outdoor firepit for cooking and rain barrels for water. Our toilet was a hole in the ground attached to a pipe that ran to a gutter at the back of the building.

The building we lived in seemed to cling to the steep cliffs. When the heavy rains hit, we never knew if our home would fall to the valley below. The roads were broken cement and dirt, and we used bicycles and mules to get around. The fields were higher up on the hills, where people grew what they could. My abuela washed, fixed and made clothes. The old men worked the fields or fixed buildings. Once the girls reached a certain age, they would go missing. The others would work the fields. Boys were runners, taking messages and supplies from place to place for the gangs. When boys got old enough, they became soldados in the gangs. Soon they would be carrying guns and doing jobs for the gang boss. Our dad was in the gangs and died when I was very young. Our mom did drugs. We rarely saw her. By the time I was eight, it had been a couple of years since we'd seen her.

Senora Vasquez let me lie in the garden writing all that day. I should have been helping the other villagers, but she told me it was a special day and I could relax. It still took me a while to see the words in my mind and put them on paper. It was late in the afternoon when Senora Vasquez returned to the hut.

"Miguel, come inside and help me with dinner." I closed the journal and went to help. "I'm going to make you ajiaco. Can you get some water to cook the rice and make the broth? I'll start cutting up the vegetables." I grabbed one of our buckets and headed to the pool. Ajiaco was one of my favourites. In Bogotá, we could only have it with corn and potatoes. In Paraiso, the soup had corn, potatoes, rice, avocado, lemon and fresh herbs. I returned with the water. "Thank you, Miguel. Now, you sit. I'll do the rest. This is your special day. Tell me a story."

"I was thinking about the day Alejandra was taken."

Senora Vasquez moved from the stove to the table to chop the rest of the vegetables. I sat holding my journal close, staring at the floor.

"I was nine … I think, when the soldados came for her. We were helping our abuela make dinner. Probably ajiaco…"

Senora Vasquez took the chopped vegetables and dropped them into a pot on the stove. "Go on, Miguel. I'm listening."

"Four large and mean-looking soldados came up to the roof where we ate. Some of the old women from the building were with us. The soldados took the food off our plates and started eating it."

Senora Vasquez was back at the table, preparing some nice-smelling herbs. She took a piece to taste.

"My abuela shouted at them, 'What do you want?' One of them pointed at Alejandra. Two others grabbed her and dragged her toward the stairs."

Senora Vasquez stopped what she was doing and focused on me.

"Alejandra was screaming and calling for my abuela. I ran for her, but one of the soldados hit me across the face and I fell to the ground. My abuela came to me. They were all gone. The other old women were crying. My abuela picked me up and sat in a chair, rocking me in her lap and singing a song I can't remember…" I closed my eyes, trying to hold back tears. The soothing smell of the soup was filling the room.

"What happened after that, Miguel? Take your time." Senora Vasquez was stirring the ajiaco.

"The next day, I asked my abuela where they took Alejandra. She just said, 'Beautiful girls all end up in the same place' and kept sewing."

Senora Vasquez brought me a glass of water, putting it on the table in front of me and placing her other hand on my shoulder. Then she went back to the stove.

"Gus, our neighbour, I asked him where beautiful girls go. He told me I don't want to know and that I should forget Alejandra. I just stared at him, kicking the dirt. He asked me to help him fix the wheel on a cart. I held the wheel while he changed some screws. Gus told me girls like Alejandra became property of the gangs. I told him I didn't understand. Gus said I was too young and to keep my head down and do my chores, and to listen to my abuela…" Senora Vasquez was still stirring the soup and the pot of rice.

"I screamed at Gus, saying I hated my abuela because she let them take Alejandra. He hit me on the top of my head, telling me to never say that again. He told me that he was friends with my abuelo…. My abuela never talked about her husband. Gus told me he died years before I was born. He fought against the gangs and was killed. Gus looked sad and told me to go help my abuela."

Senora Vasquez brought me a bowl of the soup and a plate of rice. "Gus was right. All you could do was help your abuela. I'm sure she was just as heartbroken as you when Alejandra was taken." Senora Vasquez sat at the table with her own meal. "Would you like to share any more?" I shook my head, taking my first spoonful of soup. "Do you like it?" Senora Vasquez asked.

I nodded. "It's very good … thank you."

Later that night, I opened my journal and began writing again.

A week after Alejandra was taken, I was made a runner. Each day I would bring clean water from the spring higher up in the hills to the compound of the gang boss in our slum. I couldn't carry full buckets at first and it was far up and down steep hills between the compound and the spring. Each time I came back with half-filled buckets, the soldados at the gates would hit me and tell me to bring back full ones next time.

There was a huge wall all around the compound, with guard towers that had large guns poking out of them. Inside the walls, there were a few houses. I could only peek inside from the gates and wonder what the buildings were like inside. They were made of the same stuff without holes or tarps. They didn't look like they could fall over with a strong rain or wind. There were even bigger guns on the roofs of some of the buildings. There were big black vehicles, too. Sometimes the soldados would drive them around the slum to scare everyone. I hated the people in that place.

I wasn't alone on my water runs. There were a few other boys older than me that did it as well. Most of the time, we did our work in silence, but we were a team. Javier was the oldest and biggest. He would sometimes help me carry my buckets. After my first month, I managed to return most of my buckets almost full. The soldados hit me less at that point. Each day, we would go up and down with two buckets each. We had to make the run at least five times a day. No one was allowed to take water from the spring except runners from the compound. It was guarded day and night by soldados.

One day, I asked Javier why they made us do this. Why couldn't they get water a different way?

Javier just said at least we were well fed.

About a year after Alejandra had been taken away, I was ten and very strong for my age. Javier was about to turn thirteen and was very sad. I didn't understand why, but the other runners seemed to.

We were on our way down the hill one day, when gunfire broke out near the compound. Most nights we would hear gunfire, but it seemed to always be in a distant slum and never during the day. Javier yelled at us to get off the path and follow him. We crept down until we reached a ledge, where we could see the compound. The large guns in the guard towers were firing toward one of the other slums. A couple of vehicles were on fire in the road in front of the gate. The vehicle closest was all melted metal. The gates were black and bent, and there were bodies all around. Other vehicles were moving toward the compound, firing at the towers. Dozens of men were going in and out of buildings at the side of the road.

The soldados guarding the spring were running down the path to our right and didn't see me and the other boys. More were running down the main road from our own slum, charging at the other men. Black smoke floated into the sky. All I could smell was burned rubber. I heard guns, screams and bullets hitting metal and cement. The largest vehicle from the compound forced its way out of the gate, running over the bodies in the way. Other smaller vehicles followed after with dozens more soldados. The attackers were shot down as they ran away.

When the shooting sounded far away, we left the bushes and went down the path with empty buckets. Some of the soldados left at the gate spotted us and told us to help them clean up the mess and bodies. Others went from building to building in the direction the attackers came from.

We cleared the area around the gatehouse and made two piles of bodies on the opposite side of the road, one with the attackers and one with soldados from our slum. Our soldados wore black shirts with two rifles crossed in red. The attackers wore red shirts with a pile of white skulls.

Later, the vehicles from the compound returned with soldados from our slum dragging prisoners in chains. The prisoners were lined up in the middle of the road. By now, old men and women taking a break from their chores stopped to see what had happened. Young women with very few clothes and lots of jewellery were standing around some of the nicer buildings just outside the compound. Children younger than us were also there. There were about forty prisoners. Most of them looked not much older than Javier.

The gang boss came out to address the crowd. I only caught sight of him once in the last year. He was a tall man. Shaved and muscular and he wore blue army clothes. The rest of his soldados wore their black shirts with green army pants. He was mad that the attackers tried to kill him. He called them weak vermin and cowards. All of the soldados from our slum booed. Then the gang boss said he couldn't be killed so easily. And their territory was ours now and their people would be our slaves.

Two of his soldados dragged out a corpse with rich clothes. It was headless. Another soldado handed the gang boss a canvas bag.

The boss said the corpse would feed the pigs, but the head would be on his wall. Then he pulled the head out of the bag so everyone could see it. The soldados cheered and fired their guns into the air, but the crowd was quiet.

The boss shoved the head back into the bag and tossed it to one of his soldados. He asked what we should do with these surviving vermin. He said they can't be trusted.

All the soldados started cheering and shouting, Death, death, death...

The gang boss nodded at the soldados guarding the prisoners. The prisoners were forced to their feet and dragged in front of a brick wall in plain view of everyone. The gang boss yelled, Fire! All the soldados fired at the same time. It was so loud. Then silence. The men lay in pools of blood, now with holes and red stains. The crowd lost interest and began to move off.

A soldado pointed at us and told us runners to get back to work.

As the gang boss was headed back into the compound, a woman walked out and grabbed his arm. She looked like an older version of Alejandra. I had a strange feeling it was my mother.

Five
Budapest

That day in the square where I lost everything still haunts me. It was early fall and we were heading from our farm loaded with goods to trade supplies for the coming winter. From what we had heard, things were not good in the city. There were riots and curfews. The movement my parents, Anna and I belonged to had been holding regular rallies in the city centre, demanding more equitable treatment of workers.

As we entered the city, the streets were deserted, and it was eerily quiet. We eventually found an ailing old man lying in the gutter on a side street.

"Where is everyone?" my mother asked in Hungarian.

"At the square near parliament," said the frail old man, slowly sitting up with his palms out for something to eat.

My mother handed him a loaf of bread from our wagon, and we headed toward parliament. I was nervous. Conditions in the city had been deteriorating for years, and disappearances and executions were common. Budapest's once-beautiful centre had been severely neglected. The formerly grand buildings were crumbling and overcrowded. Residents had resorted to scavenging what wood they could find from abandoned buildings to burn in winter when the power was out, which happened frequently. All the smoke from fires left the streets and buildings with an ashen hue. The streets around Kossuth Lajos square and the old Hungarian Parliament Building were filled with tens of thousands of people. While Hungary didn't exist as a country anymore, the stately and beautiful government buildings along the Danube still housed the only form of governance and bureaucratic structure that provided some semblance of order. Now that order was militarized. No one knew who was really in charge. We all just assumed it was one large bureaucracy driving the war effort across Europe.

Anna and my parents wanted to get as close as we could to the parliament building. This involved wading through a crowd consisting of downcast factory workers in dirty greys and browns, most sickly. The smell was awful. Most hadn't had a proper bath in weeks. We managed to get close to the square. Near a tent on the northeast corner, my parents spotted a United Earth flag, an adaptation of the old United Nations flag — the same sky-blue backdrop, but instead of a cartographical map of the world, it was a picture of the Earth as seen from space with two hands holding the planet up. We managed to shove our way toward the tent. The inhabitants of the city were too frail to protest. We covered the wagon to prevent anyone from seeing the valuable goods within, which could have led to a riot.

Lukas, the coordinator for the Budapest section of the United Earth movement, was speaking in German to about a dozen other members. He was tall and muscular with short brown hair and a large scar across his right cheek. I could understand German pretty well, having spent a lot of time in Vienna. Apparently, the movement had gotten their hands on a sound system and were planning to set up a stage right at the security barricades near the parliament building to broadcast a series of demands to aid the people. Anna and my parents were nodding in approval. I glanced back to the grand and magnificent parliament building, with its intricate details, many spires and tall central dome. Yet, now it was a fortress. They'd tried to hide it, but along the building were soldiers and snipers in towers. And there were anti-aircraft guns on each rooftop of the buildings around the square, and tanks preventing access to the promenade along the Danube. I couldn't remember a time since the war started that any enemy plane had made it this far west. I started to get nervous about some of the rumours we'd heard. Maybe the enemy was getting close to the Danube. Why else would there be anti-aircraft guns? Equally disturbing was the number of soldiers, snipers and tanks around this crowded square full of unarmed, tired, weak and sick people. The pessimist and realist in me wanted to leave.

"We should go back to the farm before this gets out of hand," I said quietly to my parents and Anna.

"No. It's only a few simple demands," my mother said in her usual righteous tone. "We're all unarmed. The soldiers need the workers."

"Anna, please." I knew there would be no convincing my parents, but I could maybe get my wife to safety.

"Elliott, it'll be okay. I promise there won't be any violence." Anna held my hands, squeezing my palms before turning back to the other members of the movement still discussing who would speak and what their demands would be.

"Anna, please," I pleaded, grabbing her shoulder to pull her toward me.

She spun around, glaring at me with her piercing, blue eyes. "Elliott, no," she said emphatically before turning back around, tying her long, blonde hair back.

Anna and I had met in 2063, in a small village between Budapest and Vienna. She had rallied to my parents' cause after fleeing the former Netherlands. She was way out of my league, but somehow had fallen for my boyish charm and sarcastic manner.

The United Earth movement members were finalizing the details of what they were going to say. An energetic young woman came running over to Lukas, telling him everything was ready to go. The remaining movement members each grabbed a United Earth flag and followed Lukas to the stage. I was reluctantly dragged along by Anna.

Standing on the stage, I looked out over the jumble of neutral colours and featureless faces. Lukas alternated between German and Hungarian as he spoke passionately about the past, the dream that was a United Europe, the peace and prosperity of before. The occasional murmur flowed from the crowd. *These people don't care about the past; they're only preoccupied with the present. There's no going back. Getting their hopes up won't attract more people to the United Earth cause,* I thought, but I kept this to myself. Beside me, Anna nodded and clapped. After about twenty minutes, Lukas finished to thunderous applause from those onstage and a lacklustre response from the crowd. Now it was my mother's turn. I'd heard her give speeches in the past and she was an inspiring woman. This crowd, however, was lifeless. Their eyes were vacant, their faces sallow.

My mother spoke in a similar manner to Lukas, but then took a different path in English. "Why should the soldiers get everything when we were told nothing about what was happening in the east? How can we be expected to toil in the factories and fields on scraps to supply a war we knew nothing about? This monstrosity behind us," — she pointed at the fortressed old parliament — "is sustained by your sweat and blood for a faceless and cruel machine that reports to no one."

The segments of the crowd that could understand English began raising their fists. Others were translating for those around them. Now the crowd was engaged and the soldiers were on alert. I moved closer to my mother. "Mom, please tone it down." She waved me off and my father pulled me back, telling me to be quiet.

After another ten minutes about the injustices of the war effort, a series of covered wagons entered the square. People made way for them to make it to the centre. "These wagons carry gifts," my mother said. "Please let them pass and wait for your share. The United Earth movement will take care of all of you. All we ask is that you join us."

"Anna, what's in the wagons?" I whispered.

"Just wait." Anna clasped her hands in anticipation.

Technically, I was part of this movement, but apparently, I wasn't dedicated enough to be notified of the plans. The people who had pulled the wagons in began yanking off the covers, and each was full of food. The crowd began to push forward.

"Please be patient, there's enough for everyone," my mother implored the crowd.

There might have been two hundred thousand people in and around the square and only fifteen small wagons.

I yelled at my father, who was standing beside me, "Dad, there is nowhere near enough food for everyone here. Mom is going to cause a riot. Get her down from there." I moved closer to Anna, who was near my mother on the stage. People began to run forward, pushing and shoving. The soldiers became more alert. The people trying to dispense the food were overwhelmed.

It all happened so fast.

And then shots were fired; people began running away. My mother was trying to calm everyone down, but it was impossible to hear her voice. A louder voice rose over the tumult, speaking in Hungarian and then German: "This food is being dispensed illegally in violation of proper distribution. Anyone caught with this food will be punished."

"They're trying to take away your dignity by denying you access to basic food." My mother was trying to get the crowd angrier, but no one could hear her except those of us on the stage.

More shots rang out. A group of soldiers was moving toward us.

I grabbed Anna. "We need to go, now!"

People were falling, being trampled as more soldiers came into the square. Snipers were picking off those leaping onto the carts.

"Dad, get Mom, now!" He was about to reach her, but a shot rang out and my mother collapsed. My father screamed and ran to her crumpled body. The rest of the United Earth members darted this way and that. I fell off the stage, losing hold of Anna, and Lukas grabbed me and pulled me through the crowd. I screamed for Anna and my family, but he kept dragging me away. I got free and looked back to the stage to see soldiers firing and others grabbing people and throwing them to the ground, binding their hands. I couldn't see my parents. When I turned around again, I panicked and ran to follow Lukas.

We ran for many blocks. There were still hundreds of people running every which way. I followed, crying and ashamed.

Lukas led me and three others to a small basement flat, where there were three other people already. Lukas spoke to them and then left in a hurry.

Most people seemed to be injured, and I recognized them all from the stage at the protest. I scanned the room for Anna, my father or mother. None of them were there.

"Did you see Anna or my parents leave the square?" I asked each of them in English and German. They all shook their heads and stared at the floor.

I collapsed onto the floor, sobbing and shaking. I'd left them. I'd run away.

Sometime later, someone put a glass of water and a small plate with bread and butter at my feet. I stared at it. I didn't deserve food or water, even though my body cried out for it. Lukas eventually returned with four others, none of whom were Anna or my parents.

Everyone was eager to talk to Lukas, so I waited. Eventually he came over to me.

"Elliott, how are you?" he asked in German.

"Where are Anna and my parents?"

"I don't know," Lukas said, shaking his head and staring at his hands.

The young, energetic woman from the stage, who was listening nearby, came over hesitantly. "I saw the man that was with your mother being beaten and bound by one of the soldiers."

"And Anna or my mother?"

"Your mother ... um ... I'm so sorry. She's dead."

"No, no ... you don't know that." I turned away from them and stared at the wall.

Lukas and the young woman whispered to each other, and then Lukas turned back to me. "Elliott, your mother didn't suffer. The shot killed her instantly."

I turned around, facing Lukas, shocked that he had the audacity to say this to me.

"I know that is small comfort," he continued. "If there is anything—"

"This is your fault," I said in English. "Get away from me." I fell back against the wall, turning away from everyone in the room. Lukas grabbed me and I spun around, pushing him away. "You should be dead on that stage!" I yelled. "Get the fuck away from me!"

Lukas stared at me blankly, still reaching for me to offer comfort. The young woman whispered into his ear and he pulled away. She looked at me. "He doesn't understand English."

Speaking in German, Lukas said, "We were just trying to help those people. We never thought it would turn violent."

I darted toward him and punched him square in the jaw with all my might, and he fell to the floor. Others moved to restrain me.

"Stop!" Lukas shouted, slowly getting to his feet, holding his jaw. "I'm sorry for your loss. We'll do whatever it takes to find Anna and your father."

I seethed at Lukas as he walked away.

The small, energetic woman pulled me aside. "I'm Tonya," she said. "Seven of the members that were on the stage are unaccounted for, including your wife and father."

"Would Anna know where to go in Budapest that's friendly to United Earth?" I asked.

"I'm not sure."

"There are friends of my parents that we stay with sometimes. They live on the other side of the city. I'm going to check there."

"I'll come with you. But the whole city is on lockdown. Everyone has been forced back to work and soldiers are patrolling the streets," Tonya told me.

I didn't care and left the small flat. Tonya followed me. We had to dart through alleys to get to my parents' friends. It was slow meandering through the deserted streets, but we didn't encounter anyone.

"Most of the soldiers must be at the factories keeping workers there," Tonya said.

We reached the flat, but my parents' friends weren't home. I slid a note under the door for Anna, telling her where I was.

"It's too dangerous to wait here. We can come back tomorrow if you want," Tonya said. Reluctantly, I followed her back to the small basement flat. There was no Anna and no word from my parents' friends over the next few days. By the fourth day after the protest, I was a mess. I hadn't slept, had barely eaten and hadn't showered or shaved. There were now twelve people staying in the one-room flat, and there was no running water anywhere in the city. We got used to the smell pretty quickly.

Tonya went with me every day across the city to the other flat, which was always empty and locked. On the fourth day, I decided to break in. My note was still on the ground under the door. The fridge was empty. I fell to my knees, crying and shaking.

"Stay here. This place has two bedrooms. I'm going to bring some of the others here," Tonya said, leaving me on the floor.

A couple of hours later, she returned with six others, not including Lukas. "Soldiers are going street to street looking for us. They have pictures of everyone who was on the stage." Even Tonya seemed to be frazzled, her usual sunny demeanour dimmed. "We can't stay in the city for much longer," she said to everyone in the room. Most of them had their heads down.

"We'll be safe at our farm," I said. "The soldiers won't check there as long as we give them the monthly quota. I think Anna and my father will go there if they can."

Tonya translated to the others in German and Hungarian. Since it was almost winter, the soldiers wouldn't be coming at all for the next few months. The problem would be how to survive the winter, especially if I brought back so many new people.

Six
Bangalore

A few hours later, as the sun was setting, Jahi called from the bottom of the stairs, waking Randhir and me from our afternoon nap. We both ran down to hug him. He looked more tired than usual and had a gash across his forehead.

"Are you okay? What happened?" I asked.

"Some men mugged me. I managed to get away, but they took the bags of goods I'd gathered. I had to go back and get more. I left some other bags in a good hiding spot. I'll get them in the morning."

"I'm glad you're safe," I said.

"I told you I'd be back. What did you two manage to find?"

"We got a rain barrel, some sleeping mats and a few weeks' worth of canned goods buried around the area. There are also a couple mango trees across the street," Randhir said.

"Good work. Help me carry these bags upstairs. I harvested a couple of our gardens and brought our seed packs. Did you find places for new gardens?"

"Yes," I said.

We had a rare feast that night of fresh fruit and vegetables from the goods Randhir and I found and the bags Jahi brought. Jahi fell asleep quickly on one of our new mats shortly after eating. Randhir and I cleaned up, and then he fell into a deep sleep as well, now that we were all together again. I lay awake thinking about my life.

I was six when I saw my first dead body. It was bloated and featureless, floating in a murky and stagnant river. There may have been other bodies all around it. I'd seen so many that distinguishing between any one event was impossible. I guess I was one of the lucky ones. Disease-free and alive.

That's what counted for luck in South Asia. I was the youngest of six. Before I was born, my family fled from North India during the war. I didn't know who we were fighting, but it seemed like everyone was the enemy. Millions fled the coasts, which were being inundated with rising seas. Everyone was fighting for a piece of land. Food and water were scarce, since pollution made entire areas unlivable. Then the bombs started falling. I was twelve when my mother died. She'd been sick most of my life.

I taught myself to read and write. I would spend my days reading books at the abandoned university. Books weren't exactly valuable anymore. I loved learning about the way the world used to be. The beauty of the forests and clean flowing rivers. The blueness of the sky. Art, music, literature, it all sounded perfect. I couldn't understand how we could destroy all of that. I wished I'd been born to a different time.

My family were once prominent merchants from Jaipur, and I was raised speaking English and Hindi, but my father was killed shortly after I was born. He'd been trying to organize some sort of government or system for those who had survived the diseases and war. He was trying to give out food to starving children, when a mob decided to take what he had for themselves. One of my older brothers told me this. My mother could never speak about my father.

Jahi lost his wife and children during the war. Randhir also lost his mother, father and siblings over the years. And my oldest brother died two years after my mother. After that, it was just the three of us. And for four years, we survived in an increasingly unfriendly place. We learned to fight for what was ours.

Most of the people were native to this part of India. Some helped each other and traded what they had. Some took pity on the northern refugees, but others wanted us gone. Growing food was difficult. All plant life struggled. Only the hardiest of vegetables survived, and, for the most part, they were small. The only animal life anywhere near Bangalore were pigeons and rats. But a rat made a good meal. And we carried on. For what reason, I couldn't say, but my remaining family kept on going.

Jahi would always say the disease was horrific. He said the disease spread like wildfire in the last couple years of the war. It was this that actually ended the war. There weren't enough people left to fight. If anyone caught it, they were dead within a couple of weeks. It essentially ate your insides. Most died in excruciating pain. Some of the lucky ones were killed by merciful family members. Those that survived the disease had to contend with other types of sickness brought about by contaminated food and water, the toxic air or radiation. People seemed to die faster than they could be replaced. Most people saw no point in having children. One survivor from Jaipur decided to venture back north. We'd been told by the last survivors to head south, that up there was now a toxic wasteland.

The day after Jahi returned from gathering our supplies, the weather turned foul. Jahi decided not to go and get the other bags he'd hidden. It was stormy with rain that blew down from the north and carried toxic fumes. We got this every now and then. Sometimes it didn't stop for days. We covered up our rain barrel with a tarp and stayed on the third floor of our new home and waited for the poison rain to end.

Randhir slept while Jahi told me stories. I loved his stories, even though most of them were sad. Sometimes he became particularly prophetic.

"Better days will come, Aashi. Nature is resilient and restorative. All the beauty and life that once thrived will come again. I'm sure of it."

"Is that why you carry on each day?"

He looked at me confused. "What do you mean?"

"Why do you continue to live despite all that has happened, all you have seen and lost?" I asked.

"I could ask you the same thing," he responded, grabbing my hand. "All you've ever known is this world. The world of before is but a figment of your imagination gathered through stories and the pictures from the books you love so much. Which one of us has lost more? I consider myself blessed to have been alive to know what the world is capable of being. I carry on because I believe that there's a reason for everything. You can call it the will of the gods, or fate. Things may seem bleak, but a better future is possible. I may not live to see it, but I believe it to be true and so should you."

I wanted his optimism and faith. I just couldn't understand why, if there were gods, they would allow us to survive in spite of all our sins. Why would the gods create a species that destroyed the very home they created for them? Yes, we'd created wonders and were capable of great things, but our imperfections outweighed the good.

Jahi turned to lie down and nap. The rain had let up a little, so I decided to explore. I grabbed our tools and broke the lock on a door that we hadn't opened yet. It led to another set of stairs, which I followed up to a flat roof. If we could find the materials, it would be possible to build a garden up here, safe from other people.

I looked out across the ruined core of the city. Most of the taller buildings had fallen over already or looked like they would any day now. Dead trees outnumbered the live ones. The dominant colour was grey. The river and lakes around the city were lifeless with dark, soupy waters that reeked of decay — a persistent smell that penetrated every corner of the city.

I started back down but stopped when I heard voices and footsteps coming up the stairs. I hurried to wake my cousins. Jahi grabbed a blunt metal pipe, and Randhir picked up a hammer we kept with our tools. They told me to stand behind them against the wall. I grabbed a piece of concrete that had broken off a nearby pillar.

Five men soon appeared at the top of the stairs. Two of them were armed with knives. The others had objects similar to what Jahi and Randhir held. Each of them was filthy, with torn clothing, missing teeth, visible scars and frail-looking bodies. Jahi told them to take the food and supplies and go. They continued to stare at us. Jahi tried in English.

They moved to circle the three of us, two of them grabbing our bags. One of the men with the knives kept staring and pointing at our supplies. He was the dirtiest and largest of the five and had a mean face. Jahi moved in front and kept motioning for them to leave. The largest man lunged with the knife. Jahi dodged and hit him squarely across the head with the pipe, and the man collapsed. Jahi grabbed the knife and sprang back up as the others moved in to attack.

I curled into a ball and hid my face. I could hear metal hitting metal, shuffling feet and groans. Then a horrific scream that I thought was Randhir. I got up, with the concrete chunk in my hand, but it wasn't Randhir. Jahi had just stabbed the large, mean-faced man through the chest, and he fell to the ground. Another man hit Jahi in the back of the head, knocking him down, and Randhir had one on top of him. I rushed forward, and with all my might, hit the man in the back of the head with the chunk of concrete. He collapsed with a moan. Randhir was bleeding from his shoulder and a gash on his forehead. He rose slowly and picked up a knife with his good hand, but I saw movement just behind him. I screamed, but too late. Randhir was stabbed through the back with a wooden stake. I grabbed a wrench from our tools, darted forward and swung the wrench with all my strength. The man who had stabbed Randhir keeled over but not before hitting me so hard in the gut that I collapsed, unable to breathe. Someone grabbed my hair from behind and dragged me up with a knife at my throat. Across from me, Jahi was badly wounded and was stumbling, trying to fight off two of them, and Randhir was trying to get up, grabbing at their legs. One of them kicked him in the face.

I started crying. They threw me against the wall. I hit my head hard and fell to the ground feeling dazed. With my blurred vision, I could see one of them grab Jahi, who was barely conscious now. I saw Jahi's face quickly change — he grimaced and let out a gasp. One of them had stabbed him in the back of the neck. Life drained from his eyes. I struggled to get up, but my head was spinning and someone kicked me in the side.

Randhir was trying to grab my hand, and as I struggled to reach for his, I was kicked again. Randhir tried to mumble something to me, but they kicked his face as they stabbed him in the back repeatedly. All fight and strength withered out of me and I sobbed, wanting to die too.

The men laughed. They grabbed Randhir's and Jahi's bodies and dragged them across the room. The man nearest me punched me in the face and I slowly lost consciousness. The last thing I saw was two bodies being thrown down the stairwell.

Seven
Ontario

My alarm buzzed, indicating the start of a new workweek. I reluctantly got out of bed and went about my morning routine.

Shower. Check.

Oatmeal with some berries. Check.

Dressed in the standard dark-blue pants, light-blue collared shirt, black shoes. Check.

Out the door at 7:45 a.m. for the short walk to the tram. My housing complex looked more or less the same as all the others around. Every building between ten to fifteen stories in different shades of blues and purples. Some had round balconies, others square. Between the blocks were parks, gardens, picnic areas and stores for basic goods. At the top of the buildings were solar panels and small wind turbines. The main thoroughfares had the shiny silver trams. They moved about the zone, conveying people to the Hub, the centre of all activity in Zone 4. This was where I lived, in the city now called Ontario — based on what was once known as Toronto.

I waited for the next tram at the stop closest to my apartment. My annoying neighbour, Tyra, was there with another woman from our building, whose name I had forgotten.

"Morning, Kelowna!" Tyra said, waving at me with her usual cheerful and high-pitched voice. She was short and slender with dark skin. She was always so bubbly, gabbing away about some irrelevant event at the Hub. I smiled at them both, nodding my head in their direction.

I was born in 2050, five years after the war ended. My parents had named me after a city in Western Canada that was no longer there.

"What did you do this weekend, Christie?" Tyra asked her red-headed friend.

Christie. Right, that's her name.

"Well, Saturday there was a bocce tournament at the Hub in the afternoon. Jordan was there again. We went out for drinks with a couple of people after. And guess what?"

"What?" Tyra asked, giddy with excitement.

"Jordan invited me back to his place. It was amazing. We spent all Sunday together, too. We're talking about getting genetic testing to see if we're a match."

"Yay! I'm so happy for you," Tyra said, bouncing on her little feet.

The Civic Administrators controlled everything. Every resident was assigned to a specific transect within a specific zone. Goods were rationed. People needed to undergo testing and get licensed to have children. We were taught to be grateful for what we had. That Ontario and its sister city, Michigan, where Chicago used to be, were bastions of prosperity and peace. According to the Civic Administrators, the rest of the world was uninhabitable or in complete chaos.

"So, when do you think you'll be able to get the testing done?" Tyra asked Christie.

"We're going to put the request in today and hopefully get the permit to go to Zone 2 within the next month."

As Christie was hoping for her invasive medical procedure, the tram pulled up to the stop. All the seats were already taken, but there was plenty of standing room. Everyone was wearing similar varieties of blue or purple pants and shirts. Some had patterns or black accents on their shirts, but most were plain. If it weren't for the trees and gardens, the only colours in the zone would have been blue and purple.

I headed to a car away from Tyra and Christie and gazed out at the forest ravine on the periphery, which served as the separator between Zone 3 and 4. The taller red or orange buildings of Zone 3 were visible over the trees.

Beside me, two grey-haired men were discussing the remembrance ceremonies scheduled for next week.

"It's been just over thirty years since the end of the war," the pudgier and balder of the two men said.

"Those days were hard. So many people lost. So much devastation. We thought we were prosperous and safe before the war, but things are way better now. We've built a truly sustainable future," the other man said.

They nodded at each other and continued their reminiscing. I put my earbuds in and turned on some sappy music. I was an only child and my parents rarely spoke about the war. All I knew was they had both fought in it. They did talk about the climate chaos, though. We were also taught about it in school. The climate chaos was a slow and complicated process, and it was still ongoing in many parts of the world. Essentially, sea levels rose faster than scientists had been predicting; much, much faster. Vast coastal regions that were once home to millions became covered by metres of water. Entire cities, states, countries vanished. Storms grew in intensity. Parts of the world had years of drought or became constant flood zones. Millions of people became climate refugees. Resources became scarce and conflicts spread globally. Diseases devastated Asia, making their way to other parts of the world. The Americas fared a little better, but the war eventually spread across the Pacific, and the American Southwest was quarantined. By 2045, most of the fighting in the Americas had stopped. Around that time, the Civic Administrators began building what would become the cities of Ontario and Michigan. Life under the Civic Administrators was all I knew.

The tram made its way toward the Hub. All tram lines intersected here. It was a sight to behold. Huge parks were surrounded by open square pavilions with shops, restaurants, bars and entertainment venues. The biggest buildings in the zone circled the Hub. The area was so large that special elevated monorails looped around it to get people from the tram stations at the north or south ends. There were dozens of sports fields, small ponds, running tracks, expansive gardens, heavily wooded areas and massive patios.

My office building was near the southern tram station and looked like a series of blue geometric cubes stacked at perpendicular angles. It was one of the largest in our zone, about thirty floors. The elevators were on the outside of the building, facing the Hub in tubes of lightly frosted glass, which acted as support pillars for the building's odd architecture.

I worked on the fifteenth floor and was always in my cubicle by 8:30 a.m. It was kind of funny to sit all day in a cube within a cube stacked on other cubes, at a computer, going over spreadsheets and numbers. Every floor was a series of cubicles arranged around the centre, which was split into four large glass enclosures, which served as the offices of each team lead. Each floor was divided into four teams. The central offices were raised above the cubicles by a couple of metres to remind us that our team leader was always watching us.

Gerald sat in the cubicle beside me and arrived shortly after I did.

"Morning, Kelowna, did you have a good weekend?"

"Yes, and you?" I asked.

"Busy, busy, so much going on. Ready for another week of crunching those numbers?"

"You know it."

Gerald and I had worked together for a few years, and I guess he was my closest friend. We used to go running regularly when he lived a block from me. But last year, Gerald got upgraded to a transect closer to the Hub because he was matched. Gerald met his partner through sporting events, and they underwent genetic testing to see if they were compatible. And voila. Within a few weeks, they lived in a couples housing complex, which gave them a larger apartment. And they were trying to have a child. I never told Gerald, but shortly after he got matched, I asked for permission to get genetic testing. While Gerald found who he wanted to be with first and it ended up working out, another common way to get matched was to get tested first, then they'd match you with someone else from your zone. My results were negative, so I never really tried to date anyone. It's not that I liked being alone, but I didn't really know how to relate to people.

That Monday went by like all the others. Before heading home, I decided to stop in at one of the shops in the Hub.

For shopping and entertainment, we were allowed a certain number of credits a month. I wouldn't exactly call it shopping, either. There were a surprising number of clothing stores, considering they all sold the same thing. There were also many grocery, hardware and personal products stores, each arrayed differently to present the perception of choice, when in reality they also all sold the same thing. Each store would play a certain type of music or be arranged and designed in a unique way. One of the busiest personal products stores involved a scavenger hunt. Patrons entered into a computer the types of products they were looking for and it gave them clues that led to locations with more clues, forcing them to potentially wander around the store for hours, looking in hidden crevices, in holes, behind gates — each with a puzzle to solve. The layout of the store was changed every night. I'd been there only once, as I found the whole exercise pointless, but people loved it. Some spent most of their weekend there simply looking for items that they might not have been able to get due to lack of credits.

My favourite stores were the few book and antique stores. We got very few credits for those types of items, which were considered novelties.

Most of the stores were bursting with people coming and going, but I went to one of my favourite little bookstores. A middle-aged woman with thick-rimmed glasses was behind the counter reading a hardcover book. She looked up at me as I entered.

"Welcome back," she said before turning her attention back to her book. I guess she had so few customers that I was considered a regular, popping in a few times a month. The book selection was minimal, but surprisingly, there were a great number of nature, travel and history books. I picked up a few of the nature books and settled on one about the rainforests of Central America. It was full of pictures and descriptions of the different animals and plants there.

I headed toward the counter.

"Good choice. It looks so beautiful there," she said. I put my thumb on the scanner and the display showed the requisite number of novelty credits from my account.

"Thank you, and have a good night," I said, exiting the store.

Beside the bookstore was an antique store with a painting I had been eyeing for a while. This store was filled with decorations for your home from bygone eras. Apartment furnishings nowadays were all practical, with little aesthetic value. This store had intricate vases of varying shapes and sizes. Lamps that looked more like works of art than practical lighting accessories. But the item I had been looking at for a while was a wood-framed painting of a farm beside a fast-flowing river with horses running through a windswept, grassy field. It was an idyllic scene. I had just enough remaining novelty credits to get it. I headed to the counter and performed the customary thumb scan. With my two impulse purchases in hand, I walked toward the tram station. It would be months before I had enough novelty credits for another purchase like that.

It wasn't long before the correct tram entered the station and I headed home. I was in my eighth-floor studio apartment by 6:00 p.m.

My apartment consisted of a bed with drawers underneath, a small table with two chairs, a little white-cupboard kitchen and simple bathroom. The walls were painted a light blue. There was a small closet by the door. The only other furnishing was a chair on my balcony that overlooked the ravine toward Zone 3.

I changed into my shorts, a T-shirt and running shoes and headed to the trails in the ravine. I popped in my earbuds, which were playing an upbeat, jazzy album. I returned, dripping sweat, as the sun was setting.

Tyra came prancing in as I waited for the elevator. She waved at me and I could see her lips moving, speaking at me. I removed an earbud.

"Looks like you had a good run. Great minds think alike," she said, short of breath.

"I guess so," I mumbled. The elevator door opened and we both got in.

"We should go for a run together sometime," Tyra suggested.

"Yeah, that would be good," I lied.

We got off the elevator on the eighth floor and scanned our thumbs to enter our respective apartments.

"Good night, Kelowna. Sweet dreams!" Tyra exclaimed.

"You too," I said, quickly closing my door.

I had a shower and made some spaghetti, reading my new book as I ate. Before going to sleep, I hung my new painting above the bed.

The next morning was the usual routine. I turned on the vid screen beside my table as I ate my breakfast.

"Crop yields are down in Zone 6 this year for corn and wheat. However, greenhouse production is up, so the shortages will be offset with other goods. Food credits will be unaffected for the time being," the tanned model-like female newscaster reported.

"In other news, the hit theatre production of *Over and Above* will be starting a three-month stint in Zone 4 next week after rave reviews in Zones 1, 2 and 3. Get your tickets now," said the equally tanned and attractive male newscaster. I turned the vid screen off and prepared for another day.

Eight
Budapest

It was the second day since we'd all moved into the larger flat, and we were planning to leave in the middle of the night to escape to the countryside under the cover of darkness. Luckily, the soldiers hadn't begun searching this part of the city yet. The owners of the flat had still not returned. The day before, Tonya and some of the others went to check the other safe houses, leaving me and an elderly Hungarian woman at our temporary home. Tonya said there was a chance there were even more members scattered around the safe houses than the original twelve that were crammed in that tiny basement. She said it as if she was sorry, uncertain whether my offer to bring them to the farm extended to a very large number of people. I wanted to help, but mainly I wanted to get back to the farm in the hopes of finding Anna and my dad. The truth was, there was no way I could bring back such a large group.

The sun was setting when Tonya and her search partner returned with Lukas. Our plan was to leave the city at midnight, and I was getting anxious, since the other groups still hadn't returned. Around 10:30 p.m., a young man from one of the other search parties came bolting in. He was filthy and covered in sweat. He spoke in hurried Hungarian to Lukas. Tonya, who seemed to have a grasp on all the languages spoken in the group, translated for me: "Um, he says when they got to one of the safe houses, soldiers were already there, arresting people. His partner ran toward the wagon holding the prisoners while the soldiers were distracted, questioning people. His partner managed to free the prisoners, but the soldiers saw. Some of the locals being questioned grabbed the soldiers. The soldiers started shooting and dozens of people ran every which way."

The young man was breathless and frazzled, speaking in short bursts and always looking at the floor. Tonya had to move in close to translate. "He screamed for his partner and the others to run to the alley. Then he saw his partner get shot. Some soldiers started running toward him, so he panicked and ran." The young man was now in tears, convulsing and shaking his head. He was apologizing to Lukas. He gained a bit of composure, with Lukas trying to comfort him, and Tonya continued translating when he began again: "He spent most of the day darting through alleys and hiding in dumpsters. There were soldiers everywhere. We need to leave now, he says." Tonya looked scared, too, as she stepped aside to let Lukas calm the hysterical young man down. "He thinks he might have been followed. He's right, we need to go now. We can't wait for anyone else," she whispered to me. I nodded, eager to leave as well.

They sat the young man down, and the elderly Hungarian woman gave him some water and bread.

"Start packing up. Take as much food and water as you can carry," Lukas ordered in Hungarian and German. He came over to talk to me. "How long will it take to get to this farm of yours?"

"By foot, with some of the elderly people we have, maybe two and a half days."

He looked defeated and exhausted. I don't think that was the answer he was looking for. I tried to reassure him. "Once we get out of the city, some of the closer farms may help us." Lukas nodded and continued loading some of the packs. It was another hour before everyone was ready to go.

I went over to Tonya. "The old woman I spent the day with walks with a cane. She'll slow us down." Tonya shrugged, checking one of the bags. As we were all about to leave, my fears were alleviated. The old woman sat down, addressing the room in Hungarian.

"She's not coming with us," Tonya translated.

The young man who'd lost his partner kneeled on the floor, holding the old woman's hands, begging her to come.

"That's her grandson, Tomas," Tonya told me. "She's saying she won't survive the walk and will only get us caught. She wants Tomas to go and not worry about her."

Tomas kissed his grandma on the forehead and grabbed his bag, brushing tears from his eyes. Then Lukas kneeled by Tomas's grandma, speaking with her.

"He asked if there was anything we could do for her," Tonya said. "She says she'll head to her sister's place near here with the morning crowds headed to work. She says good luck and wants us to go quickly."

Lights were out at this time to conserve power and it was around ten degrees Celsius. Seven of us would be heading out of the city: me, Tonya, Lukas, Tomas and three others I had spent the worst days of my life with, not caring about their names or stories. It took only a couple of hours before we started to reach the outskirts of the city. We hadn't come across any patrols.

"Won't there be checkpoints entering and leaving the city?" Lukas asked me.

"Definitely along the main arteries, but there's another way."

I led them to an abandoned rail line beside a small forest sloping down to the riverbank. I knew it would be tough in the dark, but we were going to follow the river's edge. In this part of the city, the riverbank was steep, but it would most likely be deserted. Our progress slowed, but little by little, buildings and infrastructure started to dwindle as we made our way north along the Danube. The sun had begun to rise and we hadn't made it as far as I'd hoped.

"We need to find somewhere to hide for the day," I said to Tonya, who had silently walked beside me throughout the night. She turned around to relay the message to the others.

We were in a populated area, one of the old suburbs of Budapest, which still had a lot of people. If anyone saw us, it would be suspicious.

"We're going to have to risk it and cross through this suburb to the farmland beyond. I know some of the farmers in the area who may help us." I addressed the group in English, Tonya translating. "Just walk calmly and don't look at anyone," I said, leading them into one of the streets. There were many people walking here and there, but nobody cared who we were or what we were doing. We didn't see any soldiers. We made it through the suburb and found an abandoned home where we rested for a few hours.

"How far are we from your farm?" Tonya asked.

"Probably two days still. I normally stick to the roads during the day, so it's been slower than I hoped."

"We'll make it. We're all tired and…"

"What?" I asked.

"I was going to say we're all sad, but I'm sorry. You have enough to think about without worrying about the rest of us."

"They're alive still. Anna and my dad. I know it," I said, hoping Tonya's past excitement would kindle some optimism on my part. She just smiled at me.

"Do you know all the people with us?" I asked.

"Lukas is really the only one I know well, but I've met and worked with each of them occasionally. Tomas you know now. One of our best informants."

Tomas was a beanpole. Tall and incredibly lean with a shaved head. He couldn't have been more than twenty and was trying to grow facial hair, unsuccessfully.

"Sitting with Tomas is Gabor, his good friend." Gabor was the opposite of Tomas, short and stocky with shaggy, brown hair and a silly looking moustache.

"The other two are twins, as I'm sure you've noticed. Tibor and Orsi. At the moment, I'm not sure which one is which." Tibor and Orsi were shorter than Lukas and Tomas but looked ten times stronger. They were pure muscle, likely in their midtwenties, with closely cropped, brown hair. Lukas had spent most of the walk, in thought, by himself. I had been harsh with him. It was obvious he already carried plenty of guilt. The bags under his eyes, his drooped shoulders and fidgeting hands were evidence enough.

After a few hours of rest, we started off again toward one of the farms in the area.

"Do you think this farmer will help us?" Tonya asked.

"I hope so. Maybe he'll give us a ride the rest of the way. It's not unusual for wagons with labourers to be on the roads."

"And when we reach your farm?"

I looked at Tonya and didn't respond. I honestly didn't know. It was a lot of people to just show up with. The problem was going to be convincing the farmer to take the time to ferry people, especially during the last couple weeks of the harvest. I would need to offer something significant to trade. Finally, around dusk, we arrived at my friend's farm.

"Elliott, welcome, welcome," Viktor, the farmer, said warmly, shaking my hand. Then he looked at everyone else with me and appeared confused.

"These are new farm labourers from the city. We need a place to stay for the night before continuing on to our farm," I explained.

"You can stay in the barn if you don't mind sleeping on hay. Where are Anna and your parents?"

I tried to control my response. "Back at the farm already. They took all the goods in the wagons, so the rest of us have to walk."

I'd known Viktor for a couple of years now but didn't know how much to trust him. We set up camp in the barn, and Viktor offered food, but I said we were well provisioned. I needed to figure out a way to convince Viktor to take us the rest of the way to my farm.

"What's wrong?" Tonya asked.

I felt like that was a loaded question on so many levels. I could have given an exhaustive list, starting with the loss of Anna and my parents, but the truth was, at the moment, all I was thinking about was the next couple of days and this group of new people I found myself with.

"I'm not sure how the farm will accommodate all of us over the winter," I told her.

"We're all prepared to earn our keep. Don't worry about that."

"Six new people is a lot. I'm hopeful Anna and my dad are there. The four other people that live at the farm may not be happy," I said.

"It'll work out. I'm sure of that. Tell me about this farm and the people there."

"It's a beautiful farm. Rolling hills covered in fields with small woodlots and ponds. On one of the hills, you get an amazing view of the Danube. The house is cozy. Judit and Zsolti are the couple who own it. Zsolti, he's a card. Always joking and telling ridiculous stories. Judit is the mother hen. Mattias and Hannah are in their thirties and hoping for a baby. Mattias is the nephew of Judit and Zsolti. They never had kids of their own. It's a good place."

"Sounds wonderful, Elliott. I can't wait to meet them."

The next morning, Victor presented a solution to showing up at the farm with so many. "Elliott, how did you manage to get so many farm labourers? I just had three picked up and sent to the Front."

I tried to think of an explanation and left Viktor waiting for a response. Luckily, Tonya was eavesdropping. She smiled and shook Viktor's hand. "For your hospitality, some of us can stay on this farm to help," she said. "All the goods go to one place, so it doesn't really matter which farm we're at. Besides, there's a surplus of workers in the city right now and the authorities are worried it's going to be a harsh winter. Additional workers are being sent to farms to help with harvest and keeping the animals for the winter."

Viktor looked overjoyed and didn't bother asking any more questions.

"So, if some of these new labourers were to stay with you, could you give the rest of us a ride to my farm?" I asked.

"Of course. Thank you, Elliott and Tonya. This is wonderful news."

Now the question was, who was going to volunteer to stay here and be separated? Tonya explained the situation to Lukas and the others. Lukas said maybe it would be best if they weren't all in one place anyway. Tomas volunteered, saying it would be closer for him to get to the city to see his grandma. Gabor decided to stay with his friend.

"You'll be well looked after if you work hard," Viktor told them.

Lukas and Tonya hugged Tomas and Gabor goodbye while Tibor, Orsi and I waved, wishing them good luck. Viktor got his wagon and horses ready and by midday, we were off.

Nine
Paraiso

"Tell me about Colombia before," I asked Senora Vasquez. Most evenings in the village, we sat on the small porch we shared, staring across the gardens with the sound of the rushing clear stream and the sight of the mountains soaring around us.

"Colombia was, and still is in many places, breathtaking. Full of riches and wonders. A land of diversity. Every corner unique. Tropical waters with white sandy beaches. The Andes Mountains that reach the clouds. The beauty of the Amazon rainforest. But, like much of the world, things changed."

Senora Vasquez was old. I'd never asked how old, but she was probably as old, if not older, than my abuela.

"Things started to get bad in the 2030s. Before that, things were good for Colombia. It had managed to settle many of its internal conflicts. But then, politicians took more and more control over our resources and wealth. Extremist groups became more prevalent. Inequalities widened. And fresh water became the new gold."

Senora Vasquez had been teaching the children of the village most of her life. "Corporations bought the rights to Colombia's vast freshwater resources and politicians got rich selling the water. But the country's poor from the cities united with the farmers and the native tribes and fought back. They were outmatched. The politicians had the army. Corporations had well-equipped security forces. Political opponents disappeared. Villages that fought back were destroyed."

Senora Vasquez took a long sip of her tea. A tear rolled down her cheek. "But the worst part was the changes to the climate and the other environmental problems we faced. Slowly, the world's institutions and governments fell apart. Colombia was no different. Now the country is controlled by a strange balance of gangs and the former elites."

"How do you know all of this?" I asked.

"I didn't always live in Paraiso. There are still ways to get news from places. You're a product of this new system of balance. You grew up in the shadow of the truce between the gangs and the former elites."

"You mean the people in the centre of the city where there are many lights at night?"

"Yes. Bogotá was once the capital of Colombia and it's still the heart of where the former elite live. They live in their gated communities and large houses, far from the slums that cling to the hillsides. The second class live in the areas around the centre, producing goods for themselves, the gangs and the people in the gated communities. They live in relative comfort and security. The other class is forgotten. The people like you, who live in the slums. They do the bidding of the gangs."

"And places like this Paraiso?"

"There are many places like this. But most of the cities and major valleys are like Bogotá. Violent and depressing places."

"Life is good here, but I worry about Alejandra and my abuela. I think about them every day. I ... I shouldn't have left them behind."

"You had no choice, Miguel. They would want you to be safe. There was nothing you could have done to help either of them." Senora Vasquez had said that before, but I still struggled with the guilt that I was safe, clean and well fed.

"Tell me what happened after the shootout between the two gangs," Senora Vasquez said. "After you think you saw your mother."

I shared my writing with Senora Vasquez every day so she could help me fix mistakes. I also found writing down the things I had seen or been made to do easier than talking about it.

"Later that night, I returned home and told my abuela what I'd seen. She didn't seem to think it was my mother. She believed my mother was dead. She grabbed me and told me to be smart. She'd lost Alejandra, but she wouldn't lose me. I told her Alejandra is alive and could come back to us. She looked at me with a pain in her eyes and told me that Alejandra belongs to them now."

Senora Vasquez refilled her tea and mine from the pot on the table between us.

"My abuela told me to never go to that place where Alejandra was. I didn't understand why. Alejandra was still in the same slum, but my abuela was serious that it wasn't safe. She told me to continue with my water duties but learn how to find food in the hills. She said one day, I would need to leave that place."

Senora Vasquez sipped her tea, staring at the starry sky.

"I didn't understand at the time, but my abuela would occasionally talk about places over the hills in the higher mountains, which would be safe. I don't know if she knew that for sure or if she wanted to believe it."

"Does it matter?" Senora Vasquez asked.

I was startled and just looked at her. "Does it matter if she knew for sure or not that there were safe places over the hills in the mountains?" I had to think about that for a bit. "Yes ... because if she knew, then why did she wait till Alejandra was already taken? And ... if she didn't know then she just sent me away."

"Whether she knew or not, she wanted you to be safe. You were both too young when Alejandra was taken."

We sat in silence for some time as the stars shone above.

"Good night, Senora."

I went to bed restless, dreaming about the day Javier didn't show up to collect water with the rest of us. It was a few months after the gang fight near the compound. Instead of Javier, there was a younger boy who was smaller than me. I asked the soldados at the spring where Javier was, but they just glared at me. The older boys on our team wouldn't answer my questions, either. When we were carrying our last set of buckets down to the compound, the gate was wide open and there was a group of soldados in the training yard with what looked like new recruits. Javier was one of them.

As I was walking home, José, one of the boys on my team who was not much younger than Javier, joined me. "Eventually we'll all be forced to be soldados," he said.

"You don't know that."

José stopped walking. I did too.

"My time will come soon. Once runners reach a certain age, they're trained to fight and kill. My brother died as a soldado when the compound was attacked." José started slowly walking again.

"I'm sorry," I said. "I didn't know."

The next week, José didn't show up to carry water either. No one seemed to know where he went. Two days later, one of the soldados called me and the other runners to a room just outside the compound. There was a boy tied to a chair with a bag over his head. He was shaking and crying.

The soldado removed the bag from his head and it was José. The soldado punched José in the jaw, splitting open his lip. The soldado turned to us, asking, "Why are we punishing your friend here?" He didn't wait for us to answer. "This rodent has tried to flee the community into the hills." The soldados never referred to this place as a slum like everyone else did.

The soldado continued, "Our leader knows and sees everything. He knows where you are and what you're doing at all hours. You belong to him. You should consider yourselves lucky that you live in a strong community. Anyone that tries to flee or doesn't do their duty is a traitor." He turned to José. "Why would you betray all of us like this?"

José was crying uncontrollably. "Please, I'll return to work."

"You can't be trusted and must be punished." The soldado took out his knife, slowly cutting off one of José's fingers. José screamed in agony. Other soldados held our shoulders and heads so that we couldn't look away. The soldado had taken three fingers when he turned to us, pointing the butt of the knife at us, looking at each of us before he stopped in front of me. He handed me the knife and pushed me forward toward José.

"Slit his throat," he said. I stood terrified and shaking. I looked into José's bloodshot eyes as he looked into mine. José's head was bobbing from side to side. He was losing so much blood.

The soldado screamed at me, "Do it! Do it now!" He smacked me on the side of the face, then grabbed José by the hair, exposing his neck.

"If you don't do it, one of them will, and then they'll kill you. There's no room for weaklings and traitors here."

I stepped forward, the blade shaking in my hand. I set the edge of the knife to José's throat. José wasn't sobbing anymore. He was too weak to even do that.

The soldado smacked me on the top of the head, shouting, "Now!"

The knife grazed José's neck, cutting it, exposing a thin trickle of blood. Blood was already pooled at the base of the chair from his missing fingers. José was passing out. The soldado twisted his ears and pulled his hair to keep him awake. One of the other soldados stepped forward, placing a pistol at the back of my head. I panicked and thrust the knife forward and across José's neck. José began shaking and choking as blood poured from the gash. His eyes rolled into the back of his head and, though it seemed like forever, he was gone in seconds. The blade was still in my hand, covered in blood.

The soldado took the knife from my hand, patting me on the head. "Good. Now run along and don't be late tomorrow." I stumbled home, falling into my abuela's arms, tears racing down my face. She never even asked what was wrong, just held me, rocking me gently back and forth. She never asked why I was covered in blood.

I'd taken my first life. What's more, it was a friend who just wanted to live a different life. I felt trapped. The same thing would happen to me unless I became like them. I wanted to find Alejandra and, with our abuela, run to the hills.

Like so many nights before, I lay in bed staring at the ceiling, unable to sleep. I got out of bed and wrote the story of the day José died. As I scribbled the words across the paper, I felt a sigh of relief. In the morning, I showed the story to Senora Vasquez.

"You wrote, *blood and laughter. I'm not like them.* What do you mean by that?" Senora Vasquez asked.

"When I have the bad dreams, I see blood and hear the laughter of the soldados as José died. I could never laugh at someone dying. No matter what they make me do, I won't do that."

"When did you decide to run away?"

"Long after José's death. I never told my abuela about killing him or the others. It became a game for the soldados. They didn't want to wait until I was old enough to make me like them."

"Tell me about the others."

I shook my head. "It's too hard."

"You're a good person made to do terrible things. You're not to blame."

"But I still killed them." I covered my face with my hands to hide the fact that I was crying.

"When you're ready, you can tell me. It will help to get it out."

"I'm not a good person. I lied and they hurt him."

"Hurt who, Miguel?"

"I didn't even know his name. The newest boy after Javier was taken. It was a few days after José died. I was so angry. I took it."

"Took what?"

"The soldados guarding the spring were eating under a tree a little down the hill from the spring. One of them had left a small bag near the spring. I took it and hid it under my shirt. It had nothing of value to me. There were some cigarettes, a small bottle of alcohol and some coins. But it felt good to steal from them."

Senora Vasquez sat in the chair next to me.

"The next day, the soldado I stole from was very angry when we got to the spring. He demanded to know who took his bag. None of us answered. He said then we would all be punished, raising a club to hit one of the boys. I said the newest boy was the last to leave the spring yesterday. The soldado grabbed him and demanded his bag back. The boy said he knew nothing about a bag. The soldado hit the boy repeatedly on the legs, side, back. The noise was terrible. Eventually the soldado stopped hitting him and told the rest of us to get to work. At the end of the day, we carried him, bruised and broken, back down the hill to his home."

"Did he survive?" Senora Vasquez asked.

"Yes, but his leg was broken. I-I'm not sure what became of him."

"Why did you blame it on that other boy?"

"They would have punished all of us."

"So instead of taking the consequences yourself, you hurt an innocent boy."

Senora Vasquez had never been angry with me before. She got up from the table and went to the stove.

"I told you. I'm not a good person." I put my head down on the table, lightly banging it up and down.

"That was a terrible thing you did, but you were angry and traumatized about José. You lashed out at the soldados without thinking about the consequences. At that age, how could you process something like that?"

Senora Vasquez came over to me and gently pulled my head up.

"Don't try to make me feel better."

She sat in the other chair and held my hands. "I'm not. I'm just explaining that you were unable to deal with what you did to José and made a mistake. A terrible mistake. Right and wrong isn't always easy to distinguish. You regret what you did, which means you don't take pleasure from the suffering of others. That's important. Are you ready to tell me about the others?"

I shook my head. "Not yet."

Ten
At the Farm outside Budapest

That first winter on the farm without Anna and my parents was tough. The others from the United Earth movement had settled in nicely. They were hard workers and earned their keep.

Zsolti, in particular, was annoyed at first that I brought so many people to the farm. Judit couldn't stop asking where my parents and Anna were. Those first few days after we arrived at the farm, I barely spoke to anyone. The sadness of not finding Anna or my father there destroyed me. Judit let the matter rest, seeing my condition, while Zsolti set about giving the newcomers jobs. Everyone was kept busy harvesting the final crops. Zsolti was confident there was enough for us all to survive.

It was a cold and lonely winter. Every day, I expected Anna or my father to return. And I started to grieve for my mother. Up to this point, I'd blocked out the image and sound of her hitting the stage; now it was all I could see, even with my waking eye. I lay in bed each night staring at the ceiling, unable to move or process information.

Everyone else gave me space and allowed me to slack off on my chores. No one really spoke to me, which made things worse. I could sense the resentment building among everyone toward me. Why wouldn't they resent me? I did little to help or earn my keep but still expected a warm fire and full plate of food. I needed some way to get out of this funk, to occupy my mind elsewhere.

One morning, I woke up later than everyone else, which was usual, but I decided to go to the chicken coops to help out. It was the easiest of the various wintertime tasks on the farm, and one that I was unlikely to screw up. I'd been out of the loop for so long on what was happening at the farm that I didn't realize Tonya was the one assigned to the chicken coops. She gladly welcomed my assistance and even offered a friendly jibe, or so I hoped.

"Welcome back," she joked.

"Thanks. How can I help?" I offered.

For the next few weeks, I helped Tonya keeping the chickens fed and warm so that we could have fresh eggs. Most of the time, Tonya would go on and on about stories she'd made up about our lives on the farm. She was quite imaginative and never serious. She never once spoke about her life or family and I didn't probe. There was no point. Whatever her life story, it was probably a sad one. Despite all that may have happened to her, she woke up each morning with a smile on her face and the energy to complete a full day's work. It may have been delusional, but if she needed her stories and jokes to get by, who was I to judge? And I enjoyed her company. As she gabbed away, it kept me distracted from other thoughts. I'd always been too serious. Even Anna would tell me to lighten up or poke me in the side when someone told a joke that I didn't react to.

Christmas was coming up and we decided to have a big feast and make each other presents. We didn't have much, but for the weeks leading up to Christmas, everyone spent their evenings locked away in some corner of the house with whatever crafts they were making. I wasn't very crafty, but I was somewhat artistic. I had an old set of charcoal pencils and enough pieces of canvas to draw something for everyone. I decided to draw a different aspect of each person's new life at the farm.

For Judit and Zsolti, I drew a landscape shot of the view from the front porch looking down toward the river in the distance. In the corner was the porch swing with the back of their heads. Judit and

Zsolti could always be found sitting hand in hand on that porch swing. Judit with her shoulder-length, curly, grey hair and Zsolti with his strange wide-brimmed hats to cover up his bald head. They'd been together for forty years and were so sweet to each other when they thought no one was around.

For Mattias and Hannah, I drew them riding on horseback across the fields, which was their favourite pastime. Hannah was the more natural rider and usually far ahead of Mattias, who was often deep in concentration trying to stay upright. Hannah reminded me of Anna. She was a similar size, with equally blonde hair and blue eyes. But when she wasn't on horseback, Hannah was more reserved than Mattias, who was boisterous and confident on the ground. He had wavy, brown hair, dark eyes and a chiselled jaw. They were an attractive couple. The United Earth members from Budapest had been with us for a couple of months now, but I knew nothing real about any of them. Tonya was the only one I really ever spent any time with, but I still knew nothing about her. I couldn't figure out what to draw for any of them. I debated whether or not to draw for each of them their vision for a united world but decided that it may upset them. Instead, I decided to draw each of them performing their daily tasks on the farm. Boring and impersonal, I know, but I couldn't think of anything else.

I drew Tibor and Orsi, the young twin brothers who didn't speak anything other than Hungarian, who I knew the least, chopping wood on the hillside between the farm and the forest. They were the strongest in the group and tended to get the most physically demanding jobs.

Lukas was a struggle, since he liked to help with everything. The week leading up to Christmas, an undersized colt got quite sick. The colt was born late in May and was weak from birth. We debated whether it would survive the winter, or if we should put it out of its misery. The colt had been weaned off its mother's milk in November and was still undersized for its age. Yet, it was a fighter. Lukas took it as his personal mission to keep the colt alive. He spent night and day with it in the barn, feeding it and keeping it warm. Two days before Christmas, the colt spurred back to life. I sat sometimes watching Lukas in there. He was a crusader, stubborn and relentless in his ideals. I envied him. For his gift, I drew him in the barn caring for the colt.

That left Tonya. Christmas Eve was coming, and I still hadn't started her drawing. I couldn't think of anything. We were sitting by the fire that night while everyone else was off somewhere rushing to complete their gifts. Tonya had finished hers, although I had no idea what they would be. Everyone knew that I was drawing something for each of them as they'd all seen me with my charcoal pencils and canvas, but none of them had tried to peek. Everyone was excited about the surprise coming on Christmas morning. Tonya sat there by the fire with a tea in her hand, staring at the flames as they flickered. The warm red glow accentuated her features and made her eyes shimmer. I could tell she was deep in thought, and it was the first time since I'd known her that I sensed the sadness within her. She normally hid it so well, but that night, sitting by that fire, she was lost to her own demons. I grabbed my pencils and last sheet of canvas and began drawing. She was oblivious to my presence. I sketched feverishly, capturing every detail and subtle emotion. Tonya had always been beautiful, but in this pensive state, she was exquisite. It must have been at least two hours of her just sitting there staring without a word.

Finally, she sighed. "Elliott, tell me about your life before this farm." Tonya was still staring into the fire, and I thought of what I could possibly tell her that she already hadn't assumed. Most people's stories were fairly similar.

"I was born in London in 2042," I said. "Both my parents were diplomats, so I spent most of my childhood in Vienna. The United Nations slowly crumbled in my early years, as global crises escalated. Yet my parents were so optimistic." I had small tears forming in the corners of my eyes.

Tonya turned to look at me. "Go on."

"In a way, I was fortunate. Even with the start of the various wars, I was able to return to England to study International Relations after high school. I'd hoped to follow up with a law degree. But by that time, things were getting worse, and the wars, diseases and economic turmoil had spread."

"I remember the riots. No jobs, no food, everyone was angry and blaming somebody else," Tonya added and then stopped.

"After the seas took London and the UN dissolved, the university shut down, so I returned to Vienna to help my parents. The United Earth movement was in its infancy."

"We had so much promise," Tonya said. "Yet history repeated itself. I remember when the Rhine Valley became a quasi–police state. I lost a lot of friends." She was staring at the fire again, occasionally closing her eyes to take deep breaths to compose herself.

"I remember getting news from different parts of the world in those days," I said. "But it was so difficult to separate fact from fiction. We didn't call it a world war, but the world seemed at war with itself. We fled Vienna during one of the largest round-ups. Any able-bodied person was sent to the Front. Everyone else was put into forced labour. We didn't even know who we were fighting at that point."

Tonya nodded. "I've been to the Front. It was years ago. A wall and series of bases that runs down the length of Poland, the Ukraine, all the way to the border with Turkey. I never saw it, but even the Mediterranean was fortified. There was fighting. So much fighting, suffering and death." Tonya turned away from me as she gently sobbed. I wanted to go over to her and comfort her, but I stayed in my chair.

"When did you meet Anna?" she asked after a few minutes.

"That would have been thirteen years ago now. She was part of the movement. There were villages along the Danube between Vienna and Budapest, which members of the movement slowly settled in, farming the outlying fields. Anna eventually ended up at the same place as my parents and I."

"Was it love at first sight?" Tonya asked.

I laughed. "She was very beautiful, inside and out."

"We don't know that she's gone. You can't give up."

I nodded and smiled at Tonya. "I was never much of a farmer. But working the fields, using our hands, growing and making what we needed, it was a good life. No matter how bleak things seemed, Anna would smile and say better days are ahead."

"She was right." Tonya got up and kissed my forehead. "Good night, Elliott."

I stoked the fire and added more logs, then finished the drawing of Tonya. I'd spent so many nights by this fireplace chatting about hopes and dreams with Anna. Those memories now made me both sad and happy.

Eleven
Bangalore

I woke up nauseous and delirious. Pain was throbbing in most of my body. My mind and heart were broken. I was alone. There were two bodies of the filthy men lying nearby in pools of blood. All of our supplies were gone. I stood at the top of the stairs, crying and shivering. My head was caked in dried blood. How could I go on alone? Where would I go? What would I do?

I was about to collapse when I remembered one of the last things Jahi said to me. *A better future is possible.* Right now, I couldn't see how, but I couldn't give up. After everything Jahi had been through, he still believed in humanity. He didn't give up. I owed it to him and Randhir to try.

I slowly stumbled down the stairs, my knees weak and wobbly. When I reached the bottom, I saw Jahi's and Randhir's broken and lifeless bodies. I cried over them and kissed them both, apologizing and telling them how much I loved them. I couldn't leave them like this but didn't have the strength to carry them anywhere to bury or burn. Outside, I gathered some small yellow flowers, which I placed around their bodies. I found a tattered tarp in an alley to cover them. They deserved better.

I sat there for hours, struggling with my own resolve to carry on. They'd been my guardians, my friends, my family, my strength. They'd never harmed anyone. Like my father, they gave to those weaker than them when they could. For their generosity, they were savagely beaten and tossed aside as if they were worthless. I struggled to remember their smiles and their words. Jahi would want me to carry on, but how? I had no faith in humanity, no hope left. A young girl could never survive in this world alone. I was about to give in, to simply lie down beside their bodies and wither away, when the sun shone through a window and landed upon their makeshift graves. It illuminated the small yellow flowers scattered around their bodies. This scene, for whatever reason, gave me the resolve to go on. I said my final goodbyes and left.

I gathered some of the food that Randhir and I had recently buried and some fresh mangoes. We'd left a couple extra bags and bottles as well. I took as much as I could carry and decided to leave the city.

I had no idea which way to go. I knew there was no point in going north, even though I was far from the worst of the devastation. Bangalore was all I knew. Only a few days ago, Randhir had suggested heading south. South had been my family's salvation before; maybe it would be my personal salvation.

The sun was setting on the horizon. I figured it would be safer for me to leave the city under the cover of darkness. I would be too easy a target if anyone saw me. Many of the novels I'd read described despicable humans as nothing more than animals. From what I'd read about animals, though, that description was unfair. What was done to Jahi, Randhir and me was done by humans, the lowest of our species. But animals don't kill for pleasure.

Heading south, it was as if my feet moved independent from my mind. I walked in a sort of dream state. I didn't encounter anyone as I left the city. The countryside outside the city consisted of overgrown fields, stumps of trees or just barren dirt. The farther I got from Bangalore, the less depressing the landscape became. The forests and grasslands were green and lush. Yet it was strangely quiet. There weren't any signs of birds or animals. I occasionally came across abandoned or burnt-out villages. I was running out of food and decided to risk travelling during the day to scrounge for food and clean water. I came upon a small pond that looked and smelled relatively clean and decided to risk it. I found wild fruits. The weather was hot and humid. I needed to find a real supply of water to drink. I still had no idea where I was headed or what I was looking for. I knew eventually I would reach the ocean, but I had no idea how far it was from Bangalore. I was very hungry. The fruits I could find sustained me but weren't really enough. My head was throbbing, the wound there oozing fresh blood.

After a few days, I came upon a village that wasn't abandoned. There were about fifty people around. They had crops and animals. I was so tempted to ask for their help but didn't know how they would react. Also, I couldn't understand their language. At night, I snuck in to steal some food and water and moved on. These people didn't seem cautious or suspicious. They had no guards, seemed well fed and almost happy. I thought about going back and trying to speak with them. Perhaps they would take pity on me and care for me. In time, I could make a new home here. Instead, I went on. The last two people in the world I truly knew and trusted were gone. I don't know how or why I kept moving, but I did.

Two days after passing the village, I started feeling sick. My energy was drained. I still had some food and water but could barely walk. I decided to rest under a large tree. I was so worried that I'd finally caught one of the many diseases around. After seeing just about every sort of disease in my relatives, I knew how to detect and treat the ones that were treatable. This was unlike anything I'd seen before. I don't even remember passing out.

When I woke up, I was in a soft bed with red blankets, in a small circular room. It was warm and clean and had a little table with two chairs. The roof was made of grass and the walls of a light-coloured wood. The floor was covered in brightly coloured rugs. The table had vibrant flowers. There was a calm and sweet scent floating around.

I felt completely refreshed. Somebody had properly tended to my wounds and I was clean and wearing a new white linen shirt and soft purple pants. I figured I was dead and had gone to heaven, and I fell back asleep.

When I awoke again, I found myself in the same room. Maybe I was still alive after all and this wasn't heaven. The pain I'd been feeling before arriving here was gone. On the table, there was hot tea and some fruit. I got out of the bed to eat and drink. It hurt to stand up and I had to steady myself against the bed. The tea was soothing and calmed my mind.

But then visions of that terrible day appeared again. I'd been too tired, sore or in shock all those days of walking to really think about what had happened. Now it all became so vivid. I saw Jahi's and Randhir's faces, their bodies. I heard the laughs of those men, felt the pain of them beating me. I fell to the bed, shaking uncontrollably.

An old man walked into the room. "It's okay, you're safe here," he said.

I curled up in bed, keeping my distance from the old man. "How long have I been here?"

"Four days now. You had a fever, malnutrition, exhaustion and infections in your cuts. But you appear to be on the mend. My name is Amar. You are?" I just stared at the man. "Where do you come from?" he asked.

I cleared my throat. "Bangalore."

"I'm from Delhi but have been this far south for many years. Most of the people here only speak Tamil. But they're kind and we have all we need. Can I get you some more food or tea?"

I shook my head and looked away from Amar.

"You're in a village near the ancient Annamalaiyar Temple. You're quite some distance from Bangalore. Amazing that you came so far alone and in your condition. I was the one who found you and managed to convince the council of elders here to bring you in because you were so young and frail. What made you leave Bangalore and journey all this way alone?" Amar asked.

I started crying and shook my head.

"It's all right. Take your time. I'll bring you some more food and leave you to rest a while."

Amar brought me more food and tea and left the hut. The plate was covered in fresh, hot food of different colours, with a bowl of rice. I ate slowly but couldn't eat very much. My stomach wasn't used to such rich tastes. I drank the tea and went back to bed, crying into the plush pillow.

I didn't wake up until Amar returned to the hut.

"It's midday. Would you like to go for a walk? The sun and air may help you feel better. There are some sandals and a blouse by the chair. When you're ready, join me outside?"

I rose and put the long purple blouse on over the white linen shirt. The blouse was elegant with red embroidery along the neckline. The sandals fit perfectly. I left the room and found Amar patiently standing outside. The sky was blue with puffs of white clouds moving slowly. The village was made up of many circular huts similar to the one I just left, with some larger wooden buildings. Well-tended fields surrounded it. Many people were out, tending to the crops. Some older women were gathered under a shelter with only a roof, making clothing or baskets or preparing food. The women all had brightly coloured clothing draped around their shoulders, descending into flowing dresses. Blues, yellows, reds and greens of many shades. The men were dressed more simply in white pants and long shirts or no shirts at all. Amar greeted each of the people we passed.

Everyone looked at me with curiosity, but no one spoke to me, nor did Amar introduce anyone. I stayed behind him, following closely. Children ran around the village, chasing each other or playing with balls. They all had plump little bellies and no exposed ribs.

Amar led me to the edge of the lush jungle that covered one of the hillsides near the village. There was a basket and blanket under a large tree at the edge of a jungle. Every direction up and down the hill into the distance was the same dark green of large trees.

Amar motioned for me to join him on the blanket. In the basket was some water, bread and fresh fruit. We ate in silence, looking back toward the village and the villagers going about their routines.

"Are you feeling better?"

I nodded.

"I had a daughter once, very beautiful. She and my wife got sick many, many years ago."

I didn't know if Amar wanted me to respond or if he was just telling me this.

"I've lived in this village for close to fifteen years now," Amar said.

"Were they here with you when they died?"

Amar paused and looked to the ground. "No, they died many years before I came here, back in the North."

"I'm sorry. My family all died too."

"How long have you been alone?"

I started to cry again. Amar put a hand on my shoulder and I recoiled from the touch, falling backward.

"I'm sorry. I didn't mean to upset you. It sometimes helps to talk about it. I'd like to help you if I can. Will you tell me your name at least?"

"I-I'm Aashi…" I took a deep breath, closing my eyes. "Two of my cousins, the last of my family, died recently. After that, I started heading south, unsure of what to do or where to go."

"What were their names?"

"Jahi and Randhir."

"The soul is eternal and ever-existing. May Jahi's and Randhir's departed souls get heavenly abode."

"Can we take a walk in the jungle?" I asked.

"Of course."

Amar led me along the edge of the jungle, down the gentle slope, with the village to our right. We soon came to a rushing creek that came out from the trees heading down the hill through some of the fields tended by the villagers.

"Take a drink. It's quite clean and refreshing," Amar said.

I bent down to the creek and cupped some cool water with my hands.

"See the path between the fields there and the small bridge that goes down the hill?" Amar said, pointing. I nodded. "That path leads to a larger road down in the flat plain in the distance. If you go left along that road, it will lead you to the temple. Many people live there. Our village trades with the temple often. I'll take you there one day if you're feeling up to it."

We followed the creek into the jungle. The air was thick, and the trees were tall. Brightly coloured flowers covered the ground. Everything was so green and fresh. There were birds flapping from tree to tree, singing to each other. I could hear — but not see — other animals. Amar led me along in silence, letting me absorb the surroundings. I became so overwhelmed by the beauty that I fell to the ground, crying again. Amar moved to assist me and I moved farther away.

"What is it, Aashi?"

I shook my head and couldn't stop crying. Amar kneeled uncomfortably in front of me.

"Randhir … he wanted to come south not long before … before…" — I couldn't get the words out, crying harder and harder — "he was killed."

Amar sat on the ground in front of me.

"If we'd just left then … they would both be here with me."

"Aashi, they're gone and at peace. You're safe now. They would want you to be happy."

My crying slowed. I knew Amar was right, but it still felt unfair that I was here in this beautiful place and they weren't. We sat on the ground together for what seemed like forever, listening to the sounds of the jungle and rushing of the creek.

"Come, it's getting late. We should return to the village," Amar said.

He stood, putting his hand out to help me up. I took it and stood, following him closely back along the creek. It was getting dark. We arrived back at the village as most of the villagers were preparing the evening meal. Everyone sat in circles in the grass near some of the larger buildings. Many villagers were busy near fire pits. I sat with Amar in a group of about a dozen other people. Several brought bowls of food, placing them in the centre of the circle. A young girl handed each of us a large leaf. The villagers were talking in a tongue I couldn't understand.

"To put the food on," Amar explained.

There were dishes with rice and coloured sauces with vegetables in them and the same type of flat bread Amar and I had earlier. Everyone used their hands and grabbed from the assorted dishes, putting the food on their leaf.

This time, my stomach accepted the fragrant and rich food gladly. I could feel myself beginning to think about Jahi and Randhir. I tried to control the tears. "Amar, please thank the people for this meal. I'm feeling very tired again."

"Of course. Go and rest, Aashi. I'll see you in the morning." As I got up to leave, Amar said, "Time heals all wounds."

As I walked back to the hut, I hoped that he was right, then I collapsed into bed, crying myself to sleep.

The next morning, I awoke with the sun. Many people in the village were already up, beginning their day's work. I wandered around looking for Amar. I found him in one of the fields near the creek, tending to some crops. He greeted me warmly. "Good morning, Aashi. Please help me gather some of these crops before we go to eat the morning meal."

"What type of plant is this?"

"Lentils. We grow several types here. We also grow rice, wheat, potatoes, carrots, radishes, tomatoes and many other crops. You'll learn about them all in time."

He already had a nearly full basket and gathered the seed pods with such skill and speed. I tried to mimic his movements. Our gardens in Bangalore were never this plentiful.

"After the morning meal, we'll head into the jungle to gather fruits and nuts. That's my main job here. Everyone has a role. For now, you'll work with me," Amar said.

We ate the morning meal in the centre of the village in the same circular groups as at evening meal the night before. Again, I was overwhelmed by the smells, colours and variety. Amar explained to me what everything was. It was all so fresh. He told me that the morning meal here was pretty much the same every day. "A good hearty meal to start the day so you have the energy to carry out your work," he said. Morning meal consisted of *dosa*, a flat bread served with coconut chutney and fruits, like mangoes, jackfruit, water apple, bananas and tamarind. Amar said these would be the fruits we would spend the rest of the day gathering.

After the morning meal, we started up the hill into the jungle with sacks on our backs.

"I've had years to learn the best spots for gathering. We'll be gone most of the day," Amar explained.

It didn't take long to find what we were looking for. In Bangalore, we would spend the day exhausted from hunger, scrounging food from our meagre gardens or hunting rats and pigeons. Here, food was everywhere. Once Amar had pointed out some of the plants for me, it was easy work. My energy levels were better than I could ever remember.

Yet still, Amar told me to take it easy. He said it would be some time before my body and mind adjusted to the nutrients and portions of food I was now getting. By midday, I began to feel what he was talking about. I felt light-headed and drained. We rested under a banana tree and snacked on some fruit and cashews. We each had a waterskin that we filled up from the creek running down the hill. Amar told me the names of more plants, birds and animals that lived in these jungles. I drifted off with his talk of this exotic cornucopia. Amar must have allowed me to rest, because when I woke up, he was gone. I called for him but heard no answer. I should have felt scared and abandoned, but I simply gathered my sack and walked up the hill in search of more food. I knew the way back to the village. In the city, I would have felt alone and scared, but here, things were safe and peaceful.

I slowly walked through the jungle, gathering food now and then while smelling each new flower and listening intently anytime I heard an animal. I would occasionally see the fluttering of birds in the canopy above. I tried to recognize some of them. Back in Bangalore, some of my favourite books were the ones about animals. I loved to look at their pictures and learn their names and habits. Jahi would tell me that many animals went extinct because of the war, but even before that, many were struggling because we'd destroyed their homes.

Eventually I stopped gathering food and just started wandering, always keeping the creek to my right so that I wouldn't get lost. At the top of a hill that flattened out, I came upon a small body of water. At its far end I saw something I'd never seen before. A group of three animals with long slender legs and white spots on their light-brown coats were drinking from the pond. I tried to recall the name of these creatures from any of the books I had read. I'd never seen such large animals before. The city really had only rats and pigeons. I crouched down in a bush so as not to startle them and watched as they drank. After some time, four large and slender white birds flew in and landed in the water. They walked in the shallows on their tall legs. I couldn't recall what they were called either. They were absolutely beautiful with their long, yellow beaks and black wings. They waded around, occasionally sticking their heads into the water, presumably searching for food. By now, the three spotted creatures had wandered back into the jungle, while other birds of different sizes and colours landed in the water.

I was spellbound. I had no concept of time and simply stared, transfixed on the miracle of life before me. *How could anyone ever want to destroy such beauty and perfection?* I wondered. Nothing I'd seen created by humans compared to this sight. It was simple and complex at the same time. Simple in its purpose, but complex in its details of colours, textures, sounds and smells. I must have sat by the water for hours, since the sun began to descend below the trees, casting shadows.

I gathered my things and walked down the hill. Amar was waiting for me at the edge of the village by the creek. "I was beginning to worry, Aashi."

"Thank you," I said, embracing Amar in a long hug.

He smiled at me. "Come, it's time to eat."

At the evening meal, I sat listening to the other villagers, trying to understand what they were saying. There were many different conversations going on at once, and the language was so different, I got overwhelmed trying to distinguish individual words from one voice. Amar smiled and laughed at the way I was craning my neck, turning my ear from person to person.

"You'll understand eventually. Most of them aren't discussing anything important. Funny stories about something a child said or did. Whether we should plant another field or two. Who is going to town in the next little while. The usual idle conversation of content people."

I told Amar about what I had seen by the pond earlier, describing the animals carefully. "Do you know their names?" I asked.

"Sounds like you saw some chital and painted storks. A good day then."

It soon began to rain and everyone hurried to clean up and return to their huts. It rained the whole night but cleared with the morning sun. The fields and trees shimmered gold with the morning light reflecting off the fresh rain from the evening. I smiled at the sight. I felt happy and at home. The pangs of guilt over Jahi and Randhir were still in the back of my mind, but I knew they would want me to be happy and safe. They died defending me; the least I could do was live my life to the fullest in their memory.

The morning began the same as the last with the morning meal. I felt so grateful for the routine, knowing that I would have a full and healthy meal to begin each day. After morning meal, Amar and I went in search of our daily haul. This time, we crossed the creek and went straight along the edge of the hill the village was on.

"It's best to change locations every day to give the plants a chance to flower again. Many other animals rely on the fruits and nuts in the jungle, too." I followed, trying to recall the name of every plant and bird we saw. "We only take what we need to survive. Stay close today, Aashi. We're going deeper into the jungle away from the creek. It's easy to get lost."

There was a narrow footpath where the plants were parted with steep hills on either side. It was still difficult walking. Branches and vines overhung the path. The air was very hot and humid.

"Amar, pardon this question, but how old are you?"

He laughed. "I'm sixty-eight."

"You move like someone half that age. I've never known someone to reach that age."

Amar laughed. "Well, thank you. You are most kind. There are villagers older than me."

"Can you tell me more about the animals, birds and plants that live in this jungle?"

"Do you know what a tiger is?"

"I've only seen pictures in books. Such a beautiful animal."

"They are. They were nearly wiped out in India before the war. Many thought that during the war, the last tigers would certainly be killed as people fled from diseases and bombs. Humans angered the gods, though, and now the tiger will be lord of the jungle again."

"Have you ever seen a tiger?"

"For decades, tigers have been missing from this part of India, banished to a tiny fraction of their former range. They were hunted for their skins or some foolish spiritual belief that their bones and other body parts cured diseases and ailments. That's the danger of spirituality, Aashi. On the one hand, you recognize the strength, majesty and power of a creature you believe to be a deity, but on the other, you believe that killing that creature and using its body will somehow impart that strength and power onto you. Imagine killing one of your gods to take their strength. No wonder the gods let us destroy ourselves."

Amar stopped to listen, looking around. "About two years ago, one of the village elders, who passed last year, was walking through this very jungle and came to a clearing with a small pond. Swimming across the pond was a Bengal tiger. The elder fell to his knees and bowed before the creature, ready to offer himself to its majesty. The tiger had no interest in the elder and swam to the other edge of the pond and melted into the jungle." Amar turned toward me and grabbed my hands. "No, I've never seen a tiger. Perhaps one day, I'll be able to offer myself as well. Still, I worry."

"Worry about what?"

"Things may seem idyllic here, but you came from one of the cities to the north. How is nature to overcome the wounds we have inflicted elsewhere? The toxins, destruction, radiation and garbage. There aren't enough of us left to clean up the mess. Perhaps in time, beyond the comprehension of man, nature will cleanse itself, but what will we lose in that time? It falls to young people like you, Aashi, to decide what sort of world you want to inherit. There are rumours of organizations near the coast that are trying to clean things up, to re-establish a government. Perhaps even with contact to other parts of the world."

With that, Amar continued on through the jungle gathering fruit.

What can I do? I thought. *I just found a safe place. I found peace and beauty. Is it really my burden to correct the mistakes of those who came before?*

It was late in the day and we began the journey back to the village, sacks full of our bounty. On the way back, Amar pointed out more plants and taught me more about what was safe to eat and what wasn't. He nodded toward some of the colourful birds fluttering about at the tops of the trees. We arrived back at the village at twilight, just as the evening meal was being served. This place was all the hope I needed.

Twelve
Ontario

At the office on Thursday, we had a team meeting to discuss the crop-yield news.

Our team lead, Victoria, was a stocky and homely woman with a habit of sneaking up on her employees and berating them for not meeting their weekly quotas. "As you've likely heard, wheat and corn yields are down this year. Directions are to cut corn and wheat rations to each zone by a quarter and compensate with equivalent proportions of lentils, broccoli and kale. You'll receive specific instructions through the intra-mail for your assigned transects. Back to your desks," Victoria said, dismissing us with a wave of her hand.

"Inspiring meeting, eh," Gerald whispered to me, nudging my elbow.

Luckily, I rarely interacted with Victoria, since I had learned a long time ago how to work the system. We were expected to perform a certain number of tasks each day. If we failed to meet the quota, credits were deducted. If we finished our work early, we were given more to do but not given any additional credits. There were some people on my floor who always tried to outshine the rest to get extra work. Often the work they did from the day before came back to them because they made mistakes. The quotas changed weekly, so it became a matter of watching everyone else. A light at the top of our cubicles flashed when we completed a task, while a virtual board at our team lead's station compared our team to adjacent ones. Some weeks, I needed to review my work only once before going on to the next task; other weeks, I triple-checked to maintain the right balance.

Within each zone, there were four quadrants that were then subdivided into six transects. I worked with a team of people responsible for ensuring the delivery of goods to all the quadrants in Zone 5. Anyone born in Zone 4 had better be good at math.

Every person was assigned a number. The first three numbers simply corresponded to location: zone, quadrant and transect. The next six digits were the individual's personal identification. If a person died, their number was reassigned to a newborn a year after their death.

My job was to make sure that any given week, residents from a particular transect were all accounted for and given what they needed. Either way, looking at 5-2-6: 594230 versus 6-3-4: 645218 didn't really get my blood boiling. That's how the spreadsheets looked — rows and rows of numbers and then columns for produce, grains, soaps and other everyday necessities.

All residents were vegetarian. The energy and resource inputs required for animal husbandry were deemed too significant long ago. I'd never eaten meat, but we were taught about older forms of agriculture and energy production to remind us how evolved our society was now. Our energy production was clean and renewable. There were community gardens for people who wanted to grow some of their own food. Some buildings had them on their roofs. Some food credits were devoted to those initiatives, so there was no real benefit compared to those that didn't grow their own food.

My thoughts were interrupted by the bell that always sounded for lunch at exactly noon.

"Headed for lunch, dude?" Gerald asked, standing at my cubicle.

"Yeah, let's go," I responded, shutting down my computer screen.

The cafeteria was located on the second floor. Everyone in the building ate lunch there, as that was the only place credits worked for lunch hour — really, a half hour.

"What do you think's on the menu today?" Gerald asked.

"Let's see … It's Wednesday. Last Wednesday was lentil soup and a garden salad. I'm going to say probably a chickpea wrap with tomato soup."

As the line of people waiting for lunch slowly inched toward the counter, the menu came into view.

Gerald laughed, "Jeez, Kelowna, bang on. What's your prediction for tomorrow?"

"Probably the lentil soup and garden salad again. The chickpea wrap and tomato soup was last Thursday."

"Oh yeah. I can't even remember what I ate yesterday, let alone last week," Gerald said.

Gerald and I carried our lunch trays to the usual assigned table with the rest of our floor.

"Want to mix it up a bit and sit somewhere else?" I asked.

Gerald had already sat down at the same table we sat at every day. "Ha ha. Very funny. You're a true rebel. Just sit down, joker."

I plopped down in the designated seat and quietly ate my lunch while the rest of our floor chatted about the weather, upcoming events or the possibility of a food shortage.

As I was tuning out the chatter of my colleagues, Gerald asked, "Hey Kelowna, do you want to go watch the game after work at the Loon?"

"Um, sure," I responded, not sure what game he was talking about.

Five o'clock was quitting time. Gerald and I headed to the Loon, a bar at the Hub with a large patio and plenty of screens. It turned out the game was a lacrosse match between Ontario and Michigan. Lacrosse, soccer and ultimate Frisbee were the main sports in the city. My parents said there used to be other sports that were played before the war. For whatever reason, these were the only three played now. For each sport, Ontario and Michigan each had a professional team that always played each other. All the athletes were from Zone 1. I never really understood the dedication to these teams when there were only two of them and each week, they played each other. One year Ontario would win the championship and the next Michigan, but sure enough, every year people in Ontario would say this is the year we're going to win two in a row, forgetting that the whole thing was probably staged.

In the zones, each sport was played recreationally by multiple teams and any resident could join. I played soccer in high school and my early twenties but was never very good.

At the Loon, the server approached Gerald and me. "Two beers and the chips and dip, please. I'll grab it," Gerald said, scanning his thumb on the server's order pad. Typically, we got credits for two beers a week, but Gerald had more because he was active in organizing zone sports and events. This was the Civic Administrators' way of encouraging people to participate in civic events. At all the bars in the zone, we had only one choice of beer and one choice of wine.

As we waited for our beers and snack, Gerald did most of the talking. "I'm organizing an ultimate Frisbee tournament and obstacle course relay. You should really come help out. It'll be fun! Lots of pretty ladies. Hey, who knows, maybe you'll get as lucky as I did," Gerald exclaimed, smacking me on the shoulder. I grinned, staring past him at all the other people in the Loon probably talking about similar things. The game had just started and the Loon was already completely full. Most of the other bars around were full as well. We were on the patio facing one of the larger hub parks. Vid screens were suspended strategically from poles around the patio. Inside, the Loon had two large floors with seating for hundreds. Our server brought us our beers and snack, quickly moving to the next table.

"You know the worst thing about living walking distance from the Hub?" Gerald didn't pause for me to guess. "I use up all my entertainment credits so quickly. That's why I have to organize so many events — to replenish the coffers."

I smiled and nodded while he kept talking. "I'm really excited for the baby. We're going to name it Toronto."

"Do you know if it's a boy or a girl?" I asked.

"No, but Toronto works either way."

Toronto was probably one of the most common baby names in the city. Gerald's partner, another Victoria, just less mean and homely, was three months pregnant.

After the game — I don't know who won — we parted ways, Gerald walking home while I waited for the tram. When I got home, I made dinner and went for a run. By the time I got back, it was nine thirty, so I read and went to bed. *Repeat tomorrow, minus the bar part. I need to think of some good excuses to avoid helping Gerald with events.*

At work on Friday, Gerald pestered me again to come to his ultimate Frisbee tournament, but I said I wasn't feeling well. I decided instead to go for a late-night run. I didn't go to the usual ravine near my apartment but instead took the tram to the adjacent quadrant, which had a large park on its eastern fringe. That was the night of my little rebellion, crossing the river and seeing the fire in the ruins. As I sat in my bed that night, heart racing with a giant grin on my face, I decided I would go again.

Saturday turned out to be cloudy and rainy. Perfect for sneaking back across the river. There wouldn't be many people out, and the ones that were would be at events at the Hub. I packed some snacks and water and put on my rain gear. I felt like one of the ancient explorers that we read about in school.

I followed the same trail and occasionally hid in the bushes, making sure no one else was around, then I crossed the river over the ruined bridge. After some time, I worked my way through the underbrush and trees up the hill to the abandoned streets. This time I went in some of the buildings, which, for the most part, had been taken over by plants and small rodents. Many of the roofs had collapsed. Each house I went in, I felt like I was invading something.

Many had framed pictures that had long ago fallen to the floor; some were heavily weathered, but in others I could make out happy families. Closets had clothes of all different colours and styles. Each home was different, but all had large kitchens with wooden cabinets and multiple bedrooms in many colours and designs. And bookshelves. So many bookshelves. Since many of the roofs had collapsed, most books were water damaged, but the occasional one was perfectly intact. Every book contained so many different stories — mysteries, adventures, dramas and thrillers. The variety exceeded anything I'd ever experienced. It seemed like such a waste. I wondered why the city hadn't made use of all these resources from the older parts of Toronto. Surely, they could use this stuff and repurpose it to meet the needs of the ration system.

Many of the people that used to live here probably still had relatives, or they themselves had lived across the river in one of the zones. Why did they just abandon all of this? Why couldn't they take these memories with them? The older generations in the city rarely spoke about the past. They were probably the most committed to preserving the tediousness of life in the city. I guess since I wasn't alive during the war and the climate chaos, I couldn't understand how things really were. But walking these empty streets, these homes and the memories in them, it seemed like it would have been so freeing. This part of Canada never saw any of the fighting and never suffered the worst effects of the climate chaos, so why change so much? Maybe that was why this was the no-go zone; it bred too many questions. And questions require answers.

Freethinking wasn't encouraged in the city. We were taught that the cleanliness, peace and order of our city was a gift. We survived the turmoil that destroyed the rest of the world because of this structure.

What good is peace and order without freedom of choice? Surely there's a way to allow freedom without resorting back to the greed, selfishness and inequalities that destroyed previous societies? With all these questions in my head, I was beginning to understand why I spent so much time alone. It seemed like everyone else in the city was perfectly content and happy with peace, order and monotony.

I found the street from the night before and decided to investigate the fire I'd seen. I didn't care anymore if it was the Civic Guardians. Maybe I could convince them I was interested in a new job. Maybe they would laugh. Civic Guardians existed in all the zones.

I found the remnants of a fire. There had been people here the previous night. Had it been Civic Guardians or were there people still living in these ruins? I couldn't control my excitement.

"Hello, is anyone there?" I shouted.

As soon as I did it, I ducked behind a car and started shaking and cursing myself. After what seemed like forever, I emerged from my hiding spot and moved on to another street that was different from all the others, wider with aged and fallen signs on all the buildings. Eventually I reached a massive structure with a huge concrete lot surrounding it. There were all sorts of signs. The massive structure was a few stories tall, extending into the distance. It had started to collapse in places, but I ventured into it and saw that it was full of stores and restaurants. Birds nested in areas where the ceiling had caved in. Parts of the roof used to be glass and had shattered, allowing easy access. Some stores had gates; others looked like they were picked clean. Squirrels, mice and rats scurried out of my way nearly everywhere. I even came across a family of racoons with a very angry mother that hissed at me.

I left the crumbling structure and continued walking on the wide street that must have been one of the hubs of old Toronto, except there were no transit points or large park pavilions that I could see, just empty buildings. Soon I came to a bridge. This one didn't cross a river or a ravine, but a huge roadway of multiple lanes. It ran as far as the eye could see. Near the corner where two large roads intersected was an opening with stairs leading underground. I decided to see what the old city built under there. In our city, the only thing underground was power, water and sewage lines and the one transit line that connected the zones. Travel between the zones was restricted to residents of Zone 1 and 2, unless you had a permit to go to Zone 2 for medical procedures.

At the bottom of the stairs was a large tiled room and a series of gates with a booth in the centre. The ceiling was slowly caving in. I jumped over one of the gates and headed toward another set of dark stairs. I pulled out a small flashlight I'd brought in my bag. As I descended into the darkness, the beam from my flashlight hit a long tunnel with tracks on each side of a platform. This must have been an old transit line. The tunnel was in worse shape than the room above. The tracks were partially flooded, and the tunnel walls were falling apart. I headed back up to the fresh air, not wanting to get trapped.

The rain was beginning to stop, and the clouds started to part, revealing blue skies. The foggy greyness that was my cover was dissipating. It was time to get back to the city. I'd been exploring for hours. I hurried back. If it was the Civic Guardians who had made that fire, then maybe they only patrolled at night.

I found the path by the hill I'd climbed earlier. The steep muddy trails and rain had left my footprints everywhere. They would know someone had been here. But even if they discovered the footprints, there was no way they could link them to me, unless there was hidden surveillance equipment. I stood at the river's edge, looking back toward the abandoned part of the city, realizing I could probably never go back. I started to tear up, wondering if there were still people living out there and what their lives were like. Then I looked across to our modern metropolis. Was it worth going back to? I could just leave and wander until I found something or someone. Unfortunately, I knew nothing about living in the wilderness or finding food. We were never taught survival skills. I didn't even know how long the human body could survive without water and food. Was I ready to disappear and most likely die just to explore somewhere new? Slowly and reluctantly, I crossed the river and returned home. Once again, Tyra entered our housing complex shortly after I did.

"Hi, Kelowna. What did you get up to on this rainy day?" she asked.

"Just went for a long hike in the ravines. You?" I asked to be polite.

"Most of the events at the Hub got rained out, so I just met some friends and went to a bowling alley. Going for a run tomorrow?" she asked as we were getting off the elevator on our floor.

"Maybe. If the weather is nice, but I'm pretty tired from today."

"Well, let me know if you do. Night." Tyra entered her apartment as I entered mine.

Sunday, I stayed in to avoid the temptation of heading east across the river.

Monday. Back to another week of work.

Gerald came in, almost skipping. "You missed a seriously great tournament. We managed to get it done, even with the rain on Saturday."

"I know; too bad. I spent the weekend in bed and am only starting to feel better now. Of course, I had to be sick on the weekend," I said, trying to cover my lie and mimic Gerald's cheeriness.

"Well, this weekend there's going to be a carnival with games and shows," said Gerald.

"Sounds good."

I wondered if he would buy the sick card two weekends in a row. Carnivals, to me, were worse than sporting events. All the noise, lights and people. Crowds made me anxious. Carnivals always had children running around screaming, "Mommy, Daddy, let's go on this ride … no, this one … wait let's play this game … Mommy, Daddy, can I have some cotton candy? … Mommy, Mommy, Mommy…" It was exhausting.

The week went by with the same amount of tedium and repetitiveness as every other week. That is, until Friday. It was late afternoon and I was finishing a spreadsheet from one of the transects when a message flashed on my screen for a few seconds. I barely had time to read it.

It said one thing: *We know what you did last weekend.*

My heart began racing again and I started sweating. It wasn't like the usual official notices through our intra-mail, which always used acronyms for events, or date and time stamps when a supervisor wanted to see someone. It was a black box with white text that flashed on the screen. Was that how the Civic Guardians operated? Who was I going to ask? It wasn't like I could have said, "Hey, Gerald, do you know what it means when a black box flashes on your screen, saying 'We know what you did last weekend'?" That seemed too cryptic and informal for the Civic Guardians. If they knew what I'd done, they would just show up at my office or home to take me away for violating the no-go zone. The "we" in that message must have meant something else. I couldn't stop thinking about possibilities. Maybe there really were people on the other side of the river. Maybe the Civic Administrators had special surveillance separate from the Civic Guardians who were always so official and by the book. Maybe I would just disappear one day.

As the thoughts in my head got more and more asinine, another message flashed: *Midnight tonight, ruined underground tunnel.*

What?

The "we" wanted me to go back there. I couldn't. Maybe they were going to drown me in that underground tunnel. Or I wouldn't even make it that far. Maybe this was a test to see how unconventional I really was. Or maybe...

"Ready to go?" said Gerald.

"What?" I said, jumping out of my seat.

"You okay?"

"Um, yeah. Sorry, having a weird daydream. Hey, have you ever had weird black boxes flash on your screen?" *Shit. Now I'd done it. Crazy moron.*

"No. Maybe there's something wrong with your computer. You should report it. Or, you're going nuts, judging by how much you're sweating."

"I'm not … um … I just…"

"Who cares? Let's go. Victoria's waiting." Gerald's partner, not our mean team lead.

I guess at lunch I'd agreed to go with Gerald and Victoria to the carnival. Gerald said Victoria was bringing a friend I may be interested in. I didn't have the guts to say I was sick again, or that according to the Civic Administrators, I was incompatible as a match. Not exactly a good pick-up line. We wandered around the carnival for a bit before choosing an outdoor restaurant for dinner. I used my credits, as Gerald and Victoria seemed to have used their monthly quota already. I think I occasionally was part of the dinner conversation and was introduced to Victoria's friend, even though I couldn't remember her name.

I couldn't stop thinking about the messages and what they meant. It was closing on 9:30 p.m. It would take at least forty minutes to get to the other side of the zone by tram and another hour to walk to the collapsed tunnel. That meant I needed to decide soon if I was going to go. I hadn't even been home yet. *Should I take supplies? How am I going to get out of "enjoying" this carnival?* Needing to lie made me nauseous.

Gerald punched me lightly on the arm. "Earth to Kelowna."

"Yeah."

"Are you okay?" asked Victoria's friend.

"What do you mean?" I said.

"Don't worry, gals. Kelowna here is the king of daydreaming," said Gerald. "I just wish I knew what he was daydreaming about."

"Do you want to go on the Ferris wheel?" asked Victoria's friend.

"Um, sure," I said.

On the Ferris wheel, Victoria's friend — *shit, what was her name?* — couldn't stop talking. She mainly talked about the poetry group she was in and the art group and the soccer team. She was a teacher, attractive and sweet, but teachers were the most dogmatic adherents to the words of the Civic Administrators. They meant well, but I just couldn't believe that teachers didn't encourage questions.

After the ride, I told them all that I had plans with my running group the next morning. Gerald knew I ran, so it was entirely feasible that this was true, and I felt especially proud of this lie. So proud, I didn't even feel nauseous. My recent rebellious actions must have been doing wonders for my weird neurosis. I thanked them all for a lovely evening and said we should do it again, to which Victoria's friend assented. *If I do it again, I must learn her name at least.*

I hurried to the tram that would take me to the eastern part of the zone. By the time I got there, it was already after 11:00 p.m. I hurried down the paths to the river, not even caring if anyone saw me. I bolted across the bridge, paranoid that if I didn't make it to the underground tunnel by midnight, the world would end. I ran so fast that even if the Civic Guardians were after me, they couldn't have caught me. It was dark, and I couldn't remember which side street I'd taken to get to the tunnel. Eventually I found the wide street with the massive structure with all the signs and the staircase that led underground. At this point I was a little more cautious. I tiptoed down the stairs. Everything was so dark. It must have been after midnight. Maybe they wouldn't wait. I could barely see on the first level at the bottom of the stairs but kept going, tripping over debris as I went. If there was anyone here, they had to have heard me by now. I saw a faint light at the bottom of the stairs and moved toward it very quietly. Upon reaching the bottom, I heard whispers. Peering around the corner, I saw two men and two women dressed in green. They were staring at me.

The taller of the two men stepped forward. "You're late," he said.

Thirteen
Paraiso, Colombia

It took time, but I finally decided to tell Senora Vasquez about the others. Instead of telling her directly, I wrote it down. She was sitting on the porch one evening, enjoying her tea, when I handed her the pages.

"Thank you. Would you like me to read them privately or with you here?" she asked.

"I'm going to read in my room and go to bed, so you can read it now if you'd like."

"Good night, Miguel."

As I left, Senora Vasquez began reading the pages:

After the death of José and the beating of that young boy, things as a water runner carried on as if normal. The slum was calm and at peace. Any gunfire was far off in the other parts of Bogotá.

Another young boy came. I kept my distance from him and the other water runners. Javier was gone and José dead. I didn't want to be friends with these boys.

Months passed with little change. I got bigger and stronger.

I would see the soldado that forced me to kill José sometimes and he would always call me Killer before laughing with the other soldados.

It was over a year before I was forced to kill again.

My abuela had thrown me a twelfth birthday party in the road around our home. There was a lot more food than normal. There was music and games. It was a lot of fun.

The next morning when I showed up at the compound, the soldado said, Happy birthday, Killer. We have a present for you. He grabbed me by the shoulder and took me into the compound. We went into one of the buildings and down some stairs. There were small rooms with metal bars full of dirty people who looked very weak. The soldado told me to pick one. I didn't understand. He demanded that I pick one. I pointed at an old bald man in the room in front of me. The soldado opened the gate and grabbed the man, dragging him upstairs.

The man had no shoes or shirt. I could see his ribs.

The soldado took the man to a corner of the compound where the walls were full of holes. He handed me a gun. The old man was sitting with his back to the wall, looking at the ground.

Happy birthday, the soldado said again, pointing at the old man.

I looked at the gun and the ground.

The soldado took another gun and pointed it at my head. Time to grow up, he said.

Five ... four ... three...

At three, I lifted the gun and shot the old man. I hit him in his stomach.

Again. Hit him in the head this time! the soldado shouted at me. Other soldados were now standing around us.

I shot again, hitting the old man in his chest. He fell to his side.

You missed his head. Get your buckets and get to work, the soldado said, taking the gun and pushing me.

I ran to the gate and took my buckets. The other boys were already coming down the hill. They didn't ask where I'd been, and I never told anyone about that day. After that, the soldado who called me Killer would talk to me almost daily. He would say I would be a man soon and should learn to shoot better. He would ask if I liked the gun or knife better.

A few times at the end of the day, he would grab me and take me to that corner of the compound and show me how to shoot. He would set up targets and tell me to hit them.

I never spoke to him but did what he told me to. It was months after the old man that he grabbed me in the morning and told me that I was no water runner that day. I thought that was it. I would be a soldado, like Javier. I should have run sooner. He took me to one of the houses with the girls near the compound and asked someone at the door something. A pretty girl much older than me came out. She talked to the soldado.

We walked away from the compound and up into the bad part of the slum. He kicked down the door of an ugly and dirty house. A woman screamed. He dragged her out of the house and gave me his gun.

The head this time, he said, moving my hand and the gun to her head. She was crying and saying she was sorry.

Five … four … three … two…

I pulled the trigger. The woman fell to the ground. Blood hit my face. I dropped the gun.

Good job. Don't be late for work tomorrow, he said and walked away. He just left her body there. No one else was around, or they were hiding inside. I walked slowly home to my abuela. When she saw me, she just shook her head and sang the same soft quiet song she always sang.

I thought Senora Vasquez would come see me once she read those pages, but she didn't. It was the next morning as we were eating breakfast that she spoke to me. "After shooting the woman. Is that when you decided to run away?"

"I didn't decide. It was my abuela who told me to leave."

"Tell me about that."

I knew I should tell Senora Vasquez everything. I knew I could trust her. Slowly the words came out. "The day after killing that woman, I came home from another day as a runner to my abuela and her younger brother sitting at a table with a map. My abuela said her brother was going to help me escape the city. I didn't want to leave her and Alejandra. I hadn't seen Alejandra in years. My abuela said she was too old and Alejandra was gone. I needed to leave the city before they made me do more bad things."

"I thought you never told your abuela what you did," Senora Vasquez said.

"She must have known. I came home twice covered in someone else's blood. Everyone knew what happened to boys once they reached a certain age."

Senora Vasquez nodded. "I'm sorry, go on."

"My abuela's brother said there were villages far to the east, away from the cities, that were safe. It would be a long and difficult walk. He told me the people there would be kind and have plenty of food. I asked how he knew this. He just told me it wouldn't be easy. He said the gangs controlled the outlying lands and anyone who tried to escape often didn't make it. My abuela said she wanted me to be free from the gangs. They explained the map to me and told me to travel only at night. My abuela's brother handed me a pack with food and water. I left later that night."

"You must have been so scared. But look, here you are. You've learned to read and write. You're an important member of this village. I'm so proud of you."

I didn't respond to that. I'd learned so much and felt safe in the village, but it was hard not to think about my abuela and Alejandra.

"My abuela's brother led me out of the slum up into the hills. In the middle of the night, he said goodbye and wished me luck, pointing out the path to follow. He told me to walk until the sun was coming up then find a place to hide. He said, remember the direction that the sun comes up and keep going that way. The path was difficult and hard to see in the dark. I didn't see anyone but moved as silently as possible. I was sure that if anyone spotted me, I would be dead. By the time the sun began to rise, I was deep in a forest following a narrow path. I found a thick area of plants along a cliff to spend the day. I realized that when I didn't show up to the compound, they would be looking for me. They would talk to my abuela and likely punish her. I almost turned around and ran back but wasn't sure I could find my way."

"She wanted you to escape. Going back would have meant becoming a soldado," Senora Vasquez said.

"I know. It's just…"

"Thank you for telling me, Miguel. That's enough for this morning. The sun is shining, and it is another beautiful day out. Help me clean up and then see to your chores in the village."

Fourteen
At the Farm outside Budapest

On Christmas morning, we all gathered around the fire with our gifts concealed in some way.

We started with Tibor and Orsi, who gave everyone wood carvings of a different animal. They did everything together, it only made sense that their gifts would be together. Their carvings were detailed and intricate and quite beautiful. They gave me an eagle, which Tonya explained was because they saw me as their saviour and hero, and that only an eagle accurately represented these traits. I was flattered and grateful.

Mattias had used scrap metal to make everyone a box for personal items. He loved working with old junk, reusing it and turning it into something else. Hannah had made everyone a different type of herbal soap. Tonya had written everyone a poem. Mine was about strength and the will to endure through loss. I actually teared up, and Tonya said that today wasn't a day for tears. And we should be happy that we have each other.

Lukas had traded in town for an old Polaroid camera that still had film and had taken pictures of different natural scenes around the farm. Mine showed the oldest tree on the lot, which stood alone at the top of one of the hills, a beautiful and gnarled tree that looked even older in black and white.

That left me, since Judit and Zsolti's gift would be tonight's dinner.

I started with Tibor and Orsi, who shared a room, so were fine with the one drawing. Mattias and Hannah loved theirs and both hugged me. Judit and Zsolti said theirs would be framed and put above their bed. Lukas teared up when I gave him his and hugged me for an eternity, saying he was glad that he had something to commemorate the success of saving the colt. That left Tonya. Everyone else was busy staring at their drawings while Tonya fidgeted. "Come on, Elliott. I want to see mine."

I took a big gulp and handed it to her, looking away as I did. I didn't see her reaction, but suddenly her arms were around me and she kissed me on the cheek, whispering in my ear, "Thank you."

After the gift exchange, everyone went about their daily chores as Judit and Zsolti prepared dinner. There was no such thing as a holiday on a farm. The animals needed to be fed, wood needed to be chopped, water gathered from the well, and various other tasks had to be completed to ensure our comfort and survival. Everyone was joyful and went about their tasks with a skip in their step. I covered for Judit and Zsolti but finished those tasks and decided to join Tonya in the chicken coops.

"Sorry I'm late," I said, walking in. "Did you get everything..." I stopped when I saw her huddled on the ground, sobbing, with one of the chickens in her arms.

She put the chicken down and wiped her face with her sleeves, springing to her feet. "Yes, everything is taken care of. You're off the hook."

"Are you okay?"

"Oh yes, just a little dust in my eye," she responded, a little too happily. As she walked by, I grabbed her arm, spun her around and kissed her. She recoiled. "Elliott, I'm sorry. I'm with Lukas."

I wanted to throw myself into the Danube. How had I been so blind? Of course she was with Lukas. They were always flirting and sitting cuddled together. I just stood there not knowing what to say.

"It's okay. I'm flattered. You must miss Anna, and this time of year is hard without the people we love."

It had only been a couple of months, and I was acting as if with all certainty I knew Anna wasn't coming back. Tonya hugged me and said, "I'm sure she's alive. We'll find her."

We walked back to the house together. I was embarrassed, ashamed and felt nothing but guilt. I had tried to use Tonya to fill the void of missing Anna.

Christmas dinner was wonderful. Judit and Zsolti had outdone themselves. I couldn't remember the last time I'd eaten so well. Unfortunately, I didn't truly enjoy it. I ate in silence while everyone else told stories of happy memories. Occasionally, out of the corner of my eye, I would see Tonya staring at me with pity in her eyes. Lukas would now and then put his arm around her and kiss her on the cheek. As the meal was completed and dessert had, Tonya stood to recite a poem about togetherness and friends unlooked for, after which everyone clapped and hugged each other. I followed suit reluctantly, still feeling uncomfortable around Tonya.

The next morning, I woke up and packed my things. I called everyone together in the living room.

"I'm leaving," I said. They all look confused.

"To go where?" Tonya asked.

"I have to try to find Anna and my father."

Everyone started shouting that I was crazy, where would I start, how would I not just end up in jail or worse?

Tonya stood to quiet them down. "I don't know if I believe in fate or destiny, but I believe Elliott is right. His father and Anna are alive. Good luck, and you know where to come when you find them. Hurry back." She hugged me and whispered goodbye.

I thanked them all and walked out the door, uncertain where to go next. For the first time in my life, I felt like one of the Valiant, though I suspected the Valiant spent less time questioning their choices and simply acted without consideration for their own well-being.

I had no idea where to start in my quest to find Anna and my father, so I simply headed back to Budapest. The only people I knew in the city had disappeared the last time I was there, and the old grandma had moved to her sister's, and I had no idea where that was.

I had two thoughts: Try to find members of the United Earth movement who still may be in the city, or get arrested in the hopes that I end up where Anna and my father are.

The first option was problematic in that most of the remaining members likely had been arrested or killed, or had left the city. Also, I hadn't bothered to help in the search of other safe houses after the protest, so I had no idea where they were located.

The other option was worse, since getting arrested could very well mean getting killed, and there was no guarantee that I would end up in the same place as my father or Anna. In all likelihood, I would spend the rest of what I suspected would be a short life in some shithole without any possibility of seeing my father or Anna again.

I'd left the farm and headed toward the city so proud that I was being brave that I didn't think to ask any of them about who I should contact or where I should go.

I decided to go to Viktor's farm and talk to Tomas and Gabor about other safe houses or where known members of the United Earth movement may be.

I arrived at the farm and was greeted warmly by Viktor. I lied, saying I'd come to check on the boys and was heading to the city to inquire about more labourers and possibly set up trades. Viktor offered me tea and some snacks. It was quiet on his farm. He asked a young woman to go and get Gabor. In the meantime, Viktor and I discussed the winter thus far and each other's Christmases. The young woman returned shortly with Gabor. Viktor explained that Gabor didn't speak German or English.

"Tomas went back to the city about a month ago to check on his grandma and never returned." Viktor said.

"Does Gabor know where in the city Tomas might be?" I asked.

After Viktor translated, Gabor shook his head. I pulled out a map of Budapest. "Can you ask Gabor if he can mark any United Earth safe houses?"

Gabor leaned over the map, marking four different locations.

"Thank you, Gabor, Viktor," I said.

Viktor gave me a loaf of bread and invited me to return on my way back.

It was late afternoon already, but I wanted to continue on. Viktor had tried to convince me to spend the night, but I knew I had to keep going, otherwise I risked second-guessing myself. I would sleep outside in the cold if I had to. I was wearing the warmest clothes I had and was quite comfortable. Winters in Hungary were no longer what they used to be.

The next morning, I continued on my way, using the main road into Budapest. I could see the city in the distance. No one so much as glanced at me as I passed through the small suburbs on the outskirts of the city. Everyone I passed was haggard and thin, with downcast eyes. I wondered what kept people going in such conditions. It seemed to be a world full of the Reconciled. The Fatalists and the Valiant were all pretty much dead. The Depraved were the ones who had luxuries or positions of authority. The Reconciled were too timid or cowardly to simply end it. That was me for much of my life.

The Reconciled were the ones who'd let the world reach this state. I hated them, wanted to grab them and shake the life out of them. It wasn't a fair perspective, considering I was just like them. Anna used to always tell me, hate is pointless. It was the reason the world was so screwed up. People weren't born to hate, they were taught to. The thought that she may be hurt, imprisoned or enslaved somewhere, losing that hope, optimism and positivity that I found so sweet and compelling, spurred me on. I had to find her. I couldn't fail her.

It was midday when I reached the city. I walked a little more cautiously now. If any patrols found me wandering the streets in the middle of the day, it would arouse questions. I should be at work. Farmers with goods to trade came on the weekend. Plus, I didn't have a cart of goods. I should have planned my heroics a little better. Luckily, the streets were deserted. The first location on the map that

Gabor had marked wasn't that far. The windows and door were boarded up from the outside, as were most of the other flats along this block. Not a good sign. I had no choice but to continue to the second location. I used alleys and narrow side streets to reach it.

The second location looked like someone lived there but was of course empty at this time of day. The windows were dirty, the furniture sparse. I cautiously knocked on the door, not expecting a response. I held my breath with my ear pressed against the door to hear any sound. Nothing. I had to decide whether to wait until the workday was over or move to one of the other locations. If the residents of this location came home, I would have to ask them if they were members of the movement. It wasn't like there was some secret handshake. If they weren't members, they could report me, and this endeavour would be for naught. The other two locations were closer to the centre of the city, about six blocks apart. The neighbourhood was the same one where I'd sought shelter the day my family disappeared. Yet I didn't think the movement would be foolish enough to remain in an area where they'd been discovered. If they were smart, they would have lain low, moved throughout the city and regrouped after some time.

The end of the workday came. I waited around the corner from the second location in a narrow alley, so I had a clear line of sight to the door. The streets were busier now with people returning to their homes. The first to enter the flat was a middle-aged woman, who was one of the numerous factory workers, dressed in the same bland grey. About twenty minutes later, another woman entered the flat. The streets were starting to seem deserted again. I inhaled deeply, ready to test my fate. I knocked on the door. The first woman answered, opening the door only slightly. I asked her in Hungarian if she spoke English. She shook her head, asking, "What do you want?"

I knew enough Hungarian to provide broken responses. Except, I didn't know how to answer *that* question. Instead, I pulled out the map and showed her the symbol of the United Earth movement. She looked at it, confused. The other woman came to the door, opening it more. They spoke to each other in hushed voices. The second woman looked at the symbol and then at me.

"Go away. We can't help you." She slammed the door.

I had no choice but to continue on. It would be dark soon and guards would be patrolling the streets to enforce curfew. I had to move quickly and invisibly. It took a couple of hours, but I made it to the third location, a large building. Gabor had written a flat number on the map. I tried the main door to the building, and to my surprise, it was unlocked. The flat was on the fourth floor. The walls were grimy with peeling plaster, the carpet torn up in places. The hallway lights flickered. I reached number 409. There was a soft glow of light coming through the bottom of the door and voices inside. I knocked.

To my relief and joy, Tomas answered. Quickly recognizing me, he pulled me into the flat and closed the door. I was in a small living room with a kitchenette to the side. There was a dingy couch and three hard wooden chairs. Tomas's grandmother, who looked about ten years older than the last time I'd seen her, was sitting in one of the chairs. She smiled and beckoned me over. I reached down to hug her. The two other people in the room looked at me warily. One was a young man, possibly a few years older than Tomas, with a dark and bushy beard. The other was a middle-aged woman with tattoos covering her arms. Tomas explained who I was. He and the others were speaking so quickly in Hungarian that I soon got lost in what they were saying.

Tomas's grandmother seemed to have fallen asleep in the short time since I'd hugged her. She was shrunken and looked as if her health was failing. The tattooed woman on the couch spoke to me in English. "Tomas has explained who you are and what you did for some of our people. Thank you. But why have you come back? It's not safe."

"I know, but I need to find my wife and father."

"Are our people safe?" she asked. "Tomas said he and Gabor were left at a different farm."

"They're safe. Tomas knows how to get to Gabor. From there I can explain how to find the others."

"Unfortunately, we can't do that. We all have jobs in the city, including Tomas now. The authorities have cracked down on labour. Too many people were leaving. They've even started raiding villages and farms looking for people who abandoned their positions. All we would do is potentially lead the authorities to them."

The tattooed woman explained to the others what we were discussing.

"Do you all live here together?" I asked.

"Yes. The authorities have emptied entire sections of the city and crammed people together into districts that they can monitor better. They claim it's to better distribute resources and provide power and water. Both of those things are out frequently enough. But we're lucky. We normally have running water."

I asked the tattooed woman why Tomas had stayed and gotten a job. She explained that he wanted to be close to his grandmother, who had raised him.

The bearded man in the flat had begun to make food in large pots on a tiny stovetop. Tomas helped his grandmother to bed while the tattooed woman and I continued to talk.

"Do you know where members of the movement that are arrested are taken?" I asked.

"Some are killed, but some are taken to the Front as labourers. Prisoners are used to mine materials, construct defences, grow food, anything really."

"How do you know all of this?"

"There's a guard in this district. Tomas grew up with him. He gave us some information. Most of the guards are good people that are in their position because they were forced to and are treated better than everyone else. I'll ask Tomas to find his friend."

After dinner, Tomas left the flat. It was near midnight when he returned. The tattooed woman explained that according to the guard, all prisoners from Budapest were transferred to Kyiv in the former Ukraine. From there, they were processed and taken to labour camps along the Front, which was formed by the Dnieper River.

"I'm sorry, but there's no guarantee you'd be put at a camp anywhere near your wife or father. Once people are taken prisoner, their identities are essentially erased. The authorities don't even bother to keep records of who goes where. Anyone who tries to escape is killed."

I collapsed on the couch.

"Go back to the farm. Your family would want you to be safe and happy."

I looked at the tattooed woman and Tomas. There was a spark in their eyes. They didn't have the same defeated look of the people I'd passed on the road into the city. They still believed the world would become a better place. But for me, the only way that could happen was if I tried to find the people who made me happy, regardless of the consequences. I spent the night on the couch preparing for my eventual prison sentence of hard labour.

Fifteen
South of Bangalore

It was the middle of the night and I awoke to screams. I rushed out of my hut to find people running about and several of the huts on fire. Women were grabbing children and running off into the jungle. Some people were carrying torches that they threw against some of the huts. I couldn't comprehend what was happening. I was about to yell at them when someone grabbed me from behind, locking my arms behind me and covering my mouth. They pulled me to behind my hut near the trees and spun me around. It was Amar.

"Be quiet and follow me."

"What's happening?" I whispered.

"Shush, we have to hurry."

Amar crouched and moved quickly toward the creek. Near the village centre I could see men fighting. There were bodies around as well. I began to weep and shudder. Amar grabbed me again and told me not to look. We stopped near some bushes. Amar, close to the ground, crept out a little farther into the field near the creek.

He motioned to me and whispered in my ear, "Run across the creek and down the hill until you reach the temple. Don't stop or talk to anyone. I'll follow."

"What's going on? I'm scared."

"I know. I am too. But you must be brave and hurry. It'll take most of the night to reach the temple. Go!"

I stumbled but did as directed, with Amar close behind. We were almost at the creek when two men came from out of the field, one grabbing me, another darting for Amar, who now had a large stick in his hand, which he swung, knocking one man to the ground. The other kicked me to the ground, pulled out a knife and headed for Amar.

"Run!" Amar screamed.

I didn't think but just got up and rushed into the night. I briefly looked back to see Amar battling the man with the knife while other people seemed to be running toward him. I ran and ran and ran.

I made it to the bottom of the hill and found the way that Amar had spoken of. I crouched and waited, but I couldn't see anyone, so I darted across to the brush on the other side and slowly began following the road. Soon I could hear and faintly see the outlines of about a dozen men. They were heading up the hill, armed with spears and other sharp weapons, which shone in the moonlight. I stumbled through the brush, with the road to my left, delirious and lost. Alone again. Why had I left Amar? I failed him, just like I failed Jahi and Randhir. Maybe he was all right. Maybe the other people I saw running toward him were villagers going to help. If I made it to the temple, maybe others from the village would arrive tomorrow. I couldn't despair or give up.

As the sun was beginning to rise, I reached the town and saw the temple about a kilometre off. The town was orderly and well kept with low-rise buildings packed tightly together. The pyramid-like temple protruded above everything else. People were out and about, but none looked at me or bothered with me. I approached the temple's metal gates, which were guarded. I said I was from the village up the hill, which was attacked, and was told to come here. The guard didn't understand me, but another ran off to get someone. A short time later, a middle-aged man with orange robes and a long beard came out with the guard. He spoke English.

"What's your name and where did you come from?" he asked.

"My name is Aashi, and I came from the village up the hill that was attacked in the night. I've been running all night. Amar told me to come here. Has anyone else from the village come here?"

"Yes, a few. Come with me. We'll get you some water and food, and then you'll need to rest."

The man led me to a large concrete courtyard between some of the towers of the temple. The monks had set up some tents. There were other people from the village there, mainly women and children. They couldn't have arrived much before me. They were all crying. The monks were doing their best to console them and feed them. The monk who spoke English led me to a cot in the shade. He passed me some water and a bowl of fruit. "Here, eat and drink. I'll check on you later."

I did as he said and must have slept half the day. When I woke up, there were dozens of the villagers around. More were coming in. Some were wounded. There were only two or three men, and these were carrying an elderly woman on a bed. When they reached the inner part of the courtyard, they gently placed the woman down and then collapsed on the pavement themselves.

The English-speaking monk saw that I was awake and came over to me. "Feeling rested?"

"Yes, thank you." I stood, stretching. "What happened? Is Amar here?" I asked.

"There's no one here by that name. The village was attacked by bandits that roam the countryside, taking what they want from whomever they want, killing indiscriminately. Up until now, they haven't come to this area because of the protection the town offers, but they must have already ravaged the surrounding area. We had no warning. I'm sorry, Aashi. How did you come to live among the villagers?"

"I arrived about a week ago from Bangalore. I thought things were better in the south." I began to cry softly, barely able to keep my head up.

"If you're hungry, there's food in the tent over there," the monk said, pointing to the largest tent by the temple entrance. I lay down and curled up to one side, crying myself slowly to sleep again.

I didn't wake up until the next day. There were about fifty villagers in the courtyard and several more of the men from the village. They were with some of the guards talking to the monks. I was hungry and headed to the food tent, where I grabbed some dosa, curried lentils and some water before returning to the shaded cot on the other side of the courtyard.

The English-speaking monk approached me. "Everyone that has survived the attack is here now. I'm sorry, your friend must have passed. Very few of the men survived. The guards we sent managed to kill or capture all the bandits. There were about forty of them. Most of the village is destroyed. Those that have survived will shelter in the town and can work in the fields around the town."

"What about me?" I asked.

"There are a few other people here that speak English. In time you'll learn the local language. The temple is for monks only."

"I don't know anyone in the town." I stared at the monk with a dejected look on my face. There was pity in his eyes. Then I remembered one of my last conversations with Amar. "Amar spoke of organizations on the coast trying to make things better. Is it true?"

"Perhaps. We don't really know. There's a large island southeast of here. We've heard rumours that there might be a group of people there with technology and connections to the outside world. Some of our monks have gone off to see if it's true. None have returned. The journey to the coast is dangerous."

"I have to try. I've already lost everything twice. All I have to live for now is to try."

"There's one of the guards," the monk said, pointing to a young man who looked about twenty years old. "His brother went off a few months ago to the coast. He speaks English. He's been planning to leave as well. I'll see if he'll let you accompany him."

The next morning, the young guard approached me and threw a large bag before my feet. He said one thing: "Let's go."

The young guard was tall and muscular, but sullen. He looked very much like a more stoic version of Randhir. That familiarity led me to follow him. He moved at a quick pace and I had to double my pace to keep up. He carried a large staff, taller than he was, made of a dark, finely carved wood. There was a shiny metal spike at the end. I had no doubt this was an effective weapon that he knew how to use. The bag he'd given me was heavy and it wasn't long before I was sore. We were heading through farmers' fields. By midday I was exhausted.

The young guard stopped and rested under a large tree on the side of a narrow path through the fields. He was eating and drinking water, seemingly unfazed by how difficult it was for me to keep his pace. "You'll need to strengthen up if you're going to survive," he mumbled.

I threw my bag down and stared at him. "I'm half your size and this bag weighs as much as me."

He took a bite out of the red fruit he was eating. "You have a few days to get stronger; otherwise there's no telling what will happen to you."

"You don't scare me. I've seen terrible things and survived."

"I'm not trying to scare you. It isn't pleasant where we're going. A young, thin girl like you will be taken as a slave or worse. Open that bag. People will kill us for what we're carrying."

I opened the bag. In addition to some extra clothes, food and water, there were bags of metallic squares and gadgets I'd never seen before. There were also several guns.

"What's all this?"

"Our passage to Sri Lanka. Those are microchips, computers and satellite phones. In high demand there. The guns are for our protection. We need to find a boat to take us across the sea. But the ruined city we're headed to is full of murderous, sick and hopeless people."

"Then why are we going that way?"

"The Ponnaiyar River to the south leads down to the ocean. At its mouth is Cuddalore, a ruined city ravaged by war and rising seas. There are many boats there. It's more dangerous to travel farther south. We have friends in Cuddalore. People who have been to Sri Lanka and can help us get there, but we have to be careful."

"The monk said none of the people the temple sent have returned."

"True, but would you if you found paradise? Hurry up and eat something, we need to keep moving. You're called Aashi, yes?"

I nodded.

"I'm Visshaly."

While I ate some food, Visshaly transferred some of the items from my bag to his. He pulled out two guns and handed me one. "I'll show you how to load and use it." Visshaly sat on the ground beside me, demonstrating how to put the bullets into the handgun and disengage the safety.

"This could be the difference between life and death. For now, I'll keep the guns, but if I give you one, be careful and remember what I've shown you." He smirked at me and I nodded. He got up, securing one of the guns to his waist.

I had eaten plenty, and I drank my fill and felt refreshed. My pack was significantly lighter. Visshaly disappeared but returned with a rough-hewn staff about my height. He handed it to me.

"Thank you."

He nodded, turning to collect his now considerably heavier pack. He hoisted it with ease. We followed a wide road through a flat landscape of overgrown fields and patches of trees. Visshaly occasionally paused, crouching or moving off to the bushes that crowded the side of the road, motioning for me to do likewise. We'd yet to encounter another person, but Visshaly seemed alert and anxious as we went. Sweat drenched his forehead and shirt. I was sweating heavily as well in the midday heat. The road had the remains of burnt-out cars and carts. We passed the occasional ruined hut or small village. The countryside here lacked the beauty of the villages in the hills and the tranquility and abundance of the jungle I'd left behind.

The sun had begun to set and Visshaly's pace quickened as he scanned the horizon for something. Ahead and to the right was a small green lake surrounded by dense trees and brush. We headed in that direction. Visshaly laid his bag down near a hut with a collapsed roof. He motioned for me to remain hidden, then darted through the overgrowth to the side of the lake. It was quiet.

After some time, Visshaly returned. "We'll rest in the trees by the lake tonight. I found a good spot to hide."

He collected his bag and walked in the direction of the lake. He pulled out some rope and flung one end over the branch of a large tree overhanging the putrid green lake. He tied the other end to both of our bags and began to heave them up into the canopy of the tree.

"Climb up to the bags and pull them so they rest on some of the branches."

I looked at him in disbelief, but he was staring up at the bags, his muscles tense from holding them up by the rope below.

I walked toward the thick trunk, trying to surmise how I was going to get up there. The lowest branch was at least twice my height. The tree's width far exceeded the span of my arms.

As I stared up at the branches, trying to solve this problem, I was suddenly lifted from the ground by the waist. Visshaly had tied the other end of the rope to another tree holding the bags in place. He hoisted me up on his shoulders. I reached the lowest branch, slowly and awkwardly pulling myself up. I climbed, fully aware of each creak and sway under my weight. The branches were thickest midway up the tree, where our supplies were dangling. I crawled out along the branch and reached the bags. I could see the outline of Visshaly far below through the leaves. I could barely lift one of the bags let alone two, unsure how I was supposed to get them between the branches. I tried lifting the two heavy bundles by the handles where they were tied to the rope, but with one arm pulling them and the other holding the branch, they barely moved. Straddling the branch, I sat upright and again tried to lift them. Nothing.

I shouted down, "I can't lift them."

Visshaly began lowering the bags to the ground. I sat there ashamed and unsure what to do. The rope began moving again, this time with only one bag. It was still too heavy to lift up while trying to stay upright and perched on the tree. I feared that if I failed again, Visshaly would abandon me. There was another large branch just opposite the one the bag was suspended from. I swung my legs out, reaching across with my dangling feet. Propped against the two branches, the bag was directly below me. Lying with my chest against the first branch and my legs against the other, I reached with both arms for the bag, pulling with everything I had. My back was tense and shaking, my knees buckling. Swinging the bag, I managed to nudge it in a narrow gap between the two branches. I shuffled closer to the trunk and pulled myself back across the gap to the first branch. I untied the bag and secured it in place. I threw one end of the rope back down to the ground, feeling victorious.

The other bag soon came up as well and I repeated my previous feat. With both bags safely propped up in the tree, I pulled the rope up as Visshaly climbed the tree. I rested against a higher branch with my back against the trunk. My knees were bruised, my back spasming and my arms lifeless, but I'd proven myself.

Visshaly congratulated me and secured the bags to the tree with the rope.

"Why do you think we pulled the bags up here?"

"To hide them and keep them close to us."

"Perhaps you do have what it takes to survive." Visshaly said this with a smile, turning back to the bags to get some food and water.

I found a spot to nestle myself safely in the tree without the fear of falling. Visshaly was out cold with his back propped against the bags, a rope secure around his waist. The night brought sporadic sleep. I'd always been a restless sleeper. Growing up the way I did, I learned to be a light sleeper and constantly alert. Any moment could have brought scavengers or worse. The village in the hills was the only place I had uninterrupted sleep and felt safe. And even that had been an illusion. The night in the tree brought no surprises. All I could hear were insects, birds and the occasional rustling in the undergrowth.

I awoke to Visshaly nudging me as the sun rose on the horizon. He lowered the bags to the ground and scrambled down the tree. I followed cautiously.

As he prepared some food, I stood nervously behind. "Can I … help?"

"It's almost done."

"Do you…"

"Pardon?" He turned around facing me.

"Never mind. Sorry." I felt safe with Visshaly, but he was still intimidating.

After the morning meal, we continued following the road. It was even hotter than the day before and it wasn't long before I was dripping sweat, constantly drinking water to replenish what I was losing. At midday, we found some shelter in a small grove of trees near an abandoned farm. As the day progressed, we veered farther and farther from the road, darting from point to point. I asked Visshaly if we were close to the river and city.

"No, but from here on we have to be even more careful, stay off the road and avoid contact with others."

By late afternoon, a wide muddy river came into view.

"That's the Ponnaiyar River that will take us to the coast and city. We'll turn east here and keep it on our right. There are many villages and towns along the river still, but I doubt they're friendly to outsiders."

We continued for a couple of hours past sunset. Far to our right where the dark river flowed, the twinkling blaze of countless fires erupted. I wondered if the people by the river were friendly or cruel. Were they just trying to survive like us? Or were they murderers and thieves?

We made camp in a small abandoned village. The area around us was somewhat tended still, but not as much as closer to the river. Visshaly wanted one of us awake at all times and I drew the first watch. It was quiet. The air was still, and even the insects seemed to have disappeared. It was eerie. Halfway through the night, I woke a groggy Visshaly and took my turn to rest.

Again, Visshaly woke me at sunrise. My body was sore, my head hurt and I was beyond tired. I could tell Visshaly was tired and sore as well but determined to continue on. After a small and meagre morning meal, we left the safety of the hut we'd camped in for the night. Turning the corner around an old animal fence, we came face to face with a man and his son or grandson. Visshaly reacted quickly by pointing his staff at them with his left hand while his right grabbed the gun at his waist. The withered man looked from Visshaly to me, putting his hands on the young boy's shoulders, pulling him behind him. They had simple farming tools with them and a bag full of vegetables. The man put his hands up as a gesture of peace, bowing his head in deference as they backed away. Not a word was exchanged, but Visshaly kept a laser-like focus on them as they slowly retreated.

Visshaly told me to get behind the wall while he scouted out the area. He came back in a hurry, motioning for me to follow and be quick. His pace was relentless as we sprinted through fields heading farther and farther from the river. Visshaly was alert, occasionally stopping and craning his neck to survey the area while he waited for me to catch up. After some time, his pace slowed as our surroundings became more forested and tended fields became scarcer. Midday came and went without a break or meal. Though his pace had slowed, my legs were weak, my shoulders slumped, and each step was a challenge. Visshaly was slumped over as well but seemed to operate on sheer determination. It was late afternoon before we finally stopped, the river now gone from sight somewhere off to the right. We were in a heavily forested and grassy area with no signs of villages or huts.

"We'll camp here for the night. I don't want to get too close to the outskirts of the city at nightfall. We'll have to hurry tomorrow to reach the city and find somewhere safe before sunset," Visshaly said.

I was relieved. It was late afternoon, which meant a good rest. I stretched my weary muscles and found a cool stream to wash in. We ate our largest meal yet and relaxed in the grass under a tree. We were on a hill that had a commanding view of the surrounding area. Visshaly napped while I lay on my back, watching the motion of the white clouds as the sky turned a brilliant orange with the setting sun. We both must have been tired since we set no watch, but the night passed without incident. Visshaly was up ready to go before sunrise and I awoke to him messing about.

"I want to get moving so we come to the city by midafternoon. We'll have to get close to the river again. This will be the most dangerous part." Visshaly handed me a gun, telling me to keep it close and hidden. He concealed his own in his waistband under his shirt. We had a quick bite to eat and were off, stumbling in the darkness toward the warm glow of campfires in the distance. By the time the sun rose, we were in well-tended fields on the outskirts of more sizeable villages with the muddy brown river to our right.

It wasn't a happy place. The fields were crops of colourless grain, the villages dull greys and browns. The river a meandering brown ooze. The people we saw had bent backs and sad faces, barely lifting their heads as we passed. Visshaly kept a firm grip on his staff with his other hand close to the concealed gun. The river soon widened, and more worn and ruined roads appeared with larger concentrations of buildings.

The smell hit us first.

Decay and death. It reminded me of Bangalore. My heart beat faster out of fear and sadness. We ate while we walked, avoiding close contact with people, which became more and more difficult. People sat on the steps of crumbling shacks pieced together by whatever refuse they could find, eyes bulging from their skeletal skulls. I could tell they were assessing their chance of robbing us. Visshaly now kept me very close and moved with a cautious purpose.

The narrow and congested streets, littered with debris and mud, were partially flooded in some places. The separation between land and water became more confused. The river seemed to be slowly swallowing the crumbling city. What little greenery there was hopelessly clung to life. Stray dogs and emaciated children fought for scraps or scavenged through the piles of garbage. Steam rose from the ever-widening pools of putrid and stagnant water.

We came to a point where the ocean and river converged, where entire portions of the city had been swallowed. In some places, only rooftops were visible, with makeshift shacks built on top. In other places, buildings simply rose out of the water. Small rowboats darted about to floating docks, which had been assembled throughout the labyrinth of canals. Along the last raised bit of land was a marketplace of sorts, consisting of foods from the land and sea. The docks bobbing in the nearby waters were filled with all sorts of supposedly seaworthy machines, many of which belched black smoke. The powered boats were larger and uglier and guarded by armed, mean-looking men; the smaller wooden rowboats rowed by defeated and expressionless souls.

Bangalore was a depressing place, but this was worse. The filth, smell and cacophony of motors, yelling and creaking buildings were an assault to the senses, but the people were truly terrifying. In a busier part of the market, men were bidding on young naked girls, others were bidding on muscular tattooed men. Weaselly youngsters darted through the crowds, looking to swipe whatever they could. Along the docks near one of the larger boats, a fight broke out that ended with two men having their throats slit and their bodies thrown into the water. Visshaly's hands were shaking, but he looked well fed and strong compared to many of the people. I stayed as close to him as possible, practically hooked to his side.

We came to a small fruit stand with a little old lady, which seemed so out of place for this market of depravity. Visshaly began speaking to her in hushed tones while I watched the chaos around us. The woman pointed to a green rowboat in which sat a young man around the same age and size as Visshaly. Visshaly thanked her, and as we walked toward the green boat, he pointed to a symbol carved into the dark wood on the side of her stall — a blue globe with a green tree growing from its top. "Look for these symbols if anything should happen."

At the boat, Visshaly handed the young man a small package from his bag and motioned for us to get into the boat. We navigated through channels of crumbling buildings with sickly looking people hanging out the windows. The water was a thick brown sludge with all matter of debris floating in it. The buildings became fewer and fewer with just the occasional rooftop poking out.

Out here, larger boats were anchored to the sea floor. Most of them were rusted with peeling paint but seemed to house a great number of people. We headed for a large, grey boat that was well maintained. It had a sleek, narrow profile but rose high above the water and was the longest, largest and most intimidating one around.

"That boat used to be part of the Indian Navy but is now controlled by us," our boat operator said. "When the government collapsed many years ago, different factions sought control of the various assets. It took years, but our group now controls a formidable arsenal and large parts of Sri Lanka." It was the first time he'd spoken. He held his head up high with a sort of pride at his exclamation. Compared to the people in the decaying city, he was clean and well fed. I wondered what led him to such fortune while countless others suffered in squalor. If this group he was a part of was so well resourced, why weren't they helping others? I held my tongue as Visshaly looked on in awe of the grey behemoth rising in front of us.

We pulled alongside it, a miniature toy next to a giant. A rope ladder was lowered from the deck towering above our heads. Other ropes with hooks were lowered to lift the bags up to the deck. The boat operator climbed up first. Visshaly told me to follow. Steadying myself on the ladder was challenging, but I was determined not to be a burden and to prove my worth. Visshaly climbed with ease in a quarter of the time it took me.

The boat operator was talking to a small group of people of many different skin colours. He shook the hand of an older man with dark hair and fair skin and returned to his little rowboat. The small group came over to Visshaly and me.

"Welcome aboard the Salvation," the dark-haired man said, reaching out to shake our hands. He was shorter than the others and spoke with a strange accent. I'd never seen people like these before. "My name is Yuki, from the island of Kyushu far to the east of here. This is Ahmad from the Malay Peninsula, Shani from Sri Lanka and Denise from Australia."

Visshaly and I introduced ourselves. Ahmad was slightly taller than Yuki, with similar features but a darker skin tone. Shani had long, beautiful, black hair with dark-brown skin and piercing dark eyes. Denise had short, golden hair, bright blue eyes and the lightest skin I'd ever seen.

"You must have many questions and there will be time for that. For now, you're in need of food, rest and a warm bath from your long journey," Yuki said.

With that, Shani escorted us below deck to our own cabins. They were cozy, with clean mattresses, linens and pillows. She showed us where to shower and where to get food. We ate first from a buffet of all types of fruits, vegetables, soups, breads and rice. It reminded me of the meals in the village. I had had no time to process what had happened or to grieve for Amar. I could feel tears welling in my eyes, but I didn't want to show any weakness in front of Visshaly. I didn't know how long it had been since I'd lost Jahi and Randhir, found and lost Amar. I felt like I was stuck on a path I had no control over.

As we were finishing eating, Shani returned with a bag for each of us. Inside were clean clothes for several days and new shoes. "If anything doesn't fit, please let me know and we can see what else we can find. You'll find towels and soap in your cabins if you'd like to clean up. After that, we suggest you rest. Tomorrow morning, we return to Sri Lanka and we can talk on the journey."

For the first time in my life, I had a hot shower with clean water. The water in the village had been clean but cool, and there were no pipes there that made it pour like rain upon your head. I scrubbed my dry, dusty skin in the running water. The soaps were luxurious and foaming with a variety of intoxicating scents. I don't know how long I spent showering, but I felt rejuvenated and, for the first time in my life, completely clean. The clothes that Shani provided were slightly big on me but comfortable. I went to bed as instructed and drifted off into a deep sleep.

Sixteen
Ontario

I stood on the platform of the tunnel staring at the two men and two women dressed in green. "Who are you? How did you contact me?"

The two men and two women each had illuminated headlamps now brightening the tunnel. The one who said I was late had a shaved head, very broad shoulders and was one of the tallest people I'd ever seen.

"We know who you are, Kelowna. Follow us. We'll take you somewhere safe," the tall man said, walking toward me. I stepped back.

"My name is Walker. This is my brother, Elgin. That's Janet and Lindsay over there."

Elgin was a lot shorter than his brother and had long, black hair. But he had the same eyes. Janet was lean and slightly taller than me, with long, braided, blonde hair. Lindsay was the smallest and youngest, with straight, shoulder-length, jet-black hair. She was the only one who smiled.

Elgin threw me a pair of green pants with built-in boots. "Put those on."

As I did, the four of them climbed down to the flooded tunnel tracks, with Walker leading the way. A moment later, I followed their light, and when I got to the bottom, Janet handed me a headlamp.

We walked through the dark, flooded tunnels for quite a while. At some points having to crawl through areas where the walls and roof had collapsed. Eventually we came to a part where the tunnel led to the outside. We were in another part of the old city. These four weren't the most talkative. They walked in single file with Walker in front and Janet behind me. As soon as we'd exited the tunnel, they turned off their headlamps and we continued on in the darkness with the moon and stars to guide us. I'd never seen so many stars. I'd never been this far out of the city. Now the lights from the city were far behind and the stars blanketed the sky. I must have stopped, because Janet nudged my shoulder and said, "Keep moving, stargazer." I had no idea how long we'd been walking, but the sun started to come up and I was very weary. I'd never walked so far in my life. Plus, I'd been up for basically a full twenty-four hours.

"I'm hungry and thirsty," I told Janet, nearly tripping over my own feet.

Janet whistled to Walker and we stopped to take a break. We were now in a forest. As the sun continued to rise, I noticed that this was a real forest, not one rising out of ruins.

"Are we out of the old city now?" I asked.

"Not quite. This used to be a very large park that was kept natural," Walker said. "The old city had a zoo here with animals from all over the world. From here, we'll be heading northeast. It's at least two more days of walking to get to our destination." His face was expressionless.

Janet opened some packs of food while Elgin and Lindsay collected wood for Walker to start making a fire. I now noticed that everything they carried was made by hand. Their clothing, their packs, even the food was wrapped in handmade linens. As the fire got going, they put some pots with water on and started to make a soup with fresh vegetables and grains. They also had apples and berries that they gave to me. As we waited for the soup, I decided to probe some of the questions flowing through my mind.

"Was it you that sent the message on my computer?" I asked.

"Colleagues of ours, yes," Walker responded.

"But how did you find me, or know that it was me?"

"We know many things that happen in the city, and we saw you when you first entered the no-go zone."

"How many of you are there and why do you live outside the city?"

"There are many of us and we live where we want, when we want. There will be plenty of time for questions when we get to the commune. Now eat and rest. We still have a long way to go."

With that, I quietly ate my soup and attempted to have a nap. The others, except for Walker, disappeared into the woods. I must have dozed off, but when I woke again, I heard muffled voices. Walker was about fifteen metres away, with his back to me. I couldn't see anyone else. It looked as though he was talking into his hand, but I couldn't make out what he was saying. As he turned around, I stirred as if I'd just woken up.

"Rested? Let's go." Even with the question, it was more a command. I slowly got to my feet, aching from lying on the hard ground and still weary from lack of sleep.

Walker put out the fire and collected our packs. He buried the ashes and cleared any evidence of us being there. The others hadn't returned yet when Walker started to move off. I followed, scared to ask any more questions. Luckily, he answered what was on my mind before I asked it: "The others have gone ahead or behind to scout."

It must have been early afternoon and we walked until about midnight, using our headlamps once the sun went down through the overcast sky, and snacking while we went. We were now in an overgrown field. Along the way, Walker had collected additional wild foods and shown me what to look for. I could tell that he'd been raised in the wild. Here and there we saw remnants of houses, roads and other strange structures that Walker explained used to be farm buildings and equipment. Every so often, we had to wade across small creeks. All the anxiety I had about leaving the city was gone — I felt like I was on a real adventure. I was overjoyed that there were people outside the city and that they were taking me to their home. Perhaps one day I could learn everything Walker knew about survival. Once we stopped walking, Walker simply lay down in the overgrown field and went to sleep. I pushed down some of the tall grass to make the ground a little more comfortable and dozed off.

Walker was up before I was and had some food prepared for me. "Hurry up so that we can get moving." His tone hadn't improved in our time together. This whole enterprise seemed like a burden to him. Even when he was explaining and showing me things the day before, it was like he was talking to a child.

It was sunny and warm. The landscape was pastoral and the most beautiful place I'd ever been, with gently rolling hills interspersed with woods and fields. Even the ruined farms possessed their own sort of beauty, the way they blended perfectly with the natural landscape around them. There were birds fluttering around that I'd never seen before. There were birds in the city, but there was far more diversity out here. Wildflowers grew at the base of trees in a dazzling array of colours. The sun pouring through the canopy of the trees highlighted the green of their leaves. The textures, smells, colours were like nothing in the city. Even the parks in the city felt ordered and sterile. This was true nature as it was intended. The sheer diversity was overwhelming.

About two hours into our walk, I spotted a large grey dog.

"Have dogs out here gone wild?" I asked. Some people in the city had them, but none were as big as this one.

"That's a coyote. But wolves are moving south again and breeding with coyotes, so it could be a mix."

An hour later, we spotted six deer grazing in a field. Again, Walker had to tell me what they were. They spotted us and pranced off. I wanted to run after them and just watch them. I asked Walker what else was out here. He told me there were many different types of animals and each year they were becoming more and more common. Nature was reclaiming what humans had once tried to control.

We continued on for about five hours, when we met up with Elgin and Lindsay again. Walker said we were close to the commune, maybe another hour. We were on the top of a low hill that was the highest point around. I could see a large lake down below. I gazed at the tilled fields and small village on the shore of the lake. There were people moving about and smoke rising from some of the buildings. Further along the lake, I could see the ruins of another town, much smaller than the old city of Toronto.

"The name of the commune is Port Perry, after the abandoned town to the north," Walker explained. "That's Lake Scugog."

As we walked down the hill toward the new Port Perry, we had to pass through the fields of crops that the commune grew by hand. I knew nothing about agriculture. I'd never been to Zone 6 to see how the residents there produced all the food for a city of millions. But I knew that Zone 6 had a larger population than Zone 5, by virtue of my job. Based on the number of people I saw in the fields, I could tell it was hard work to grow food. I got more and more excited to learn about all of this. As we went, my three companions waved and greeted everyone we saw. It was the first time I'd really seen any of them smile. A small girl ran up to Walker and he picked her up, kissing her cheek as he carried her the rest of the way.

The buildings in the commune had all been built by hand and they were beautiful. They were made of coloured bricks with wooden roofs. There were wind turbines and solar panels on some of the roofs.

"We produce everything we need right here in harmony with nature," Walker explained. He was a little warmer and less rigid now, bouncing the giggling girl on his shoulders.

Everywhere were giant barrels that held water. Each house had a little garden with flowers and other plants. Birds, bees and butterflies fluttered around. Children were playing games that I couldn't understand. The adults were all working at something but laughing and smiling as they did it. Everyone seemed to know everyone else.

There couldn't have been more than a couple of hundred people. Was this what Walker meant by many of us? Or were there many places like this? If only people in the city knew about this.

Walker led me to a circular house near the shore of the lake. We entered and the house was simply one large circular room with nothing but benches arranged around a firepit in the centre. The walls were beautiful murals of landscapes, flowers, birds and animals. I'd never seen such vivid works of art. Most art in the city consisted of abstract shapes, patterns and lines. A bald man with a short, grey beard sat on one of the benches. He patted the seat beside him as Walker left the house. I sat next to him and he extended his hand to mine. "I'm Henry, one of the commune's councillors. Do you know the truth about what happened to your parents?"

I pulled back from him, arching my eyebrows and scowling. How did these people know so much about me? Somehow, they'd gotten a message into my computer, one that was untraceable for the Civic Guardians. More and more questions were circling in my mind, but Henry was watching me so intently, all I could do was answer his: "My dad died when I was eighteen, in a transit accident that killed five other people. My mother died less than a year later, of a heart attack."

"And you're twenty-six now?" I nodded.

Henry took a deep breath. "That's the official story of what happened to your parents. The truth is, they were killed by the Civic Administrators."

I stared at him, dumbfounded. *Not possible.* My parents were the epitome of conformists.

Henry could see that I was uncomfortable and suspicious. "The truth is, your parents were spies for us. I knew them from the war. We fought together. As the war was ending, decisions had to be made on what a new society would look like. We'd lost so much. Infrastructure and resources were scarce. To survive, we had to make hard choices. The remnants of the government decided to set up the zone structure as a means of control and order. Many veterans of the war wouldn't stand for it. They believed that we didn't fight and sacrifice so much just to bury the past. The government believed the only way for peace and security was to isolate and forget the rest of the world. Many of the most outspoken veterans disappeared mysteriously in the years after the war — before you were born and before the new city structure was officially established."

I was still trying to process what Henry had told me about my parents. I thought back to conversations with them.

Henry looked sad and thoughtful. "Of course, most people knew exactly the way things were before the war, but they were so scared and traumatized by everything that happened, they were willing to embrace this new societal experiment and more than willing to forget the past. Your parents couldn't forget. They, along with a group of others, including myself, decided the best way to fight this new system was to undermine it covertly and to eventually remind people of the aspects of humanity they'd lost. Your parents volunteered to be inside elements in the city. In those times, many records were lost and it was hard to keep track of who anyone was, so it was easy for your parents to get in. The Civic Administrators were cautious of any veterans except the lowliest soldiers. Your parents weren't just any soldiers. Your father was a hero of several battles and your mother was a genius intelligence operative."

Another bombshell dropped. My parents were heroes, geniuses. My entire childhood was a lie. I was getting more and more agitated. I was facing away from Henry, repeatedly tapping my foot and shaking my leg. Henry sighed, reaching for me, before pulling his hand slowly back. "But we managed to hide their true identities and give them new ones. We'd hoped that they would get placed in Zone 1 or Zone 2. Unfortunately, they were placed in Zone 4, which is why we suspected the Civic Administrators knew more than they were letting on. As the city was being established, tests were administered on the population to see their aptitude for various tasks and to match them with the duties of specific zones. We believe your parents scored too high and frightened the Civic Administrators. Little did we realize that no one got into Zone 1 that wasn't already fundamentally involved in establishing the city. Zone 2 was reserved for intelligent, technical and scientific minds, like your parents, but with one obvious difference, they also had to have malleable personalities. The Civic Administrators didn't want freethinkers in Zone 2. That zone was going to be the arm that would keep the city running efficiently through technological advances, health care, genetic diagnostics. They couldn't have residents questioning the very wisdom of that system. Your parents were guilty simply because their unconscious minds were freethinking. They sought to bury that characteristic by placing people in meaningless tasks while giving them a certain level of personal comfort they didn't have during and before the war. It was an elegant solution to prevent conflict."

It was starting to make a little more sense. Bits were coming back. I started to remember distinct times I would wake up to my parents arguing, my father wanting to leave the city, my mother saying they had to stay and continue their work. I tried to remember subtle hints of the parents Henry was describing, but unfortunately, he gave me no time to process anything.

"Now, I don't hate the Civic Administrators. Most of them are good people just trying to prevent further chaos. They're trying to protect some semblance of human society. That's noble. Their means are what we question. Humanity accomplished so much that they're willing to forget simply because of all the horrors we unleashed as well. We don't have the best track record of learning from our mistakes and preventing history from repeating itself. The Civic Administrators believe that if you erase that history and make people believe that Ontario and Michigan are all that's left of humanity, then we can't possibly repeat our past mistakes."

Henry paused, shrugged and looked down at the floor. "Maybe they're right. I've seen terrible things done by one person to another, and by many people to the world. Yet I can't reconcile one of the basic needs of sentient humans: freedom of choice. Humanity has been fighting for true freedom, or the idea of freedom, for millennia. Elites have historically subjugated the majority of society for their own personal gain, robbing most of humanity of that freedom of choice. Slavery, inequality, racism, sexism were all too common in most human societies. Is the zone system in the city any different? It's just hidden better. Wouldn't you agree?"

"I … um … I…" I couldn't think of anything to say. My eyes were starting to tear up.

As I listened to Henry, his story made so much sense to me and confirmed much of what I secretly believed. The part about my parents was the most confusing. I'd spent so long believing they were dull and distant because, for the most part, they were. The idea that they were freedom fighters just seemed outlandish.

Henry nodded. "Kelowna, you must understand, the parents you knew were the spies putting on an act to prevent detection. They loved you immensely and wanted to tell you everything so many times. The plan was to bring you here or to one of the other communes, after they'd accomplished their mission. They could tell that you didn't belong in the city. But they knew they were being watched, as everyone in the city is. The Civic Administrators are very clandestine. The Civic Guardians are the face of public order, but they don't monitor for outliers like you. They don't understand those that would question authority. In a way, their society is perfect. Never in human history has there been a society with so few inequalities and injustices. There's no crime, no hunger and no poverty. Yet, the better things seemed, the more worried the Civic Administrators got. They worried about people like you; people who would get bored by comfort and monotony. That's why there's been so much focus on entertainment and activity pursuits in each zone over the last five years. Distraction. The city now has enough resources and infrastructure to operate efficiently, freeing up time for—"

"Henry, this is all fascinating, but what does it have to do with my parents and how they died?"

"Your parents' job was to infiltrate the city's network so that we could keep an eye on things and know more about what was going on. As I said, your mother was a genius intelligence officer. The problem was they lived in Zone 4. The network server controls were all in Zone 1. All your mother could do was insert bugs in the system to cause disruptions in other zones' networks. Your parents kidnapped two Zone 2 technicians a few months before your father was killed. With our other operatives, your parents managed to change their identification to match the Zone 2 workers they'd kidnapped. They knew they had to move fast as their disappearance would not take long to discover."

Lindsay walked in, carrying a tray with glasses of water and some fruit. She put it down between Henry and me.

"Kelowna, please help yourself," Henry said, grabbing one of the glasses of water and a piece of apple. I grabbed the other glass and slowly took a sip.

"The Zone 2 workers were supposed to repair the Zone 4 network glitches and go to Zone 1 to reboot the network. Your parents took their place. All went according to plan. Your mother managed to install the encoded monitor into the city's network so that we could access surveillance and Zone 2 data. Zone 1 was still locked out. Your parents risked discovery trying to access it. They got away clean."

Henry paused to grab some grapes. I took another drink.

"From what we gathered, their slip-up came when they released the workers. We'd managed to get them a drug so that the workers would remember nothing. They were only gone for two days and were found in a maintenance shaft below a building in Zone 2. They were questioned but could remember nothing. Your mother was smart enough to erase the surveillance footage from where they'd been so that they couldn't match their faces to the identification of the two missing workers. The Civic Administrators found what they believed to be the bug installed by your parents. Your mother managed to install a separate program that would mess with ration data. The Civic Administrators believed that was the plan all along, to create disorder in the perfection of their ration system. Your parents had no idea they'd been discovered. We still don't know how they figured out it was them."

"Then how do you know they were both killed?"

"Because your father and the five other people killed in the transit accident were all informers of ours. They were on their way to a meeting. Your mother was to meet them there. It was late and they were the only people on the tram. They weren't sitting together. It was foolish for them all to get on the same tram, but since we could tap into the city's surveillance network, we believed that we were fine. When your mother found out what happened, we begged her to escape with you and come back to us. She said there was still more that she wanted to learn about the network. We told her it was too dangerous. Your mother did manage to feed us more information, but all of it was false. They knew what she was doing and used it to hack into our networks. We had to shut down for four years. Fortunately, your mother's program was still in place."

I sat with slumped shoulders, cracking my knuckles, staring at the floor. Henry placed his hand on my shoulder. "I'm sorry, Kelowna, but there was nothing we could do to save them. We managed to save the surveillance footage of your mother being injected with the serum that caused her heart attack. It was at a busy tram station and didn't take long. She didn't die in pain."

I didn't know what to say. I was crying softly. My parents weren't the boring stiffs I thought them to be. I spent so long resenting them. My parents had been killed by an organization that professed to have created the perfect society. A perfect society that had never made sense to me. I suppose I was a product of my rebel parents. Subconsciously, they must have imparted more on me than I thought. The only home I'd ever known was the exact place that I couldn't go back to.

A scowling man with a tight, sweat-stained T-shirt entered the room.

"Kelowna, this is Ares, my son," Henry said. "He's here to escort you to a safe house. One of our sanctuaries where the Civic Administrators can't find you. You'll be able to rest comfortably there."

I didn't respond and simply got up to follow Ares. We walked north, along the shore of the lake. We reached the ruins of Port Perry after at least an hour and headed toward a building on the outskirts of town. There were several other people nearby. The large sliding door on the building was open and inside was a flying machine. I'd seen flying machines overhead occasionally in the city, but Zone 1 was the only place they came from or went to. This one was small with blades on its roof.

"This is a gyrocopter and our ride," Ares said.

"Where are we going?"

"North."

Ares put on a greyish-green long-sleeved shirt that matched his pants. He got in the front of the gyrocopter next to a woman with spiked short black hair and numerous piercings in her ears. She was dressed in the same greyish-green fatigues. I got in the back. We began to move forward out of the building. Soon we were airborne in a smooth, seamless motion. The landscape, which hurried by as we went, didn't seem to change much. I wondered how fast we were going. Ares and the young woman had headsets that they seemed to be using to communicate with each other. They didn't give me one, which I took as a sign they didn't want to talk to me. Ares did hand me some fresh warm bread. My seat was too far back to hear what they were saying despite the fact the gyrocopter was surprisingly quiet. Instead, I watched as we flew over endless forests, small lakes and, here and there, the remnants of farms, towns and roads. About an hour into the ride, the sun set, and as it got dark, my head started to droop. Even with all the new information running through my mind, the exhaustion from everything I'd been told and all the walking caught up to me. I awoke to the gyrocopter slowly descending into a large pit. There were buildings and huge equipment scattered around the edge of it. At the bottom of the pit, under a large rock overhang, were two sliding doors that opened into an immense cavern. Ares propelled us through the doors, where there were other gyrocopters and machines I'd never seen before. The lights were a faint yellow, and it took time for my eyes to adjust to the gloominess.

Ares and the young woman got out of the gyrocopter, greeting others that were all dressed like them. Most of the people around looked at me, but no one spoke to me. Ares ascended a staircase to a control room without a word. The woman went off to a room at the side of the cavern. I was left standing by the gyrocopter wondering what I was supposed to do. I was unwanted and useless to these people. Despite what my parents did, I could offer no equivalent support to whatever their end goal was. The Civic Administrators would be looking for me. I would be declared missing; any known associates would be getting questioned. Gerald would perhaps be the only person worried.

If Henry was telling the truth, the Civic Administrators would know who my parents were. Did that matter enough to have constant surveillance on me? If so, why had they just let me leave?

Ares came back down the stairs, whistling and motioning for me to follow. He handed me a bag with some matching clothes in them. We followed a long and wide corridor. At the end was a large elevator. We got on with a few others and began heading down.

"Welcome to the bunker," Ares said in his typical direct and gruff manner. "This place used to be a metal mine. During the war, it was turned into a base, even though the war never made it this far east. It's capable of housing thousands. An underground river provides water. We have wind and solar generators on the surface. We grow enough food in some underground greenhouses. Scattered communes provide the rest."

Ares's demeanour was brisk. He clearly hadn't volunteered to give me the tour and seemed anxious to be done with me.

"But why? Surely the Civic Administrators know about this place. Why hide underground when they don't seem to care about the villages on the surface?" I asked.

"We aren't hiding; we're preparing. There's more to this world than just Ontario and Michigan."

Preparing for what? I thought.

As we descended, others got off and on the elevator at multiple levels.

"Living quarters are near the bottom. Labs, greenhouses, storerooms are on the higher levels," Ares explained.

We got off the elevator at Habitat Quarter F. Each hall leading off the main corridor was numbered: 1, 2, 3, and on and on. At the end of the main corridor was a large cafeteria and common area.

"You can get food and relax here," Ares told me as we moved around at a jogging pace.

There were games, books and probably about fifty people there at the time. We turned at 4 and came to door 46.

"This is your room," Ares said, pushing the thick metal door open.

There was a small dresser and bed, nothing else.

"There's a shared bathroom at the end of the hall." Ares was standing at the door looking impatient.

I had the room to myself but couldn't believe how stark it was.

"Get some food and rest. I'll check on you in the morning," Ares said, walking off before I had a chance to ask any more questions. I wondered how I was supposed to know what time it was down here.

I had left monotony and the colour blue for drab greys in the bowels of the earth. I went to bed without food. I couldn't go back to the city, but I definitely didn't want to stay here. The village by the lake or another place like that farther away, on the surface, would be preferable.

I tossed and turned in the lumpy bed, thinking about my parents, trying to recall their faces and any hints of the people they really were.

Seventeen
Paraiso, Colombia

After telling Senora Vasquez about the night I left my abuela, she thought it would help if I wrote down how I got to the village. I spent many nights writing the story of how I escaped Bogotá…

I was so tired and sore, scared and sad. I felt anger too — at the soldados, my abuela, my mother, myself. I spent the next day in the bushes beside the trail. I still hadn't seen or heard anyone. I wanted to see more of where I was with the daylight. I climbed up a part of the hill with few trees. In every direction was forest and hills. The sun was behind me, so I kept it to my back and followed the trail. I was told to travel only at night, but the trail was so hard to see. The forest was too thick.

I walked for hours, even as it got dark. I'd eaten only a small amount of my food and was very hungry. I didn't know how long it would take me to get somewhere safe and didn't want to run out of food. I found fresh streams to fill my water.

After two days and nights of walking, with brief periods of rest, I found a paved road. The map my abuela and her brother had given me showed the trail and road meeting at a town called Choachí. I followed the road but stayed to the side, in the forest. I still hadn't seen or heard another person. The road went down out of the hills on a winding path. At one point, the hill had no trees and there were empty huts that were falling apart. It was dark again when I reached that part. Far below at the bottom of the valley, I could see lights and fires. I kept moving that night, since I knew there would be people nearby. I would find somewhere to hide during the day. As the sun was rising, I reached another clearing. I could see up and down the valley. There were fields everywhere and large pits carved out of the hills. There were many towns and villages. The largest town was to the east of where I was. If I was following the map right, it would be Choachí.

There were people coming out of houses and moving along the road near me now. I went deep into the forest and found somewhere to hide for the day. At night, I crossed the road and headed through some fields on steep slopes. I could see the lights ahead. I reached the edge of Choachí as the sun rose. I had to keep moving. By the end of that day, I reached a large bridge that crossed the nearby river. At the other end of it were houses built right against the steep banks of the river. The water was fast-moving and a dirty brown. The bridge was the only option I could see to cross. The map showed the river heading long distances in both directions.

There were many people moving across the bridge. They were dirty, each with their heads down. At each end of the bridge were small huts with armed men inspecting the goods and pushcarts of the people. I didn't know how I was going to cross it. I needed some rest and would have to wait until it was fully dark to see if I could cross without someone finding me. I found a small ditch with tall grass and got some rest.

I woke up a few hours later. The moon was covered in clouds and the only lights came from some small fires across the river and the guard posts at each end of the bridge. There were gates across the bridge and guards walked back and forth across its ends. The riverbank on this side was steep with lots of bushes and small trees. I walked along it. My heart was racing, waiting to see a beam of light or hear a gunshot. I'd reached the bridge.

There were at least four armed men that I could see on this side of the bridge. There was no way I could get across without being seen. I thought about following the river. Perhaps farther down it would be easier to cross. I only had enough food for a few days. I was sure I could steal food from the farms if I could get across. I didn't know how to swim or if the river would be easier to cross somewhere else.

Under the bridge were metal beams that formed Xs. It looked like I could crawl across them if I could get to them. I crept slowly down to the spot where the bridge joined the riverbank. There was sharp wire covering the ends of all the beams. I had to find a way to get through it.

I emptied the smaller canvas bag into the larger one to the point that I could barely close it, then used the empty bag to spread some of the wire apart. Under the main beam there was a thin cable that ran the length of the bridge. Using the rope I had, I tied my bag to the cable and pushed it through the gap in the wire. My stuff was now hanging safely on the other side. But the cable wasn't strong enough for my weight. My small canvas bag had separated the sharp wire, but I didn't think it would stop me from getting cuts. I had no choice. I found some wood on the ground and used it to protect my hands and to pry the wire farther apart. I made it halfway through with only some rips in my clothes, but the wire was bunching up as I crawled through. There was a metal beam about a metre in front of me with no sharp wire. I needed to jump to it to be clear of the sharp wire. If I missed, I would fall into the river or get all cut up.

I took some deep breaths and jumped. I hit the beam hard but held on. I heard voices on the bridge. I climbed up the beam to get as close to the bottom of the bridge as I could and began to crawl upside down along the beam, dragging my supply bag by the rope. At the end of the bridge I saw a small light and two shadows. They were searching the area. I froze, hoping their light wasn't strong enough to reach me. After a few minutes, they went back up to their post.

At the other end of the bridge, there was a place where the sharp wire had sunk down toward the river and there was a wide opening. I crossed over a little too quickly, cutting my left arm badly. It wasn't until I felt and saw that blood that I realized my head was bleeding too. I hit it hard when I jumped. I climbed down to the riverbank and tied a shirt around my arm. There was nothing I could do about my head right now.

I walked slowly along the riverbank. This side of the river wasn't as steep as the other, but it also had no trees or bushes. The houses were close together. The riverbank was muddy and covered in garbage. It was hard to move fast, but I was too out in the open. I reached a gap in the houses and ran through it toward the fields. No one was following me.

There was a wide dirt path that headed toward the mountains in the distance. The map said to follow it. The path was very uneven. There were many dark huts along it. There were fields on both sides. I needed to get to where the hills started again before the sun rose. I hadn't slept enough and was moving very slowly. The bandage on my arm was soaked and red. My head wasn't bleeding as much, but I felt dizzy. I had to keep going.

I reached a hill that still had some trees. As the sun began to rise, I saw another large town and a place where the dirt path crossed a wider road. There were more gates at that point blocking the road. All around were fields and huts. I hoped the small grouping of trees on the hill would provide enough cover.

I found the largest tree and started to climb it. When I was little, I would climb all over the buildings and roofs in the slum. I made it to a branch big enough to lie down on. I used the rope to hold me and my bag. It wasn't long before I fell asleep.

I woke up with the sun still up but far to the west. My head was hurting. I drank the rest of my water and ate a lot of my food, hoping it would help. I climbed down. I was running out of food and had no water left. There was a tree on the hill with round yellow fruits. I didn't know what they were, but I ate several. They were sour but juicy. I filled my bag with more of them and rested again on the ground.

A loud horn woke me up. The sun was setting. I went to the edge of the hill and could see people leaving the fields, heading to huts and moving along the dirt path. A vehicle filled with guards was heading up the road toward the gate. The guards got out and replaced the ones that had been there during the day.

I needed to stay away from that road so decided to follow a small creek that came down out of the hills and into the fields. I filled my water several times.

My feet were like bricks and I fell a lot just trying to keep moving. As it got dark, the only lights or fires were far away. I kept heading to the mountains, but my legs didn't want to move, and my head was so sore. There was a rough footpath ahead of me that climbed up.

I reached the top and could see all around me. The hills got higher and higher near the mountains. Some were covered in trees, others in fields. Some had small villages. Others had huge holes carved out of them. Smoke rose from the camps near these holes. The mountains were still far away. It would take days to reach them and I was losing strength.

I set down my pencil and closed the journal. I would have to finish the rest later.

I lay on my mat in Senora Vasquez's home, thinking about the first person who helped me on my way. I had found a small hut with a caved-in roof, where I'd drunk the last of my water and eaten my final piece of fruit before falling into a deep hunger-filled sleep. Sometime later, I was woken up to someone shaking me. I leaped up, banging my head against a collapsed beam. It was an old man. "Who are you?" he asked. I didn't speak. "What are you doing here?"

I looked around for something I could hit him with. I was bigger than him, but he had an axe in one of his hands and I was so weak and tired.

Our eyes met. "I'm not going to hurt you," he said. "You aren't from around here, are you?" He looked at me with sympathy. "Come on, you can help me carry some wood back to my farm." I had no choice but to follow him. If he wanted to hurt me, he would have already.

"I'm Pablo. We aren't allowed to take wood from these forests, but my family needs something to cook with."

"Is it the gangs that run things around here?" I asked him.

He laughed. "Who knows? Whoever they are, they aren't kind people." Pablo had thin, dark hair with patches of grey. He bent forward slightly, with a noticeable hunch to his back. His skin was dark from too much sun. "Where are you from? What's your name?" he asked again.

I didn't know whether I could trust him, but he could have killed me if he'd wanted to. "I'm Miguel. I'm from Bogotá."

"You aren't the first person to show up around here from the city. You're lucky I found you and not someone else. Otherwise, you'd be put to work on one of the farms or the mines."

Pablo was pushing a cart loaded with blocks of wood. I helped him steady it on the rough path by holding one of its sides. "Don't worry. My place is isolated enough that no one really comes around. It's just me, my wife, three children and two grandchildren. We give away most of what we produce to be sure we're left alone, so we don't have much, but we're comfortable."

He stopped and took a drink from a bottle strapped to his side. "That's a bad cut on your head and arm. Come. Let's go get you cleaned up."

We arrived at a cozy, single-level, well-kept dwelling made of stone, with glass windows, wood floors and a real roof. Inside was a wood stove, large table and a couple of sofas. There were three small bedrooms off the main living area. Pablo had brought a few pieces of the wood from the cart inside and laid them in a pile by the wood stove. "Out back is the outhouse. We get water from a nearby well. Come, I'll introduce you to my family."

He led me to the table, which several people were setting for dinner. "Miguel, this is my wife, Sofia." Pablo's wife shook my hand. She was a very thin woman with curly grey hair and was missing a few teeth. "This is my oldest son, Carlos, and his wife, Tania," Pablo said. Carlos nodded at me while Tania chased around two young girls. Carlos was a younger version of his father with less hair.

"The two little gigglers over there are my granddaughters, Grace and Isabel. Don't worry, I can't tell them apart either." Pablo whispered that last part to me as we watched the twins play. Even their clothing and hairstyle were the same.

Then Pablo turned toward a young woman. "This is my daughter, Andrea." She was a younger version of her mother and looked a few years older than me. "And finally, my youngest son, Christian."

Christian came over to shake my hand before returning to the kitchen to help his mother. He looked to be around my age. Andrea set an extra place at the table for me.

"Miguel, please follow me and we'll get you cleaned up." Sofia grabbed my hand and led me to one of the rooms, which had a large tub. Tania brought in some buckets with warm water. Sofia was pulling some items from a cupboard and went to another room. She came back with some clothes. "Please, Miguel, wash up. Here is some soap and a brush. Christian's clothes should fit you. Your clothes are all torn up."

It was true, my shirt was ripped and full of holes and my pant legs had frayed at the bottom.

"When you're done washing, let me know and I'll tend to your cuts," Sofia told me, leaving the room and closing the door.

I sank into the warm tub and scrubbed the dirt from my body. It had been a long time since I'd had a warm bath. We rarely had real soap or enough clean water to fill an entire tub in the slum. I must have been taking a while, because Sofia knocked at the door.

"Is everything all right, Miguel?"

"Yes, thank you. I'm nearly finished."

I finished scrubbing and got out, drying myself off. I put on the pants Sofia provided and called to her. She came in and washed the cut on my head and arm again before putting a soothing paste on them both.

"There, that should prevent any infection and help the cuts heal. Come. Dinner is ready."

I put on the shirt she gave me and followed her into the main living area. The table had many different types of food and the room smelled very good. At the end of the meal, I began to cry. Everyone just looked at me. Sofia grabbed my arm, whispered, "It's okay," and offered me more food. After the meal, I offered to help clean up, but Sofia and Pablo told me to sit. I watched from one of the sofas as the family cleaned up. I felt better already. The bath, the paste on my cuts, and the meal had given me energy.

When everyone was done cleaning up, they all sat around the wood stove in the living room as Carlos got a fire going with the wood Pablo had brought. Pablo asked, "So, Miguel, tell us your story."

These people were kind and caring, the likes of which, other than my abuela and the others in our small apartment building, I'd never met. "I had to flee before they made me become one of the soldados. Any boy my age becomes a gang member. My abuela made me leave so I wouldn't have to do terrible things." I didn't tell them about Alejandra or the terrible things I'd done already. "I was told there are villages in the mountains that are free from the gangs and violence. Is that true?"

Pablo responded, "There are small villages up in the mountains that keep to themselves. The people around here that control everything don't go there. Their vehicles can't reach them."

"And they don't bother you?" Pablo had already told me they gave away most of what they had, but I didn't understand why he didn't take his family into the mountains.

"My family has farmed this land for generations. I grew up with one of the people in charge around here. We have an arrangement.

We trade most of our goods in town and they don't come on our land."

"Why not go farther into the mountains?" I asked.

"This is good farmland and home."

I nodded. "Thank you for everything. I don't know what to say."

"You're very welcome. In the morning, Christian will take you to a small village east of here. A friend of mine collects wood and goes into the mountains for days at a time. He'll take you where you need to go."

I didn't know what to say and had nothing to offer in return. I thanked them again. Sofia prepared one of the sofas for me to sleep on and I slept better than I had in a long time.

In the morning, the family prepared a large breakfast with bread, eggs and fruit. After breakfast, Christian said it was time to go. The rest of the family was already doing various chores around the farm. The two grandchildren were playing in a flower garden. Sofia filled my bag with more food and water. I hugged each of them, thanking them again.

Christian was waiting by a large cart filled with goods. "You're an orphan from Choachí that my father brought to help on the farm if anyone asks." I nodded.

The cart was so heavy, it needed both of us to move it. We pushed it across rough tracks and fields for most of the morning. Soon we had a small river on our right. Christian said this led to the village that we were heading to, and if Pablo's woodcutting friend, Daniel, wasn't in the town, I was to continue to follow this river up into the mountains.

We arrived in the village in the early afternoon. Daniel was home. He was outside his shop getting his horse cart ready. Christian greeted him warmly and explained the situation.

"Today is your lucky day, Miguel. I know the perfect place and I happen to be headed that way," Daniel said.

I said goodbye to Christian and sat at the front with Daniel. He had two horses to pull his large cart.

"It's a four-day journey to the village. It's deep in the mountains and very isolated."

The journey was easy and uneventful. I slept most of the time in the cart as we followed the river into the mountains. On the third day, we left the cart behind and rode the horses.

"I've never ridden a horse," I told Daniel.

"Well, the cart won't fit on the paths from here and it'll take too long on foot. It's not hard. The horse will do the work."

Daniel was right. The horse knew where it was going, and I just needed to hold on. We hadn't really spoken much on the journey. Daniel didn't ask me any questions and I didn't ask him any. Midway through the fourth day, we arrived at the mountain village, Paraiso, and it truly was a paradise, set in a lush and narrow valley, framed by soaring mountain peaks, with fresh mountain streams and ponds and towering trees. When we arrived, Daniel was greeted excitedly by many. The first person he introduced me to was Senora Vasquez.

Eighteen
Budapest

I was thrown roughly into a dark and damp room, with my hands tied behind my back. There was no bed and only a small drain in the corner. It was a concrete box that reeked of human misery. They questioned me with a black bag over my head for hours. When I didn't provide answers, I was punched in the stomach. Eventually they worked up to my face. Finally, they punished me with jolts of electricity. I couldn't see my face, but I could feel the swelling and bruising. I'd lost at least a couple of teeth and could still taste the blood in my mouth. I collapsed to the floor, still convulsing from the electric currents that had passed through me.

What was I thinking? I was more likely to die than be sent east. I knew they could sense my weakness and that I would break.

Eventually I passed out from pain and grief, dreaming of Anna. Her image slowly drifted from my mind. My last glimpse was of her looking at me with displeasure. I called to her, apologizing. She turned her back to me and was gone. Anna, who was so strong and inspiring. What had she seen in me? I had failed her.

Tomas had arranged for me to meet with his guard friend after I convinced them that I was going through with this foolish plan. We'd met the day before my incarceration — at least I think it was the day before. Tomas explained to the young guard what I was hoping to accomplish. He looked to me with pity in his eyes, shaking his head. He tried to dissuade me, the same as Tomas and the tattooed woman had. There was no guarantee I would end up anywhere near Anna or my father. No guarantee I would even be transferred to the same place as them. But I couldn't be dissuaded. The young guard arrested me, taking me to a central police station. He explained to his superiors, from what I could understand, that I was a member of the movement who had been in hiding and trying to rally supporters. He had caught me after hours banging on doors, trying to solicit sympathy to our cause. His commander didn't even look up from his desk, simply telling the guard to take me to processing. I was strip-searched. They cut off my hair and forced me to wear an itchy, grey jumpsuit. From there I was transported to the core of the city, in the old parliament district. When the truck came to a stop, that was the end of seeing anything. My last look was of the square where I'd lost everything. I was handed from one set of guards to another. This new group was even rougher than the previous and put the black bag on my head.

The hours of interrogation and torture had taken their toll. I couldn't move and lay in that dank cell awaiting what I thought would be my eventual execution. It felt like days — maybe it was — but eventually the cell door opened. They jammed the bag on my head again and dragged me through hallways and up staircases. Eventually we were outside. I could feel the sun and the breeze. I was placed in a truck and off we went. I had no idea where we were going, but the smell of many unwashed bodies, including my own, wafted through the truck. The only sounds were the noise of the truck, the occasional whimper from one of the other people or the thud of a guard hitting someone, who then screamed out in pain. Eventually the truck stopped, and we were shuffled off, still blinded. There was a brief relief from the stench when we felt a cool breeze, but that quickly transitioned to hot and stagnant air. We were loaded into another vehicle, our hands freed, only to have our torsos and ankles restrained against seats. They removed our hoods. I was surrounded by dozens of others in dull grey wool, all of us along the edge of the carriage, facing each other. There were large windows with heavy iron bars set horizontally. We were on a train. My spirits lifted. I was the only fool in this train car with a smile on my face.

The train slowly pulled out of the station. They didn't even bother leaving guards in the train car. None of us could move. Anyone who had to go to the bathroom went in their seat. I had some stale bread and porridge that morning with a glass of water, but that was it. It would be hours before we reached Kyiv, if that was in fact where we were going. Some of my fellow passengers looked as if they wouldn't last that long.

Once we left the city, we travelled through the peaceful Hungarian countryside, occasionally passing through small, seemingly abandoned villages. I drifted off to a laboured sleep. I dreamed of Anna and my father, believing I would soon be reunited with them.

Hours passed and the train eventually stopped. We were in another city, not as large as Budapest. Guards in masks entered the train car, passing out water and bread. Many people begged to use the toilet, but the guards just moved on. One old man near the end of the car was unresponsive. The guards kicked and smacked him. When the man didn't respond, they unchained him and dragged him by his feet off the train car. Everyone else focused on their meagre helping of bread and water. No one cared that we'd just witnessed the end of a man's life. It was like he'd never existed.

It was night when we left. I'd lost track of the days or time, wondering how long we'd been travelling and how much farther there was to go. I was thankful that I'd not soiled myself yet but wondered how long my weakened system could hold out. I drifted off again to the rocking and swaying of the train.

As the sun rose, we passed ruined and desolate villages. The landscape had the signs of war, but a war that had ended some time ago. The first wall was a large concrete monstrosity with anti-aircraft and gun emplacements along its top. It stretched to the horizon, standing at least ten metres high. We passed through a heavy metal gate and continued on our way. Beyond the wall, the scene was even more stark, with rundown wooden hovels surrounded by razor wire fences. Labourers were shuffling along rutted gravel paths to various points in this bleak landscape. The very air seemed to have a deathly quality. The people working were human shells — skeletal with skin tones that matched their garb. My earlier euphoria had turned to despair. Even if I found Anna and my father alive, they would likely be nothing more than walking corpses.

The train reached the outskirts of a ruined city. Half the buildings were bombed out. Half-naked children caked in dust and dirt played among the ruins. The buildings that were standing had black smoke spewing from stacks on their roofs. They must have been converted to factories. The centre of the city was in better shape but lacked any of the old stately elegance of European cities. Instead of old buildings, there were massive concrete fortresses lined with weapon placements. Everything was ordered and purposeful with no unnecessary decoration. The train stopped in a large square surrounded by fenced yards and smaller trains running in every direction. There were guard towers everywhere.

Guards came aboard, unchaining us from our seats and ordering us out the door. Each car had been attached to a chain-link tunnel leading to separate buildings. Once inside, men and women were separated. We were ordered to remove our clothes. Standing in a white room with a central drain, we were hosed off with puncturing pressure and cold water. Buckets were thrown into the centre of the room with coarse brushes and soap. After scrubbing down, we were rinsed off.

Next, we were led to an adjoining room with the same grey wool jumpsuits and black boots neatly arranged on a table, though these ones were fresh. There were guards with clipboards in front of three doors. The guards asked what languages we spoke, asking in numerous languages themselves. Then we were asked what professional or labour experience we had. After that, we were told which door to go through.

When it was my turn, I couldn't think of what to say for professional experience. Something told me this wasn't the time to mention I'd spent most of my life trying to reform international institutions. So, I simply said I was a farmer. It was what Anna and my father would most likely have said as well. I was told to go through the door on the right. We were finally given the use of a toilet, but like many others, I had already gone in the shower room. The next room had long tables with bread and water and bowls of soup. There didn't seem to be portion restrictions and everyone ate as much as they could. I knew that overeating would only make me sick after having so little in the last few days. I finished a bowl and two small pieces of bread. No one spoke. What was the point? We didn't know what would happen next. The room slowly filled and the door from the preceding room eventually shut.

Guards appeared at the other end, ordering us to line up. We were shuffled back outside through another chain-link tunnel and loaded onto a small tram. Once full, the tram moved off. Once out of the city, we stopped in every village. Though I suppose they weren't really villages anymore. Each one looked like concentration camps from one of the darkest chapters of European history. At each stop, three or four prisoners were ordered off before we continued. The sun was setting as I was off-loaded. I could see part of a river behind more concrete walls and military installations. My new home was surrounded by a five-metre-high chain-link fence lined with razor wire. The barracks were long wooden shacks with crooked roofs. The largest building was concrete and appeared to be where the guards were stationed. It had a tower that gave it a commanding view of the camp. There must have been hundreds imprisoned here.

I was led into a long hall that served as the dining room, where dinner was being served. None of the guards spoke to me, but the prisoners here were speaking to each other. Some were even laughing. I surveyed the hall for any sign of Anna or my father. Some people on the benches were eyeing me suspiciously. I was new meat. I grabbed food and walked along the outside of the hall. Anna and my father weren't here. At the end of the hall, people at one of the tables were speaking English. I asked if I could join them. There were four men and two women. They welcomed me and continued their conversation. I ate my food in silence, absorbing the conversation around me. These people didn't seem downtrodden or depressed by their circumstances. It was idle chatter, as if nothing was out of the ordinary.

"How long have you all been here?" I asked.

One of the men, the most boisterous of the group, who seemed to be around my age but was taller with dark hair and a muscular build, responded. "I've been here four years. This place is heaven compared to where I was before. I'm William." He shook my hand.

"Elliott."

"How did you end up here?" William asked.

"I'm looking for my father and my wife, Anna."

"What makes you think you'll find them?" William asked.

"I was told most prisoners are transferred this way."

"Where were you arrested?"

"Budapest," I responded.

"What did they arrest you for?"

"Um … I, uh … I asked to be arrested so I could find them."

The group started laughing, William loudest of all.

"Oh, Elliott, that's fresh. You may be the first person I've met that purposely wanted to come out here," William said, still laughing. "How long ago were your wife and father taken?"

"A few months. Where do most prisoners from Budapest end up?" I asked.

"They could be anywhere, hundreds of kilometres north or south of Kyiv. On farms if they're lucky. Better than the mines or factories from what we hear."

"So that city was Kyiv? Where the train unloaded?"

"Most likely. This camp isn't far south of Kyiv," William responded.

We spoke long into the night, mainly William and I. For the others, English wasn't their first language, but they were comfortable in it and William seemed to be a sort of group leader. There were no assigned bunks, so William led me to the barracks he stayed in with the others. There was a total of twenty-four people in the barracks, including me. Some were couples. William explained how life worked here. "As long as you show up to work the fields, the guards don't care what you do," he said.

"How long have you been here?" I asked.

"I've been all over the Front for years, this camp the last couple. Things are easier now than they were. The fighting seems to have stopped completely."

"Then why the camps?"

"Good question. Even the guards don't seem to know much. Rumour is, there's no one left east of the river to fight."

We spoke of his family, mine, the farm and the movement. He had lost his wife and kids in one of the few disease outbreaks to breach central and Western Europe almost a decade ago. After that, he turned more political and militant. After working in the factories, he'd experienced fighting on the Front. That was the worst period of his life. There was no method to the war. Every day, thousands from the east would try to cross the Front with bombs from both sides exploding everywhere. Most were unarmed but were gunned down anyway. It didn't seem like a war from William's perspective. Their job was to keep people from the other side out, and that's it. There was no organized invasion force or well-equipped army by the time William arrived. It was pockets of broken soldiers led by vengeful commanders and civilians with nowhere else to go.

As we were getting ready to go to sleep, I asked, "Is there any way to locate people at other camps?"

He shook his head. "Once you're assigned to a camp, you don't leave."

William climbed into bed and quickly fell asleep. I lay down, staring at the ceiling, depressed with the knowledge that I'd likely never find Anna and my father.

Nineteen
Near Sri Lanka

I woke to soft chiming bells and the subtle rumbling of the ship, with a deep murmur from decks below. Someone was knocking on my cabin door. I opened it to find Visshaly.

"Did you sleep well?" he asked.

"Yes, thank you. It's been a long time, if ever, that I've felt so refreshed."

"It's time for the morning meal and then we've been asked to join Shani and the others. The ship has already started moving."

"I'll get changed and meet you in the meal room."

The selection of food was again overwhelming. There were so many items unfamiliar to me. The colours and textures were vivid. I chose some red and yellow fruits with some dark crispy breads and joined Visshaly, who was already nearly finished. The meal room was almost empty, but many dishes were stacked in the corner. The halls were filled with people coming and going to various duties.

I had so many questions circling in my head about who these people were, why they seemed so prosperous, where they were from and what the rest of the world was like.

"What do you think our place will be here?" I asked Visshaly.

He just shrugged.

"Don't you want to know everything about these people and where we're going?"

"I just want to find out about my brother and the other monks."
Visshaly moved to clear his tray. "Eat quick. I'll meet you on the deck.
I need some air," he said, leaving the meal room.

I was alone with my questions. I'd forgotten that Visshaly's
brother had left for the coast as well. I hoped they would be reunited
soon. For all the talk of danger before and on our journey to the coast,
we'd managed to find what we were looking for. If Visshaly's brother
was anything like him, I was sure we would find him safe and sound
on this island called Sri Lanka. I began picturing a lush green expanse
rising from a crystal-blue ocean, the veritable paradise that had been
promised. Tears welled in my eyes and guilt clutched at my chest.

"Why do you cry, Aashi?" Shani came to my side and grasped my
hand, then kneeled beside me with pity in her eyes.

"I was thinking of those I've lost along the way to get here and
was sad that they're not here."

Shani nodded and paused for some time, searching for words of
comfort. "The world is full of uncertainty and misery, yet through
that struggle, the good virtues of humanity have endured. Mourn
those you loved that are now gone. Our sorrows and tests can make
us stronger and more empathetic or they can make us weak and
cruel."

"I'll try to be strong to honour their memory." I regained my
composure, breathing in deeply, and smiled, thinking of the precious
moments of joy I'd had with Amar, Jahi and Randhir.

"Come, it's time we joined the others. We have much to discuss."
Shani pulled me gently by the hand and led me up to the deck. The
morning was cool with a lifting fog, but we were out in the open sea
with gentle waves crashing on the sides of the metallic behemoth that
ploughed through the glistening waters. This water was a dark and
menacing blue. A slight grey haze was all that was visible of the land
we'd left behind. The other noticeable change was this water seemed
pure, rather than the brownish-black sludge along the coast. Even the
air tasted cleaner.

Shani led me to a staircase near the front of the ship, which led up to a large outcrop of small windowed decks rising from the main body of the ship. We entered a narrow room with a large table. The walls were covered in maps. Visshaly was with the others who had greeted us the day before, with his head down and a great sadness on his face. Somehow, I knew it was about his brother. I wanted to go and comfort him, but Shani led me to a seat at the other side of the narrow table, where Yuki sat. He smiled and greeted me warmly. Ahmad stared intently as if questioning my worth, while Denise shuffled through sheets of paper in front of her. I was across from Denise, who had yet to lift her head. Visshaly was beside her.

"I hope you slept well and are feeling refreshed," Yuki said, looking at me.

"Yes, thank you. I've never experienced a hot shower."

Yuki nodded. "Yes, there are many luxuries we take for granted here, but we work hard to maintain those simple pleasures. You'll have to work hard, as well, to enjoy them. Now we'll discuss what you can offer to stay among us."

Yuki launched into a recap of the last thirty years of human history, detailing places and events I'd never heard of, that had led humanity to this particular point in time. He detailed technological marvels and scientific discoveries, which passed over my head with words and concepts foreign to me. I became more and more lost in his monologue, but he never once looked at Visshaly or me but off to a point on the other side of the room. I scanned the faces of the others while he spoke. Denise was still fixated on the papers in front of her. Ahmad had his eyes closed and his arms crossed, possibly asleep. Shani must have sensed my gaze and turned to look at me, smiling, before turning back to Yuki. Visshaly looked just as lost and confused with the arched eyebrows and perpetual frown I'd become accustomed to. His face seemed more pained than before and his strong shoulders were slumped. I wanted to ask what had happened. I wanted to console and comfort him, tell him I understood loss and grief. Yuki was still going through mundane details but was now focused on present-day activities. His voice became background noise. He never once let anyone else speak or ask a question. After what must have been an hour, he turned to Ahmad and Shani, telling them to help Visshaly and me to "acclimatize and discover our worth."

Ahmad led Visshaly out of the room without so much as a glance at me. Shani led me to a smaller, adjacent room.

"You probably didn't follow much of that. Forgive Yuki, he takes for granted that the rest of us aren't geniuses. But he's a great man. He's responsible for countless discoveries that have contributed immensely to our mission."

"And what mission is that?"

Shani laughed in a sweet way. "Why, to save the world of course. Things are still bad in a lot of places and there's a lot of work to be done, but we've accomplished a lot. Forests and oceans are healing, and species we once thought were lost are recovering. Every day, more and more people join us. In time, everyone will come to understand our true purpose."

I looked at Shani with skepticism. The places and people I knew didn't care about the forests, the oceans or the creatures that called them home. They were simply trying to survive. If that meant taking down anyone in their way, then so be it.

"I've been more fortunate than you, it's true," Shani said. "I grew up safe and healthy. I know little of the dark places of the world, except what I learn from people like you. Now we have to discover where your talents lie and where you can be of most use."

We sat at a small table. Shani held an electronic pad and began using her finger to swipe across the screen.

"Is Visshaly okay? Did he get news of his brother?" I asked.

"You can ask him yourself, later."

"But why can't we do this together?"

"It's standard practice for one person to assess each newcomer. We're free to choose different paths here based on our strengths and weaknesses. I myself have been training for a new path. That's another perk; you aren't forever stuck in one role. Many among us choose one role for a couple of years and then try something new. But we must start somewhere. Can you read or write?"

"Yes, I taught myself."

"Good. And I'm guessing you know how to grow food and scavenge supplies?"

"Yes."

Shani was tapping the screen on the pad as she asked me questions about various skills and experiences. I answered far more noes than yeses. My life, up to this point, had been about finding food and staying hidden. I'd had no time for other skills. Reading and writing were useless, except that I wanted to know what things were like before. I wanted to know what the books, which we often had to burn to cook or stay warm, said. Reading had let me escape reality, if even for a moment. But it hadn't taught me how to be braver or stronger. It hadn't saved Jahi, Randhir or Amar. It hadn't proved helpful with Visshaly. But it did offer escape. Somehow, I thought reading would not prove entirely useful to these people either.

"We'll find a way for you to contribute. I promise, Aashi."

"Thank you. I'll help any way I can."

Shani nodded, tapping more information on the pad.

"We're headed to Sri Lanka, where I'm from." Shani showed me a map of a large island not far from the coast of India on her pad. "We're reclaiming paradise. Sri Lanka is beautiful but, like many places around the world, has experienced deforestation, pollution, war, famine. The government collapsed about twenty years ago."

Shani showed me more maps of Sri Lanka broken into different sections with different dates on them. "About fifteen years ago, a militant faction dedicated to restoring what they called *communalism* had taken control of large parts of the south of the island. They were a well-equipped and resourced faction made up of scientists, engineers and freedom fighters dedicated to fixing the mistakes of the past. They had cells throughout the larger islands of the Indian and Pacific Oceans. Sri Lanka became a key base of operations."

Shani scrolled to pictures of various people on the screen. At the bottom of each picture were names and dates. "Once this group took control of an area, they began reforestation projects, soil and water remediation, wildlife conservation programs. They practised organic farming and participatory democracy. The societal structure consisted of small communes, no more than two hundred fifty people each. They followed a collective charter of policies and rules, operating largely independently but in constant communication and resource sharing with other communes."

"Is there peace now?" I asked.

"There have been struggles and violence. Battles are still being fought in the northern part of the island. Now leaders are groomed and educated from a young age. Soon paradise will be restored. Wait till you see what we have done, Aashi."

Shani showed me more photos, this time from the sky looking down on fields, villages and jungles. "You'll soon see what we have built. The waters run pure, the hillsides lush with green again, children running through the fields laughing and playing. There's no hunger, no suffering."

"It sounds wonderful. What's your role, Shani?"

"I've had many trades. Currently I'm responsible for acclimatizing new personnel like you. But soon I'll go on our most ambitious expedition yet. We have a series of research and scientific vessels that are going to join numerous other vessels that have been travelling the oceans in an effort to restore coral reefs and remove the tonnes and tonnes of waste that previous societies so casually discarded. We won't finish in my lifetime, but the hope is that one day, the oceans will cleanse themselves and schools of fish, dolphins, turtles, sharks and whales will once again flourish."

"I read about coral reefs. I've seen pictures. They're beautiful and so colourful."

"Sadly, the pictures you saw showed the way things were. There are few healthy reefs left, but we hope to change that. There are still dolphins, whales, sharks and turtles, but too few, given the size of the ocean."

Shani shook her head in dismay, gazing at the floor before returning to her cheery self. "Our project is ambitious, and there aren't enough of us or enough resources to cover the area we need to. Yuki and some of the other key leaders are trying to connect with like-minded groups around the world to see what we can do about stemming the tide of pollution still making its way into the oceans. They believe if we can stop further inputs, then maybe we have a chance to catch up. I'm hopeful. I witnessed the changes on Sri Lanka. Not too long ago, the commune I was born in was surrounded by bare hillsides and the creeks ran brown and low. Now the hillsides teem with life and the creeks are clean. I hope that one day that picture of the reef you saw will become a reality again."

"I would like to help with that, join this expedition if I can. I want to see the wider world, the open oceans, a whale! Maybe even learn to swim."

Shani smiled at me and held my hands. "I'll speak to the others and see what they say. We could be gone and at sea for quite some time and we'll have to teach you to swim and scuba dive. But I know many of the crews still need people, so I'm sure they'll agree."

I was excited and scared at the same time. I had no idea what scuba diving was, and this was the most time I'd ever spent on a boat. Living on land hadn't worked out too well for me, so maybe the sea would be different. I wanted to find Visshaly to see if he would join as well. He wasn't in his room or in any of the common areas. I went up on the deck to watch the ship glide through the waters, waves breaking against its metal sides as it lurched forward. On the horizon ahead were dark shapes. Another crew member pointed and said, "Home."

As most of the crew stood at the front of the boat staring into the distance as the faint outline of land gradually came into clearer view,

I still couldn't find Visshaly anywhere. I searched the cabins and the common areas again and went back up to the deck. I found him leaning on the rails at the rear of the boat, staring at the water below.

"I've been looking for you everywhere."

He looked at me briefly before turning back to the water. "Sri Lanka isn't far now. You can see it from the front of the boat."

I could see that he was upset, but he also looked angry. "Visshaly, what's wrong?"

He sighed deeply, looking across the horizon. "They don't know anything about my brother. All they know is that he never made it to any of the safe houses or Sri Lanka."

"So, he could still be out there somewhere?"

"You don't honestly believe that, do you? Someone like you should understand what that means."

I knew that in all likelihood his brother was dead but couldn't think of anything else to say. "I'm sorry. Is there anything I can do?"

"Like what? Go stare at your new home like everyone else."

"I want to help. I owe you. Have you decided what you want to do yet? Shani thinks I'll be able to join some of their ocean expeditions to repair coral reefs and remove waste. I'm sure they can use someone like you if they're willing to take someone with no skills like me."

Visshaly smiled at me, putting his hand on my shoulder. "You're stronger than you know, Aashi, but that isn't the path for me."

He walked off, heading below deck. Other smaller boats were now close by and details of the island were becoming clear. I could see green hillsides scattered with patches of forest and fields. Straight ahead was a large assemblage of buildings of many different colours. The engines on our ship slowed and the crew moved to drop the anchors.

Shani found me on deck. "We have to anchor out here. This ship is too big to get closer. We haven't had time to build a new harbour. The coast has changed too much. We'll use small boats to get to land. Come. We need to go help pack supplies."

Shani led me below deck where everyone was busy packing up goods or cleaning out cabins. Everyone seemed excited and happy to be going to Sri Lanka. Truthfully, I was too. Despite everything that had happened to me, the people here were kind and happy. I'd been wary at first, but the excitement of what was to come blocked out past trauma. Perhaps I'd finally found a safe place.

Twenty
In the Bunker outside Ontario

I awoke to the sound of bells, but they were more like obnoxious tones, pulsing robotic moans. I got dressed in the greenish-grey fatigues rather than my usual blue and headed to the common area to see what food was like here. While Zone 4 was monochromatic, at least there had been the sky and trees to look at. Here there were grey walls, grey ceilings, greenish clothes and yellowish lights. There was no art, no architectural details, simply a dull bunker.

I reached the common area, which was full of people coming and going, most with trays of food at tables. At least there was laughter and smiles. There didn't seem to be any order to where or with whom people sat. I guess that was one positive sign. The food, on the other hand, looked bland. Some fruits, oats, cereals and breads. A far more limited selection than what was available in the city. I was about to head to one of the lines in the cafeteria, when a woman approached me.

"Kelowna?" I nodded and looked around, confused as to how she knew me. "Relax, I can always spot a newbie. You have the lost-puppy look. Besides, Ares told me to meet up with you. I'm going to show you the ropes. My name is Nadie." *I guess Ares pawned me off on someone else.*

"I was just about to eat something," I said, grabbing a tray and heading for the bowl of oats. Nadie followed.

"Of course. I'll join you if that's okay." She had also grabbed a tray, heading instead for some bread.

We sat at an empty table and Nadie looked at me inquisitively. Nadie was a rare beauty — tall and slim with black hair, tanned skin and striking hazel eyes. She had long earrings made of silver in the shape of feathers and a beaded necklace with the pattern of yellow flowers surrounded with blues and greens. "Tell me about the city, Kelowna. What is it like living around so many people? Did you like it?"

Nadie was still staring at me while nibbling on some bread and fruit.

"The city is … it's clean. It's actually quite beautiful … but … it's just so … predictable." I didn't know how to answer those questions, since compared to what I'd seen so far of this bunker, the city was preferable.

"My people have lived in this region for thousands of years. I prefer the quietness of the woods or the openness of the shores of Lake Huron. But I've never been to the city."

"Would you like to go?"

Nadie shrugged. "Who knows? Maybe I'll get to go soon."

We continued to eat in silence for a few minutes, Nadie waving to some of the other people coming and going about their day or politely smiling at me.

"I know the bunker must seem pretty drab in comparison. Don't worry, we only spend two weeks at a time down here and then two weeks in one of the communes. It's important to see the sun and the stars," she said.

"That's good." It was all I could think of to say.

Thousands of questions were racing through my mind. As if sensing my thoughts, Nadie said, "I'm sure you have lots of questions and they'll be answered in time."

Another set of tones rang out through the halls.

"That one means it's time to go to assigned duties," Nadie explained. She grabbed my tray and motioned for me to follow.

As Nadie returned the trays, she continued to explain life here: "Level F is one of five habitat levels, each capable of housing a thousand people. Most of the time there's only about half of that. Levels A through D are operations, storerooms, the greenhouses and the hangar, which you've seen."

We were walking along the main corridor toward the elevator, along with everyone else. There actually were several elevators wrapped in a circle that formed the centre of each level. Each corridor and hall branched off from that central point.

"Levels J and K are the maintenance, power, water and waste levels. The systems here are self-sustaining. Waste water is purified and reused. All other waste is composted, turned into energy or repurposed. The city uses similar technology. One of the positive outcomes of the resource wars is that societies have finally developed clean technologies that produce little to no waste."

We got on one of the elevators and Nadie took me down to Level J, which was an immense cavern with huge reservoirs and machines. It was hot and noisy. Many people seemed to work on these levels. There were large pools of water, a maze of pipes, large devices called turbines and other machines I couldn't comprehend, despite Nadie's explanations. My life had been books and spreadsheets. I wondered if I would be expected to work down here. I couldn't imagine what use the people here would have for a numbers geek.

As we continued our tour, we skipped the other habitat levels and went up to Level D.

Level D smelled like the village by the lake. It was filled with greenhouses and animals.

"The chickens give us eggs. The goats give us milk, which we use to make cheese, yogourt and butter."

Level D was livelier and more colourful than anywhere else I'd seen so far in this labyrinth. The greenhouses contained a multitude of plants. The animals lived in enclosures with grasses and small bushes, which were thriving underground.

"The lights on this level operate on the same spectrum as the sun. This level uses the most energy, but we produce enough food to feed everyone here and many of the communes in the winter. We can feed thirty thousand people year-round."

As we walked around Level D, Nadie explained the different crops. I walked around, absorbing the scene of all this life around me in an otherwise lifeless place. "How did you get this all down here? We're underground surrounded by tonnes of rock, yet it seems like we're on the surface."

"It's impressive, isn't it. It took a long time. Most of the soil is from the composting facilities. The botanists keep extensive seed banks from plants above ground and artificially pollinate the crops. There's a lot I don't get about it either, but this is my favourite level." Nadie led me back toward the elevators.

"Let's head to Level B. Level C is off limits until we figure out what role you'll be given."

"What's your role here?" I asked.

"At the moment, tour guide. Welcome to Level B."

Level B was a series of storerooms and control areas with screens covered in maps and other items I couldn't comprehend. At the end of a corridor, there was a circular room with a large, round table. The walls of the room were covered in blank screens. As we entered, I recognized Ares, but there were four other people. One, an older woman with short grey hair, blue eyes and only the faintest signs of wrinkles, stood to greet me. "Welcome, Kelowna. Please sit," she said, pointing to a place at the table. Nadie left the room, closing the door. Ares and the others stared at me.

"My name is Elizabeth, and I'm one of the council members here. Ares, you know."

She introduced the other three, but I was barely listening. Instead, I was surveying the room and the giant blank screens. On the other side of one of the glass walls was a room with numerous computers and people working away.

"The communes have council members as well. The council makes decisions as a collective. I've been elected to speak on behalf of the council today as the eldest member." The screens around the room began to light up with images. "These are live satellite images of the Earth. After the wars, the satellite network was neglected, since most central governments had collapsed. Our organization manages to control many communications and surveillance satellites. The Civic Administrators control some as well."

Elizabeth had a remote, which she used to flip through images from around the world. "Every part of the world fared differently against the combined factors of climate chaos, wars and diseases. Some parts have no central organized authority anymore and have limited technological capabilities. Our organization is slowly growing worldwide."

She pressed a button, changing the image again. "This image is a nighttime extrapolation of the eastern and western hemispheres, combined from satellite data taken over the last year. As you can see, Ontario and Michigan are not alone. In North America, there are still hundreds of large cities. For the most part, they operate independently with little outside contact. Ontario and Michigan are the largest and most advanced. The Civic Administrators from both operate very closely and are starting to exert control over other cities."

Another click, another set of images with side-by-side photos of coastlines around the world before and after the climate chaos. The images were shocking. Entire regions were now under water. "Many of these areas were once heavily populated. Based on what information we've been able to gather from similar organizations around the world and current satellite imagery, we estimate that at least two-thirds of the human population has died over the last thirty to forty years."

Elizabeth continued to show different images from different parts of the world. The story was largely the same. "The Sahara Desert has doubled in size. Europe has lost about half of its population and has no centralized governance structures. Australia is a dust bowl. The Americas have been least affected, losing about a third of our population. Large parts of Central and South America are controlled by violent gangs. Sadly, Ontario and Michigan represent the closest thing to a stable government anywhere in the world right now."

Elizabeth switched the screens to black again and sat at the table, staring at me. There was so much information to process. So much about what I thought I knew about the world was wrong.

"We aren't telling you all this to depress you. We simply need to erase the doctrine that the Civic Administrators have ingrained into you. They have their reasons for telling the people that they're the only ones who have survived. It's a simpler explanation and suits their purposes. However, it isn't true. It's taken years to re-establish a global network. We still don't have enough people or equipment to do all that we hope to do. That's where we think you can help. Will you help us, Kelowna?"

I was stunned. How could I possibly help these people? They knew more about the outside world and its problems than I could ever hope to. I sat with a furrowed brow.

The others left the room, leaving Elizabeth and Ares across from me, staring. Ares leaned over to Elizabeth and whispered in her ear. He was still staring at me and frowning.

"I knew your parents," Elizabeth started. "I was in the army with them and was in intelligence with your mother. They were wonderful people. I wish I could have saved them."

"Why didn't you?" I fired back, more aggressively than intended. Elizabeth looked down at the table, then back at me, hurt. I didn't look away.

"They knew the risk and took it on willingly. We would have saved them and you sooner if we could have. After your mother's death, we tried to get you out, but it wasn't the right time. You were being watched closely. We couldn't risk exposing ourselves. And after that, I'm sorry to say, but we'd other matters and forgot about you until recently."

"Why recently?" I asked.

"That's why we wanted to talk to you." Elizabeth pressed some buttons on the remote. "This was shot a couple of months after your father's death," she said, as a video appeared on the largest screen. A video of my mother.

I gazed at the screen in shock, tears welling in my eyes. My mother looked tired and frail. She began to speak: "Our mission was … a success … but somehow we were … discovered." She began to explain some codes and technical jargon that I didn't understand, gaining her composure as she spoke. She seemed in her element now. "I've embedded an untraceable program into their network but have been unable to hack into Zone 1 to bring the entire system down. I'm hoping One Earth, with these codes, can initiate the program to gain control of the entire network."

Her video then turned into a message to me. "Kelowna, I'm sorry that your father and I never told you any of this, but we weren't sure how much we were being watched. Understand that we love you very much and that everything we have done is for you. You're our hope. Our friends will help you. There are codes embedded in this video and in you that will help to complete our mission. Goodbye, my son."

She blew the camera a kiss and shut her eyes before the video ended.

"Wait … um … this … did she … know she was going to die?" I stumbled, trying not to cry.

Elizabeth turned to me. "When your mother's program was discovered, the Civic Administrators gained access to our networks. We had to shut down for four years, but we still had access to their networks, though we avoided using them until we figured it was safe. When we did log back in, there were new firewalls and security features. It took another two years to rediscover your mother's program. She was good, very good."

A tear ran down Elizabeth's cheek and she looked at the table, shaking her head. She steadied herself. "They thought they'd deleted it, but it was still there, lying dormant. It was only a few months ago that we discovered this video file embedded within some of the dormant program. Your mother was too good. We don't have anyone with her coding skill. We're still trying to activate and decode her work. Once we obtained this video, we began looking for you again. I wish our motives were purely for your benefit, but we need to know what information your mother gave you."

I looked at her as if she was nuts. I was still focused on the last part of my mother's video. I couldn't remember either of my parents saying they loved me. That video represented the first time seeing my real and honest mother.

"Considering how difficult it was for us to find this video when we knew what to look for, it's nearly impossible that the Civic Administrators have discovered it. Your mother wouldn't have said that there are codes embedded in this video and in you if she didn't mean it. There must have been information she considered too important to embed in their network."

I was still trying to process that video and everything that Elizabeth was saying.

"If you're right, then my parents used me as some sort of carrier. I think I would remember something like that."

"It would be small, something they could have put in your food or a drink or injected while you were sleeping. I know this must make you sad or angry, but they wouldn't have done it unless they had no other choice. Whatever information you possess could make a significant difference in our cause."

At that, Ares spoke up. "Listen, I know you didn't know your parents the way some of the people here did, but this is important. Do you remember the Civic Guardians questioning you at all after either of your parents' deaths? Did they do any tests on you?"

"I don't know, I don't think so. Give me a minute; this is a lot to take in."

Ares, exasperated, got up. "I told you we should have just drugged him and extracted it," he said, storming out of the room. I looked at

Elizabeth, stunned at Ares's outburst. My knees started to shake as I realized how trapped I was here.

Elizabeth stood, walked around the table, sat in the chair beside me and grabbed my hands. "I know this is a lot, Kelowna. I'm sorry for Ares, but he's impatient. The truth is, we've been struggling to unravel the mystery your mother left. Most people here believe the codes embedded in that video and whatever is in you is the prize we've been waiting for, that her program will somehow solve all our problems. I'm not so optimistic. I'm sure it's important, but it will only be another tool in our struggle. It's not fair to you. You've been given no time to adjust, to learn about this place, about the world outside Ontario. You need time to absorb this information about your parents. We can return you to a commune if you would like."

I sat in silence, trying to edge away from Elizabeth. While on the tour with Nadie, returning to the village by the lake or somewhere else seemed so appealing. But with the new-found knowledge of the world and my parents, I wasn't sure what I wanted. Elizabeth sat patiently, awaiting a response.

"No, I want to know what it is. I want to know why my parents died."

Elizabeth smiled and nodded at me, squeezing my hands. "Follow me." She led me down the corridor through a control room with more computers and screens. A door at the back of the room led down another corridor. On the left was a large laboratory. There were two other people there. Elizabeth introduced them. One was a doctor and the other was their main nanotechnology specialist. They hooked me up to a series of cords and machines, explaining that they were going to monitor my neural patterns and heart rate.

"We suspect the Civic Administrators questioned you extensively and we need to know if they discovered anything."

"Honestly, I don't remember ever being questioned."

"There are ways to alter a person's memory, but if we find what your mother put in you, it should mean they didn't," Elizabeth explained.

The doctor turned to me. "Kelowna, with your permission, we're going to run you through a series of tests."

"Okay," I replied, anxious and shaking.

They injected me with something and the rest of those tests were a blur.

I regained consciousness some time later. Elizabeth explained that I'd been out for a couple of hours.

"Did you get what you were looking for?" I asked.

The nanotechnology expert leaned over me. "Yes. Your mother managed to hide her own nanochips under the standard chip. Every person in the city has a nanochip embedded behind their left ear when they're born. Luckily for us, the Civic Administrators didn't examine yours further. Your mother used their own technology to mask what we needed."

"Thank you, Kelowna," said Elizabeth. "It will take us some time to decipher and make sense of how this nanochip fits in with the codes embedded in the video. I suggest you return to your quarters and rest. I'll ask Nadie to escort you back to the habitat level."

With that, Elizabeth led me out of the laboratory to where Nadie was waiting. Nadie guided me to the elevators, and we went to the cafeteria for food. She was giving me space and silence. I'd stared at the floor since leaving the laboratory, cracking my knuckles and fidgeting with my pockets. The cafeteria was full of other people. We grabbed some trays and I picked up some salad and penne.

"Am I allowed to eat this in my room?" I asked Nadie.

"Yes, just return the dishes and tray. Do you want company?"

"No, thanks. I'd prefer to be alone right now."

"I understand. I'll check on you in the morning, Kelowna."

I left the cafeteria, returned to my closet of a room and ate very little of my food. Before going to bed, I went down the hall for a warm shower and processed the day's events.

Twenty-One
Paraiso, Colombia

One night, months after I'd arrived in Paraiso, Senora Vasquez and I were sitting drinking tea outside our hut. I was thinking about the people who had helped me get here, particularly Daniel, who led me into the mountains on horseback. "Do you know Daniel well, Senora?"

"Yes, I've known him for many years. A good man."

Daniel had come back to Paraiso a few days earlier. Before he'd left again, he'd approached me while I was tending a garden and asked how I was liking life in Paraiso. I told him I was grateful to be here. Daniel was an imposing man with a deep voice. Everyone in Paraiso seemed to know and adore him.

"Tell me about him," I asked Senora Vasquez.

"You spent days travelling with him."

"I slept most of it. He didn't seem to want to talk."

"Daniel, like many, has had a rough life."

"Did he escape from the slums too?"

"No, nothing like that. It was many years ago. Daniel was an important man in the valley far below. At that time, the villages were safe, and trade was easy. Slowly, other groups tried to take control of the area. As they got more violent, Daniel encouraged people to fight back. Many died."

Senora Vasquez grew very quiet and still, staring at the teacup she held close with both hands. "One day when Daniel was out patrolling the roads, some men came and grabbed his beautiful wife and two young children. When Daniel returned, he found his house empty and ruined. Some of the other villagers told Daniel where they went. Daniel gathered as many villagers as he could and headed in the direction the men had gone. At one of the crossroads, Daniel found a group of over a hundred men, all armed with guns. They had his family. There were only about fifty villagers with Daniel, armed with pitchforks and axes. The leader among the men with guns explained to the villagers that they controlled the valley now. Everyone would be safe as long as they provided what was asked of them. Daniel refused, telling them to leave. The man shot Daniel's wife in the head."

Tears were rolling down Senora Vasquez's cheek and she was sobbing but trying to control it.

"Were you there?" I asked.

"Yes. Most of us tried to convince Daniel to accept the terms so he could get his children back. Daniel agreed, but the man refused, saying the children belonged to him now and to remind everyone about what happens when they resist. Daniel ran at the men holding his children. They shot Daniel in the leg, but he pushed forward, throwing an axe at one of the men, hitting him in the chest. The leader restrained the rest of his men from shooting Daniel. Instead, they grabbed Daniel, punching and kicking him. Another man hit Daniel in the back of the head with his rifle, knocking him out. They took Daniel's children away."

"Why didn't the rest of you do anything?" I didn't mean to sound harsh, but my question caused pain for Senora Vasquez.

"I think about that day often. We were scared. They had more men and guns. We would have all died. Maybe that would have been better. Maybe not…"

Senora Vasquez refilled her teacup. "Either way, there's a happy ending. I looked after Daniel and helped him regain his strength. Other villagers tried to find out where they'd taken his children. No one learned anything. The men came often to our village and told us that Daniel was never to leave or his children would be killed. Daniel was a broken man for many months. He barely ate, never spoke. There was confusion in the valley for many days as new groups fought for control. Daniel's children escaped with other prisoners from the town. Daniel was reunited with his children. It was then that we decided to escape into the mountains."

"Why doesn't Daniel still live here then?"

"He did for many years. But his children are grown now, with children of their own. Daniel comes often, but he returned to the valley several years ago to help others, like you. He is a saviour to many of the people here."

After I'd arrived in Paraiso, Daniel hadn't stayed long. I didn't get a chance to see or thank him before he left. I saw him many more times as the years passed, but I spoke to him only that one time when he asked how I was liking life in Paraiso. The few days at a time he stayed in the village, he spent in the forest with his grown children and young grandchildren.

For four years now, I'd lived with Senora Vasquez and listened to her wonderful stories. But she never spoke about herself and her own story. It was obvious she was well respected in the village. I asked her once about herself and she responded, "The past is gone; it's better to look to the future." I tried asking other villagers about her, but they also refused to discuss her life story.

The village would often have communal gatherings to celebrate different events, whether it was the completion of a new hut or a full moon. There was joy, comfort and community here. And laughter. I'd never heard laughter so often. Paraiso was home to 138 people, 47 of whom were younger than me. The oldest person was a ninety-six-year-old woman, who despite having no teeth, laughed more than anyone. A child rolling down a hill, a joke or someone slipping harmlessly in the stream would cause nearly everyone in the village to laugh. Everyone except Senora Vasquez and I laughed constantly. While Senora Vasquez often had a smile on her face, it was the gentle smile of a kind woman.

About a year after I arrived in Paraiso, and before I told Senora Vasquez about killing José and the others, I told her about how the soldados prepared new recruits.

There was one day I remembered in particular. It was months after José's death. We returned to the compound with the last of our buckets. At least ten recruits were standing in the yard, naked, as soldados threw stones at them. The soldados at the gate ordered us to watch. Most of the recruits had red cuts all over their bodies. Suddenly, one of the recruits was hit near the eye and fell to the ground. One of the soldados yelled to stop and the throwing of stones ceased. The recruit that fell to the ground slowly got up. The soldado who yelled the order to stop approached the recruit, pulled out his pistol and shot him in the head. He told the other recruits that they had passed the test and could go clean themselves up. I remember staring at the dead recruit until I was smacked on the top of my head by one of the soldados at the gate, who told me to go home.

After that, one of the runners would get hit every day for no reason. It was a game to the soldados. One day, the smallest boy on my team returned with full buckets for the first time since he started being a runner. Instead of congratulating the small child, the soldados dumped the buckets over his head and told him to do it again. He started crying as we climbed back up the hill. I yelled at him to stop and told him to do as he was told, or he would face worse.

Another time, on a hot and dusty day, one of the boys, who was slightly smaller than me, tripped as we approached the gate, spilling one of his buckets on a soldado. He was beaten so badly that one of his eyes swelled shut and I was certain he'd broken some ribs. The rest of us were told to carry him home. The next day, he limped his way to the gate but fell, spitting blood, on the first climb up the hill. One of the soldados guarding the spring saw and came down the hill asking what was wrong. The rest of us didn't speak. He grabbed the broken boy and told him to get up. He managed to stand up briefly before convulsing and coughing up more blood. The soldado flung him to the ground with a look of disgust and told the rest of us to get back to work. On our second climb, one of the younger boys leaned down to see if he was okay. Before the soldados saw, I yanked him up and told him there was nothing we could do for the injured boy. On our last trip down, the soldados were changing shifts and they told me to check if he was alive. I bent down and turned him over so that he was face up. He wasn't breathing and had gone stiff and white. The soldado carried my buckets and told me to carry the body. There was a pile of garbage out behind the compound where I was told to throw the boy; the dogs and vultures would take care of him, they said. All of these events blurred together, and I don't know why I told Senora Vasquez some after a year and the rest after four years. It was only as more time had passed in Paraiso that I remembered them all fully.

When I was seventeen and more confident in my reading and writing, and I considered Senora Vasquez family, I was ready to tell her about the worst night, the event that gave me more nightmares than killing José or the others, carrying that dead boy and throwing him in a pile of garbage or watching that naked recruit die.

As we always did at night, Senora Vasquez and I were sitting in front of our hut looking at the stars and listening to the sounds of the night.

"I did see Alejandra one more time before I fled," I said.

"Oh? Do you want to tell me about it?"

"It happened about a month before I left. I never told my abuela I saw her. It keeps me up at night."

"Take your time, Miguel."

My leg was shaking, and I had to close my eyes. "We'd just delivered our last buckets when the soldado that called me *Killer* led me to one of the houses where there were many soldados drinking and eating while young naked girls danced for them to loud music. The soldado led me upstairs, saying there were other things I needed to learn to truly be a man."

I began to shake and cry. Senora Vasquez pulled her chair closer to mine and put her arm around me. "It's okay. It's not your fault."

I struggled to tell the rest of the story. "In the room were two other soldados. Tied to the bed was a young naked girl. It was … it was … Alejandra. I tried to leave, but the soldado blocked the door. I tried to force my way out, begged him to let me go. The soldado smacked me across the face, saying she was a pretty girl. Alejandra looked up and saw me. She struggled to get out of her bonds. The soldado holding me asked if we knew each other. I told them that she was my sister."

I had to stop and was shaking and crying. Senora Vasquez tried to comfort me.

"One of the soldados removed his pants and climbed over Alejandra. I tried to turn away or close my eyes, but they hit me every time. They forced me to watch. Alejandra never screamed or cried. I wanted to grab their guns or knives and kill them. I wanted to do something, but they were too big and strong. I understand why you couldn't help Daniel save his family all those years ago."

I buried my head in Senora Vasquez's shoulder, holding her tight.

"Miguel. You're not to blame. There was nothing you could have done. Sometimes the world doesn't make sense. Sometimes people do horrible things to each other. There are good and bad people in the world and there always have been. It doesn't make it easier, but you're safe now."

"And she isn't," I said, angry.

"No, she isn't." Senora Vasquez had nothing else to say but continued to hug me.

Around two weeks after telling Senora Vasquez about that night, some new arrivals came to the village. There were around two dozen of them, all fairly tall and strong, dressed in dark green. I was off upstream of the village when they arrived. As I walked back into the village, I found Senora Vasquez in front of our hut. "Who are they?" I asked.

"Many of them grew up in this village but had left to go south and join a large resistance movement."

"Resisting what?"

"The gangs. This movement has been getting stronger for some time and controls large parts of southern Colombia now."

"What are they doing here?"

"I'm not sure yet."

Later that afternoon, there was a meeting with a few of the key villagers, including Senora Vasquez, who brought me along. A tall, middle-aged man with dark skin addressed the assembled villagers and newcomers. "Good afternoon. We have good news. We now control a third of the former Colombia, as well as all of Ecuador and parts of Peru. More importantly, we've made contact with like-minded groups in other parts of South America and around the world. Our next target is the valleys in and around Bogotá."

Target? I thought. *For what?*

"We'll restore democracy and equality to all of Colombia," he continued.

The gangs won't give up control. They're too well armed.

The man must have sensed my thoughts. "We don't want a long, bloody conflict, but don't expect the gangs in this region to just give up control. They'll likely try to paint us as invaders. But we do have allies already in the area. And spies. We've spent years learning the strengths and weaknesses of the various gangs. They don't know it yet, but we already have them surrounded." Senora Vasquez looked worried. The other assembled villagers were nodding. "We thank you for your hospitality and will not stay long."

I walked back to our hut with Senora Vasquez. "How long have you known about this movement?"

"For years. But it isn't one group with any one name or purpose. I used to be very involved. It took a long time to bring everyone together."

"I want to help."

"I figured you would. I won't stop you, but you'll have to convince the commander to let you join."

Over the next few days, dozens of heavily armed fighters began arriving in the village. They, like the others before, were young, fit and energetic. Everything was orderly and calm without the hint of fear. Senora Vasquez kept to herself more than was usual and rarely engaged with any of the newcomers.

"Why aren't you more involved in all the discussions going on?" I asked her.

"My part in this struggle has ended. I did all that I could with the hope that this time, things would be different."

"I don't understand. Anything is better than the way Bogotá is."

"History has a tendency of repeating itself, Miguel. Perhaps human nature is fundamentally flawed. Generations of social engineering are not that easy to undo. This group, this movement, whatever it started out with — the right ideals, worthy goals — now it's an amalgam of various ideologies and purposes, egos and leaders. My fear is that the stronger this group becomes, the more territory they control, the more likely they'll become another version of the tyranny they sought to overthrow. Paraiso is all I need now."

"Do you really believe they'll be just as bad as the gangs?"

"I hope not." Senora Vasquez pointed at the tall man that gave the speech on the first day they arrived in the village. "See that commander over there? He was responsible for the takeover of Cali, a city in the south. One of the first things he did was execute most of the gang members who controlled the city and enslaved the rest. What would you call that?"

"Justice."

"I'm sure that's how most of the formerly oppressed felt as well. An eye for an eye. The problem with that approach is it leaves each of us with only one eye or completely blind."

Senora Vasquez walked away and began tending one of the gardens. She had to be wrong. Even if everywhere couldn't be like Paraiso, it would certainly be better than what most places were like. None of the newcomers seemed evil or inherently violent. I'd grown up with people that took pleasure from others' pain. The young fighters here seemed kind and just. They could never commit the kind of violence I'd seen. If the soldados in Bogotá were killed by them, then the world would be a better place.

A fighter around my age, but shorter and thinner, approached me. "Are you Miguel from Bogotá?" she asked.

"Yes."

"Come with me, please."

"But who are you? Where are you taking me?"

"I'm Maria. We've been told you want to help. I'm taking you to one of the commanders."

I followed Maria to one of the tents that had been assembled in a vacant field north of the village. There were dozens of large canvas tents. Even more had been set up on the other side of the stream. Another camp had been set up about a half day's walk west of the village, on the narrow path that would lead down into the valley. Most of the fighters were encamped there.

I was led to the largest tent, which was covered in cables, satellites and other equipment I'd never seen before. There were two guards at the canvas door. Inside the tent were a series of screens with young fighters dressed in the same dark green, intently speaking into communication devices while examining maps and images. There was a large table in the middle with stacks of paper and larger maps. There were several fighters sitting around the table, speaking in low murmurs. The young fighter that led me into the tent went over to a middle-aged woman with dark hair and whispered in her ear. The woman looked at me and nodded before walking to the back of the tent, pulling aside a flap and disappearing. Maria and I followed her. Behind the flap, a middle-aged woman was sitting behind a neatly organized desk. In front of the desk were two chairs. The woman motioned for me to sit. Maria sat in the other chair.

"I'm Rosa. I understand that you grew up in one of the slums in Bogotá and worked as a runner for one of the gang bosses."

I was surprised. Senora Vasquez must have told them about my past. I was angry that she'd done that. The surprise must have shown on my face.

"Listen, I don't know any more about you than that and you aren't responsible for anything you might have done. We're hoping that you can help us with intel about that area, the gangs' capabilities, potential allies in the slums, those sorts of things."

"I thought your focus was the valley below?"

"It is, but that will be over within the week. Most of the gangs have already moved out, since they take their orders from Bogotá anyway. Our network in the valley is strong. Bogotá is the real challenge. Without securing it, the surrounding valleys that provide much of the city's food will be under constant threat. Luckily for us, things in the city are already destabilized. One of the gangs has taken over nearly seventy percent of the city already. A few years ago, the leader of that gang made an uneasy alliance with the people who live in the gated communities, in the core of the city, to increase his own power and wealth. One by one, the other gangs were exterminated. The remaining populace continues to suffer. Now it seems the remaining gang and the people in the core have turned on each other. The gang leader has thousands of troops, a lot of weapons, vehicles and territory. The elites in the core have their own private army with better weapons and equipment. Food, water and other goods are already in short supply in the city as the gang has shifted their tactics to starve out the centre. Riots and close-quarter battles are strangling the city. The death toll is catastrophic. We didn't intend to move on Bogotá so quickly, but we have a responsibility to the thousands of innocent people caught in the crossfire, and to be honest, this chaos presents an opportunity. So, are you willing to help and return to Bogotá?"

I was shocked at how much they knew and now more worried about my abuela, Alejandra and everyone else I knew in the slum. "I do want to help, but I'm not sure how."

"Any detail may help. Key gang members, locations, how many of them guard those locations at different points in the day," Rosa said.

"I only know things about the compound in the hills near my neighbourhood. I don't know anything about the rest of the city."

Rosa showed me a map and some pictures.

"That's the compound in my neighbourhood," I said.

She then showed me pictures of people. "This is the leader of the gang that now controls most of the city," Rosa said.

"That's him. The gang boss from the compound I ran water to."

"Based on our intelligence and surveillance, he's still living at that compound and has fortified the hillside and entire neighbourhood. The compound has been expanded significantly. These are recent satellite images. Do you recognize anything?"

"Not really. This looks like the layout of the original compound. But all of these other buildings are different. The roads have changed. This doesn't look like my neighbourhood."

"If you recognize the leader of the gang, then I assure you, it's the same place," Rosa said.

"Then I can't help you. It's all so different. I don't even see the building I lived in with my abuela. It was up the road from the compound, but that's all changed."

"You can still help. You'll recognize people. They might recognize you. There might be a chance to find some of your friends or family. It's up to you."

I paused, looking at more of the photos and maps. I had to try to find my abuela and Alejandra.

"Yes, I'll help."

"Good. Maria here will get you equipped and explain your training."

Rosa returned to her desk and Maria led me out of the large tent. "We'll start training first thing tomorrow morning," she said. "Come find me at the open tent by the creek over there."

Maria walked off to talk to some other fighters, and I headed back to my hut, nervous of what was to come next.

Twenty-Two
At the Camp outside Kyiv

The next morning, we awoke with the sun and had a simple breakfast of juice, cereal and fruit. People were well fed, and the camp seemed to operate with very few guards. After breakfast, it was time to head to the fields and barns. William told me I could join their group. The gates to the camp were left open, and farming tools left outside the gate. Fields were all around the camp. There were no fences beyond the fields, just forest and burnt-out villages. I could see the wall along the river in the distance, but other than that, the only wall was around the camp.

"William, why don't people escape? The guards don't seem to care, and no one is watching us. You could go anywhere."

"Where would you go? Back to Kyiv, west to the outer wall, north or south to another camp? As soon as anyone came upon you, you'd be shot. No one escapes because there's nowhere to go. Besides, why bother? We have food, clean water, shelter. We keep most of what we grow. The guards aren't cruel. This is a better life than most places."

"Is that all we can hope for now? We're still prisoners. Still not free to make our own choices."

"You'll figure it out soon enough. Those days are over."

There was something in the way William spoke that reminded me of me. That's the way I used to speak to Anna and my parents. They were the idealists striving for a better world. I was the realist, accepting our situation and trying to just survive. Losing Anna and my parents had changed all that. Survival alone wasn't worth it.

I couldn't figure out what we were supposed to be doing. It was the middle of winter. The temperature was hovering around zero and there was a light dusting of snow on the ground. Winters in this part of Europe would have been cold and difficult once, but those days were gone. The fields were barren, but people were turning the dirt regardless. There were some greenhouses around the camp where food was still being grown. There were barns with animals and feed. Others were headed to the woods with axes. Yet our group was tilling the partially frozen fields.

"What's the point of this?" I asked.

"Some days we work in the barns, the forest or the greenhouse. Other days we till the fields, even in the winter. No one can sit idle in the camp all day. If we till the fields now, it'll be easier in the spring," William said.

I knew that it didn't matter whether we tilled them now or when temperatures climbed but didn't bother saying anything. They'd been here for a while, and I was new. I had to make do and figure out my next move.

At midday, soup was served outside the gate. Everyone was given an hour break. In the afternoon, we went to work in one of the chicken coops, cleaning the pens, gathering eggs, stocking the feed and water. It was easy and slow work. There were hundreds to do the work and a crew had already done it in the morning. My family had operated a farm much larger than this, with fewer than ten people. If the war was over, why bother keeping these camps operating? What was the point?

Days turned into weeks, weeks into months. Spring planting went well, and the summer was warm with frequent enough rain to nourish the crops. Some of the prisoners started to notice that the trams stopped coming. They used to come every week or so, dropping off one or two people or replacing a guard. It had been at least two months since the last one.

The guards had noticed as well.

It was late August when everyone woke up one morning to the gates open and the guards gone. Everyone gathered in the dining hall; many seemed confused and scared, while some of the more senior prisoners gathered at the front, whispering to each other. William was one of them. Others had gone into the guard barracks and the central building to see what they could learn.

William came over to our table to explain what had been discussed. "Apparently, there are riots in Kyiv. The guards started them. There were messages left on the computers in the central building. Most guards across the Front are abandoning their posts and returning home. The outer wall has been abandoned, gates left open. One of the guards left a note for the prisoners. It said we're free."

At this point, most of the same information had been relayed to all the other tables. There was shouting and confusion across the dining hall. An old Ukrainian man stood on a table at the front of the hall, shouting for everyone to quiet down. The old man spoke with authority. One of the women in our group spoke Ukrainian and translated for us.

"The old man has been the longest resident of this camp," she explained. "He says that we have a good life here. We have fertile fields, clean wells and comfortable shelters. We could build a community here. If the war is over, so be it." Our translator paused, straining to hear the rest. "Most of us have nowhere to return to. We don't know what we would be returning to or how we would get there. Why risk it?"

Others were shouting him down. This was still a prison. Some were scared that the people to the east would begin attacking again when they realized everything was undefended. The disease could spread again.

William whistled with his fingers in his mouth, one of those shrill, ear-piercing and powerful whistles. "We're free. That means everyone is free to choose their own path. Stay, go, it's up to you."

Each table reverted to quieter conversations.

"I thought those days were over," I said to William.

"Freedom was always an illusion. We believed democracy made us free. We were slaves to the pursuit of money. When that failed, we were slaves to those in positions of power. Now, if there's no money, no government, no power, I guess we're truly free."

"What will you do?"

"I don't know. See what's out there, I guess."

People spent the day deciding what they were going to do next. One of the couples in our group decided to stay. The other three decided to head south. They had no reason, they just wanted to see the Black Sea. I was tempted to join them but knew where I had to go.

William was strangely quiet as the others explained their chosen paths.

"And you, Elliott?" someone asked.

"I'm going to go to Kyiv. If I know Anna and my father, they'll want to know what's happening there and help. If I can't find them, I'll return to our farm outside of Budapest and hope they're alive and will head there too."

The others wished me luck and went to make their arrangements. The couple that were staying joined another group of people that had decided to remain at the camp. It seemed like at least half of the people in the camp would make it their home.

William still didn't move or speak for some time. I stayed with him, realizing like so many others here, he'd nothing to drive him or give him hope.

"Is she worth it?" he asked. I nodded. "Then I'll help you find her. Any woman that can convince a man to do what you did is worth meeting." He smiled at me and patted me on the shoulder.

We spent the evening gathering extra clothes, food and canteens and packing it all into bags we found in the guards' barracks. The people that were leaving decided to wait until first thing in the morning. Numerous maps had been found in the barracks, which were distributed based on which way people had decided to go. William and I had a map of the Front with Kyiv at its centre.

Before going to bed, I faced William in the bunk beside me. He was lying flat on his back, staring at the wood panel ceiling.

"Thank you," I said, turning onto my side and going to sleep.

I woke to William shaking my shoulder. He looked haggard, like he hadn't slept at all. "Time to go."

Most of the other people in the barracks were already gone or up moving around. The dining hall was quiet. Many people left before sunrise. I guess it was easier than saying goodbye. Many of the people that were staying had already gone about their usual chores. After a light breakfast, William and I double-checked our bags for the essentials and were on our way.

No one was at the gate to wish us well. A few others who were also heading to Kyiv had left shortly before us. It was likely we would meet up with them. The easiest thing to do was follow the train tracks that delivered us to the camp. It was a warm day with a light breeze and the fields were full, it being near the end of summer. Despite all the uncertainty around what would happen next, the walk was peaceful. William was sombre and quiet. He was normally so gregarious.

We estimated that Kyiv was at least eighty kilometres away, based on the amount of time it had taken the train to reach the camp. Walking all day with very little rest, we hoped to cover the distance in three days. Halfway through the first day, we passed another farming camp that appeared deserted. We managed to catch up to a few of the other people from our camp heading to Kyiv, greeted them kindly and continued past them.

We found a village a few hundred metres off the tracks to the east, beside a small creek heading toward the river. Most of the houses were in serious disrepair or burned, but one of the larger stone houses still had a roof and seemed like as good a place as any to camp for the night. We gathered some wood and had a fire in one of the rooms where the roof had caved in. Our dinner consisted of some bread, cheese and fruit. The water from the creek seemed fresh enough and we took our fill. William had still not said more than a few words all day.

After dinner, as he was readying himself for bed, I cleared my throat awkwardly. "Is everything all right?"

He looked at me hesitantly. This man, who once had all the confidence in the world, now appeared like a scared and lost child.

"I don't know. For so long now, my life has been dictated by others. I'm not sure what to do next."

"You're still young. There are many things you can do now."

"Perhaps."

"If we don't find Anna or my father in Kyiv, I'll head back toward Budapest. Come with me. The farm we live at is beautiful. You can make a home there."

"We'll see. Good night." He curled up on the floor under one of the blankets we'd brought.

"Night."

William was a former Valiant, crushed by circumstances beyond his control; now he was somewhere between the Reconciled and the Fatalists. If Anna were here, she would know how to invigorate William. She would know how to motivate and inspire. I lay awake that night wondering where in the world Anna could be. I knew she was alive. Not out of any misguided faith, but just a belief that her sheer strength of will was enough to keep her going. It was entirely possible that she was in the thick of things in Kyiv. She'd probably founded a new chapter of the movement and was trying to restore some semblance of governance in this destabilized part of the world.

I was finally at a place where I fully believed in what she and my parents had spent their lives trying to create. Now I would give my life to protect her and to fight for a better world against anyone who would try to set us back. How could I make William see? He needed something to believe in again. Kyiv would have the answer one way or another.

We travelled all the next day and camped that night just outside the city. Smoke covered the central parts with pockets of glowing oranges and reds, but it was quiet. We assumed it was people burning what they could for light. The electricity seemed to be off. The next morning, entering the outskirts of the city was beyond eerie. The walls and towers were broken in many places. The outlying areas, which before were a hive of activity, were deserted. William and I looked at each other nervously.

As we entered the central part of the city, we began to see people. Haggard, dishevelled and dirty people.

"Likely factory or mine workers. Poor bastards," William said. They avoided eye contact and scurried into dark alleys the moment they saw us. As we got closer to the central square, with its large concrete buildings and monumental fortifications, we could hear the chants, cheers and commotion of thousands.

Or tens of thousands. Every section of the square was packed. Trucks and trains were covered in people all dressed in the drab grey that defined a prisoner. Some of the buildings were equally full of people hanging out of windows or on balconies, in the towers and on rooftops. The main building at the end of the square was a different story. It had the highest walls and guard towers. This one appeared to still be guarded.

A makeshift stage had appeared in the centre of the square near the buildings that once processed all the prisoners. The chain-link fences and pens had been dismantled. Fires burned in some of the outlying buildings. This scene was too reminiscent of that day in Budapest, nearly a year ago. I thought of my mother's speech that day and of my panic and guilt.

But in Kyiv, many of the prisoners had weapons. There were naked and mutilated bodies piled beside the stage. The former prisoners in and around the stage now wore bits and pieces of guards' uniforms.

"What now?" William asked me.

I shook my head in disbelief. It wasn't safe here. It was too familiar.

Groups of former prisoners had begun assembling tents and pavilions of their own along the outside parts of the square. They'd strewn together bits of flags or symbols of different locations and organizations.

"We need to find the United Earth tent." I grabbed William's arm and rushed headlong into the sea of humanity. We passed tents for different countries that no longer existed and ones for political movements that were outlawed long ago — communist, fascist, neo-capitalist, among other ideologies. I needed to get a better vantage point. With everyone dressed the same and the square packed to the point of bursting, it would take hours to walk around the whole thing, checking each pavilion. Near the central stage, one of the trains was left in place. It seemed as good a place as any to get a better view.

William followed, surveying the area with military precision. The train had a few armed men around it with no obvious affiliation. I spoke to one of them, near the end of the train. He was armed with a club.

"No speak English."

I tried German, broken Hungarian. He shook his head. We went to the other side of the train and tried a different man. This one had a gun. And he spoke German. When I asked to climb the train to get a better view, he told me to get lost. William was losing patience. He scanned the area, then with lightning speed propelled his fist into the man's nose, grabbed his gun, wheeled behind him and proceeded to knock him unconscious. He grabbed the man's hat and flak jacket, a knife and extra ammunition. He found zip ties and tied the man's hands and feet together before sliding the body under the train.

"Well, get up there and take a look," he said to me. I began to climb a ladder at the end of the train car. "Don't stand on the top where everyone can see you. And be quick about it," William shouted.

I tried halfway up the ladder but only had a view of about a third of the square. I climbed a little higher, hovering over the top rung.

There were hundreds of pavilions. In a corner of the square, not far from the still-guarded main building, a tent was painted blue and green in the shape of a circle. It was hard to make out, but it had to be the United Earth banner. I rushed down the ladder and told William where to go. He led this time, carrying his newly acquired weapons.

At the centre of the square, people were pressing toward the stage as a man spoke through a poorly assembled sound system. The sound was bass mixed with static. Yet people were eager to hear what he had to say and continued to press forward. Not a single word could be made out in any language. A path cleared along the edge of the square. We pushed our way through, going the opposite direction of everyone else.

As we got closer to the pavilion with the blue-and-green circle, it got more distinguishable. There was no question; it was United Earth. My pace increased, a smile across my face, a jump in my step. There were dozens of people still hovering around this pavilion. I didn't recognize any of them. I began to shout, "Anna!" and "Peter!" — my father's name. I pushed my way through some of the crowd, still shouting. Near the edge of the tent, a woman stood on a box. She screamed, "Elliott!"

I collapsed to my knees, crying. She ran toward me and I got to my feet in time to catch her sailing into my arms. Anna, at last. We hugged and kissed, falling to the ground. Others around us were clapping and cheering. When we finally composed ourselves, I introduced Anna to William. She led us into the pavilion. Unsurprisingly, she'd already established herself as a leader here. She introduced me to some of the others around a table with maps, photos and pamphlets. I only had eyes for her. After the introductions were made, I pulled her aside, kissing her.

"Have you seen my father?"

She shook her head. "I'm sorry, no." I hugged her again.

"What are you doing here?" she asked.

"I came to find you."

She looked at me like I was a foolish child, putting her palm on the side of my face. "You always were a fool, but you're my fool." We embraced and kissed again. "Come on. We have much to discuss and do here." There she was. Anna the activist, the fighter. Whatever happened to her in the last year hadn't weakened her resolve.

Some of the other members around the table were explaining that they had to rebuild, to be a central part of whatever new structure took place in and around Kyiv. They had control of the building behind them, which served as a communications centre. The building still had power. Some of their tech people had established contact with other members of similar movements around the world. They were discussing tactics, available resources and manpower.

The discussion turned to what was going to happen here. Things were tense. One group had killed many of the guards, who had laid down their weapons. These people had been anarchist political prisoners for years. Most of them had been mine workers or worse, working in deplorable conditions, forced to fight and lied to for years. They wanted vengeance and nothing more. Those who were left of the military leadership from this sector had barricaded themselves in the central building, which was still heavily guarded.

There had been some exchange of gunfire and casualties the first couple of nights, but things had quieted down. Many people had already left the city in search of food and clean water, which were becoming scarce. More would leave in the next couple of days. They didn't care what happened here. Most of the people around the table were worried about what would happen if these violent anarchists took control. They believed we would be exchanging one violent regime for another. I couldn't take it any longer.

"Let them have control of Kyiv. What do you really think you're going to accomplish by opposing them? You'll get people killed. Centralized governance isn't coming back. People can go back to learning to grow their own food and live in small decentralized communities. What's wrong with that?"

Anna grabbed my hand and told me to be quiet. The rest basically ignored my outburst. I stormed out of the tent with William in tow.

"You're right, you know. Do-gooders have no place in the world anymore," William said.

I laughed. "Unfortunately, Anna is the ultimate do-gooder."

Anna came out shortly after, with that pitying look I'd seen so many times.

"I'm sorry," I said. "I just got you back. I won't lose you again."

She held my hand. "After all these years and you still don't get me. I'm not content with a comfortable life. We can make this world a better place. Can't you see that?"

"All I can see are angry people pointing guns at other people scared for their lives. Words aren't going to solve that."

"No, but most of the people here want something new and different. Those people with guns may take control for a day or two, but then the majority will overwhelm them."

I faced the crowded centre of the square before turning to the heavily guarded main building at the end of the square. "Why can't we go back to our farm? The movement is still active in and around Budapest. That's our home."

"We will soon. I promise." She let go of my hands and moved toward William, who was staring at the guarded building. "William, what's your part in all this?" she asked.

William shrugged. "I told him that I would help find you. Honestly, I never thought we would. I didn't think past that point."

"You're welcome to come with us anywhere we go," I said. William nodded, then turned away to face the latest commotion.

The man from the stage was now in front of the gate at the main building, surrounded by his own armed supporters. He had a megaphone. The press of people had followed closely behind.

He was speaking Ukrainian and we couldn't make out the words. He was angry and agitated. There was no answer from inside the main building. He began to confer with some of the other people around him.

Suddenly, there was a bang and he collapsed to the ground. Gunfire from the guard towers rang out. The people with guns outside the wall returned fire but were too exposed. I grabbed Anna and pulled her to a sheltered doorway in the building behind us. William followed, alert with his own gun ready.

Two of the guard towers protecting the gate exploded as rockets from somewhere in the crowd hit them. A heavily armoured truck came into view, its gun spraying across the top of the wall. It sped straight for the metal gate, indifferent to the living and dead bodies it hit on the way. It buckled with the hit but stayed in place. The truck reversed. Another rocket hit the metal barrier. The truck rammed again and the gate broke. Dozens of armed people who had sought protection along the wall spilled through the opening. More armed and unarmed people followed, some being mowed down as they ran. Anna ran back to the United Earth tent before I could grab her. I followed.

Everyone inside was unharmed and discussing what to do next.

"Anna, please, we have to go," I whispered, grabbing her hand. She pulled away, so I left to survey the scene outside. There were hundreds of bodies around the broken gate. Sporadic gunfire rang out from inside the main building, and hundreds of people were still running away from the square, while others hid behind trains or in the doorways scattered around the square.

Some of the people outside the gate were injured. Others that had sought safety were starting to come to their aid. William and I grabbed what water and materials we could find to help some of the injured. William and I helped transport those with serious injuries to a tent near the stage, where other injured people were taken. Afterward, we helped those with more minor injuries. Lastly, we carried the dead to another area set apart. By the end, my arms were lead, my back aching. I'd stopped counting the dead at twenty-eight, and those were just the bodies *we* carried. There were many others helping. The area for the deceased was overflowing with bodies, easily over a hundred.

By this time, gunfire from inside the building had ceased. A group of people were exiting the main door, cheering. They were dragging two chained and bloody men who looked like military personnel. A press of people had returned and waited anxiously at the broken gate. Anna and the other United Earth members moved toward the gate to learn what had happened. I was too tired to listen to whatever came next. I returned to the United Earth tent and found a flimsy cot.

It was dark outside by the time Anna woke me up. A few small lamps provided a faint glow inside the tent. "There's going to be a debate, tomorrow at noon. A council of sorts is being formed by the various political factions remaining in the city."

"And what happens to the two men dragged out of that building?" I asked.

"There will be a trial. Those men commanded all the prison camps in this area. The people that needed vengeance got it."

I snorted. "So the people with all the weapons and power now are just going to give up control to others?"

"They're too few," Anna replied.

William remained silent. I turned to him. "What do you think?"

"You were right. Anna's optimism is infectious. I agree, though. I don't believe the people that captured those commanders are going to give up power. History has never worked that way. If anything, they'll insist on becoming a military or police arm of whatever you plan to establish here. The safest thing would be to kill them."

"You're not serious." Anna looked disgusted. "They were treated as slaves, beaten, made to work in deplorable conditions. They can't be blamed for what they've become."

"No, they can't. But any semblance of humanity they once had is lost. You can't recover that. These people have no place in the new world you're trying to create. They'll simply continue the old one."

"Do you want us to give up on you too?" I asked William.

He looked at me, pained. He thought long about his next words. "Perhaps. Beating that guard felt good. When the shooting started, I wanted to run and join. The camp restrained all that because I was a prisoner. That freedom you spoke of, it terrifies me."

Anna still looked perplexed and flustered. She lay down in my arms with her head on my chest. She didn't say anything, but I could tell she was nervous. She was always so brave and strong. The circumstances of her life had to be wearing down her hope. I had no words of comfort. I could only hope that she would come to the realization on her own that our best and only chance was to give it all up and return to the peace and tranquility of our farm. If father wasn't here, he had to be there.

The next day, the leaders of the various factions held a council in the main building. Three older representatives of United Earth attended. Hundreds that had fled the square the day before returned to see how things had turned out. Thousands more had left the city for good. Anna and I spent the day discussing the time we'd been apart. She had little to say, wanting to focus on the times before. William disappeared for most of the day. I conveyed my concern for him to Anna, telling her of his life. She could offer no words of comfort.

The day was hot and sunny. In the afternoon, we took a stroll through the centre of the city. The area near the river was still walled with large fortifications and gun emplacements. If there was any access to the river before, it was gone now. Entire blocks were bombed out, countless charred ruins, never rebuilt. The rest of the central part of the city had been rebuilt with imposing square concrete structures. It lacked any of the beauty that must have existed in old Kyiv. This city had been the central point of a warzone for a long time. The buildings were, for the most part, deserted.

As the sun was setting, we returned to the square. William was sitting on a small staircase beside the door of a building that United Earth had claimed, cleaning his gun.

"Any word?" I asked him. Anna looked nervously from William with his gun to the main building, which had been taken over by more armed guards from extremist factions.

He shook his head. "We should leave before it's too late," he suggested.

Anna implored, "We have to stay for now, to ensure a peaceful transition."

William laughed in derision. "Look at how many armed guards there are now. Most of them are from anarchist groups or worse. Those black arm bands with the white symbol, that's a neo-Nazi group. The red headbands, a communist group. They may have a common cause for now, but how long before they start fighting each other? The pacifist and democratic groups, like yours, will be caught in the crossfire."

"Why would they spend the day talking if anyone wanted more bloodshed?" Anna asked.

I had to agree. No one group seemed dominant. It would be too difficult for any one of them to take complete control. Perhaps they recognized that a sense of unity was important.

It was early evening by the time the leaders from United Earth returned. They seemed agitated and exhausted. An old Ukrainian woman with grey hair and a stiff posture spoke to the rest of the group. She seemed to be the overall leader. One of the younger men translated to English. Everyone present seemed to speak one of the two languages.

After a day of talking, no agreement had been reached. They decided that there would be a vote on three options. Option 1 would be installing a democratic government with representation from each group, centralized in Kyiv, which would oversee the entire Kyiv zone. The Kyiv zone being, for now, the area that had previously been used for military purposes, stretching hundreds of kilometres north and south between the wall and the river. Under this option, reinstating electricity, water and train service would be the priority. Armed groups would act as defence and security in case the situation on the east side of the river deteriorated. Goods would be traded equitably. People would be assigned jobs based on their experiences, but living conditions and working hours would be improved. Those elected would decide among themselves on an overall leader.

In Option 2, each group would take control of a section of the zone, free to govern their own affairs. There would be mutual defence agreements, but otherwise each group would provide for their own. Sections would be broken up by specialty to ensure power, water, timber, metal and food were produced in adequate quantities. Trade agreements would be established based on production rates in each of these specialty zones.

Under Option 3, people would be free to choose where to go and what they wanted to do. There would be no formal agreements or defined zones. Individuals would trade goods and govern their own affairs however they chose.

Once the old woman had explained the three options, everyone began shouting questions. Which groups seemed to be in favour of which option? How were the options decided? Who would be responsible for electricity and water in the various scenarios? What if no one wanted to be farmers? The three leaders who had been present at the meeting tried to calm people down and answer each question one at a time, but they seemed less than thrilled with their own responses.

Finally, the old woman indicated Option 1 was their preferred choice. Obviously, numerous details would need to be worked out. She expressed concern with some of the more militant groups. She would not tell people how to vote, but she believed that Option 1 was the only way that the ideals and principles of the United Earth movement could begin to influence others to join their cause. Many of the other groups were looking to United Earth for guidance, since many of its members were scientists and engineers who would be needed to restore basic services.

Anna, William and I left the tent while questions, debate and a general feeling of unease spread through the group. Anna had a look on her face I'd seen often — the look of a mathematician calculating a complex formula. She was weighing the situation in her mind and assessing all potential variables.

William was harder to read, sitting and staring at the main building. "None of the options will work," he said.

"What do you suggest?" Anna asked, incredulous.

"I suggest we leave and head west, to your farm. Elliott has talked it up so much, I'd like to see this place."

"You're free to go," Anna said. "I have more faith in humanity and would see the scars in this region erased." William's rational pessimism seemed enough to reignite Anna's passionate optimism. I suspected William was right but hoped Anna would prevail. I'd often been torn between wanting to be an optimist, like the people I loved, and accepting the reality that the world was not a fair place. I sat silently, looking from one to the other. Something told me William didn't want to leave alone. Whether he wanted it or not, our fates were now entwined. I knew there would be no convincing Anna. William knew I wouldn't try to persuade her to leave. He grabbed his gun and went into the building behind us without another word.

"Why does he stay?" Anna asked.

"He has nowhere else to go. He promised to help me find you and he's done that, but he's alone. You can't fault him for wanting to get as far away from here as possible."

"And what do you want?"

"I want you. I want what you want. Even if William is right, I'm not leaving you. And this time, I'll protect you."

Twenty-Three
Sri Lanka

It had been over a month since I last saw Visshaly on the ship. Shani kept me busy and distracted with various routines. Things here were different from what I was used to. The communities were very organized, and everyone had assigned daily duties and roles. The scars of past wars and poverty were still visible.

We were south of what was once the capital of the country known as Sri Lanka, on the outskirts of the city. They'd taken me into the city during my first week on the island, but most of it was in ruins and no one lived in it. The people said one day they may restore it and improve the layout and design, but other work was more important.

South of the city, everyone lived in small compact communes surrounded by lush fields. The idea was for each community to be self-sustaining. They weren't far apart, but each was limited to two hundred fifty people. Each community had a council with one person chosen to represent them on a larger council that decided communal affairs for the whole island. It seemed idyllic, but I'd very little time to get to know anyone or experience life here.

Every day I was trained in the operation of the ship and other tasks. I learned about marine rehabilitation technologies and geography, plus I had swimming lesson. I'd become quite proficient at swimming and enjoyed it; there were clear streams and placid lakes with safe and clean coastal areas.

After the first week, though, I began to buckle under the pressure. The pace and volume of information was relentless. Shani was always very kind and patient but frequently explained that I had to learn all of these things before we departed. If the group leader of the expedition wasn't confident that I understood what would be expected of me, then I wouldn't be able to go.

I became frustrated one day and screamed at Shani, "You don't understand. This is all new to me. You've never known what it's like to live in constant fear, be sick from hunger and witness unimaginable cruelty!"

Shani was taken aback. "You're right. I'll never understand, but that doesn't mean I won't listen if you want to talk. You've been given a rare opportunity here. That makes you lucky."

I couldn't look at her. I was still seething, but I was also disappointed in myself. "Why me? Why not the thousands of people in India and around the world that need help?"

Shani reached for me, but I crossed my arms and pulled back. "Building a new world takes time," she said. "Not everyone can be saved. Frankly, not everyone is worth saving. But Aashi, don't squander this opportunity. I'll help you in any way I can." Shani waited for me to respond, with her hands behind her back.

"Um … thank you. I'll try, I promise."

As tired and frustrated as I was with everything that was being thrown at me, Shani was right. I owed it to Jahi, Randhir, Amar — and even Visshaly — to not give up.

Later that day, Shani took me to the new capital, which was around a lake lined with several of the communes not far from the coast. In the centre was a large lotus-shaped canopy, supported by intricately carved wooden beams.

"Each beam represents different cultures from around the world. This meeting place is for everyone," Shani told me.

Around the lotus canopy were dozens of white homes with colourful gardens adorning their sides and roofs.

The lotus canopy had an enormous round table in its centre, surrounded by tiered seating, which was slowly filling up with people from around the area. Yuki, Denise and several other prominent members of the organization were already seated. There were speakers playing soft and calming music.

Shani and I took a seat, and she handed me a small circular device. "These are translation devices. Put it in your ear," she said. "Every gathering consists of many different languages." She put her own in her right ear. "Important decisions are going to be made today, including the day of departure for the latest expedition."

Six ships were scheduled to depart and join nearly a dozen others at points around the Pacific Ocean. Other similar organizations in the Americas, New Zealand and other Pacific islands also had ships. It was expected that a coordinated effort consisting of nearly a hundred ships would be spending more than a year at sea, gathering data on current ocean conditions, removing waste and conducting bioremediation programs and coral reef restoration projects. It was said to be the largest joint effort by people from so many different places in more than thirty years. The planning, coordinating, logistics and resource requirements for such an effort were immense.

At the commune gathering, they decided that the ships would leave one week from tomorrow, at first light. Crews were told to say their goodbyes, report to their superiors and gather supplies. I'd made significant progress and learned so much that the captain of the ship Shani was scheduled to go on had accepted me as a technician. That meant I would provide support and assistance to some of the research scientists and project managers. Mainly, I would be organizing gear, collecting samples, cleaning equipment and doing other simple tasks. Even that required significant training.

There was only one person I needed to say goodbye to, and I had no idea where to find him. I asked Shani if she knew where or how to find Visshaly. She said she would find out.

The week came and went quickly, each day filled with last-minute training and outfitting the ship with supplies. We were scheduled to leave the next day and I still hadn't seen Visshaly. I'd barely seen Shani either. We were all given the afternoon off to spend with family or friends before departing first thing in the morning.

Shani found me and said she knew where to find Visshaly. He had been farther inland for quite some time and had only returned last night. He was south, near a newly built harbour and large warehouses. Shani gave me directions to a building in that area where I could find him. Shani was spending the day with her family.

I was on one of the trains that ran up and down the coast connecting the various communes. As the train got closer, I could see large grey warehouses with green vehicles, helicopters and countless weapons. People were also dressed in green, marching in straight, rigid lines, conducting athletic drills or shooting at targets. The train stopped and I was in the midst of a bustling sea of dark greens and imposing greys, dwarfed by monstrous metal machines. All the warehouses were numbered and orderly. I walked in the direction of the one I was told Visshaly would be at. There was a guard posted outside and I explained who I was looking for and what I was doing. He didn't understand me and motioned for me to stay put. He went off to talk to someone else. Sometime later, a woman approached me and told me to follow her.

We found Visshaly cleaning and assembling guns at the back of the warehouse with several other young men and women. He was dressed in all green as well. The woman told me I had ten minutes. Visshaly stood at attention, back straight, chin up and saluted the woman as she left. He escorted me out to the yard behind the building where other people dressed in all green were loading trucks and helicopters.

"You look good," Visshaly said.

"What's all this? What is it that you're doing?"

Visshaly looked at me and smirked. "Sometimes change for the better requires force. Do you think everyone is just going to agree that the commune life is the way it should be?"

"But who are you fighting?"

"For now, there are still northern parts of Sri Lanka where warlords control everything and everyone. First, we'll regain complete control of Sri Lanka and then slowly turn attention toward India."

"You don't have to do this, Visshaly. You can come on the ships."

"I want to do this. I want to stop people like those warlords once and for all, so that people like you can go and save the world." He smiled at me and ruffled my hair.

I was crying and went to hug him. He loosely hugged me back. I pushed away, looking up to his eyes. He was so proud and sullen.

"Be careful," I said, embracing him one last time.

"You too. Who knows, we may see each other again one day."

He walked back toward the warehouse. I looked around at all the young men and women in green. They probably all believed, like Visshaly, that their cause was just and righteous. I'm sure all soldiers throughout history believed the same thing. How many wars had there been where it was sworn this would be the last one? Yet, the cycle continued.

The train ride back was a whirlwind of emotions. I was excited about this adventure, apprehensive about the future, scared for Visshaly and anxious for myself. The realization came that Shani was about to be the only person I had any connection to in the world. The ship we were to depart on was called the *Horizon*. It too was a large military ship converted into a research vessel. Around a hundred eighty people were going to call it home for the next year or so. I'd been too dependent on Shani and only just realized that this course I was now on was because of her. I'd never asked about other options, never tried to connect with anyone else. I spent my whole life clinging from one person to the next only to lose each.

Shani was kind and comforting, only a few years older than me, but I'd no idea if she thought of me as a friend or a little sister or had simply been asked to find a place for me. Cynically, I believed I was nothing more than a burden.

I boarded the ship as the sun was setting. It was a warm, humid morning and the sea was placid. The crew were excited and moving about the ship, tying down gear or going below to find their cabins. My small, dark cabin was at the aft of the ship, with the faint hum of the engines vibrating the room and only a soft light on the wall illuminating two lockers at the end and two bunks on one side. My cabin mate had already claimed the lower bunk and organized their things but was off doing something else on the ship. I hung my clothes and went on deck to watch the ship depart from Sri Lanka. I had no work for the first couple of days. The ship was headed to some of the southern islands that were part of a large grouping of islands once known as Indonesia. We would be spending months doing coral restoration work, but first the ship needed to traverse the open ocean for some time to get there.

Those first few days were dull. I mainly assisted some of the marine biologists and coral specialists in monitoring the health of the coral nurseries on board the ship. One of the labs had massive tanks filled with dozens of species of corals and fish awaiting transplant. I would check the water temperature, pH balance and oxygen levels every couple of hours and enter the data in a computer. It was monotonous but essential work. Some of the research scientists taught me the names of the different species and explained that this diversity only represented a fraction of the corals and fish that used to call these reefs home. Other ships had other species, and the hope was that one day the oceans would return to their true beauty and diversity.

One of the older scientists had videos of dives in the same locations over a span of forty years, and the changes were drastic. He watched the videos with me and explained in detail the causes of the changes. Sometimes he would cry as we got toward the end. I couldn't help but cry as well. The early videos were filled with colourful large corals of different sizes, shapes and textures, which were matched in their vibrancy by the schools of different fish, as well as rays, turtles and sharks swimming among their bounty. The later videos were dull greys, whites and blacks, looking like graveyards with fish swimming lethargically and alone.

"But we're going to change all that," the older scientist, Mateo, would exclaim. "I won't be around to see it, but I hope that you get to see what the oceans were meant to be one day."

My cabin mate was a middle-aged woman, born and raised on Sri Lanka, who was also serving as a technician, but on a schedule opposite to mine, so I rarely saw her and only spoke to her once. I saw Shani now and then, but she was part of ship operations, so she had a cabin in the higher decks with a different meal room and common area. I spent most of my time with the scientists, but we never spoke about personal matters, hopes or dreams. They were all business, except for Mateo. Some of them were young, some old, some white, some black or brown, men and women, but they all spoke English.

About five days into our voyage, we came upon a bad storm. The sky was black with torrential rains, constant lightning and thunder and winds stronger than any I'd ever experienced. Everything in the labs had to be tied down and the tanks constantly monitored. The waves crashed onto the deck as the ship rocked against the angry sea. Few members of the crew were functional, as whatever food they ate came violently up. My stomach and head felt every movement, as if the waves outside were hitting my insides. I wanted to vomit, but nothing came up. The ship lurched forward, angling up the massive waves, only to come crashing down the other side. The deck was off limits, but through the windows I saw waves cresting over the sides of the ship, an angry ocean lashing at its high, strong steel sides.

It took two and a half days to pass through the storm. By the end, I was exhausted and weak, having barely slept or eaten. Most of the crew was in equally rough shape. The captain ordered a skeleton crew with minimal operations and told everyone else to recuperate. The doctor and two nurses on board were just as tired and sick as the rest of us, but they were adamant about treating everyone else first.

The specimens in the tanks had fared poorly, too. All the crashing back and forth and up and down had rattled the precious life in those tanks. Sadly, about a third of the specimens were destroyed.

We arrived at our destination two days later. Three other ships were already there as part of the reef restoration expedition. It was expected we would spend at least three months among a series of small and larger islands on the southern Indonesian archipelago. We were anchored between the narrow island of Kri and the large island of Waigeo, which was a green blur on the horizon. The four ships would spend a few weeks together conducting restoration work around Kri and its neighbouring small islands before breaking apart with one ship headed west and the other two south. Our ship would be journeying east for a long open-ocean expedition.

The first few days, the crews of each ship were busy with their various assignments. Some crew members had taken smaller boats to the various islands to talk to any locals to better understand their current situation and, it was hoped, to recruit them to the cause. Other crew members were removing waste and debris from the waters.

The team I was assigned to spent the first few days taking water and sediment samples and analyzing the results. My job was to help collect the samples and monitor equipment. I tried to understand the tests and analyses the scientists were conducting, but most of them, if they bothered to explain at all, did it in such a hurry that I was soon lost.

Mateo was the only one to explain things in terms I could understand.

One bright, sunny day, we were both on the aft deck taking a break and enjoying the cool ocean breeze.

"Mateo, how do you carry on each day with all that you've seen?"

"Nature is resilient, Aashi."

"But the challenges seem so immense."

"We have fallen far, but now we're waking up. I'm confident future generations will not revert to past mistakes. I have to be," Mateo explained with a smile on his face and a pat on my shoulders.

Immediately, after any statement like this, he would go back to explaining a piece of equipment or some experiment. "So, based on our monitoring, it looks like conditions in the area are stabilizing and improving. Here, look at the readings of temperature, pH and dissolved oxygen. Tell me what you think it means."

Mateo showed me an electronic pad with decades of water-quality data, which he had plotted on a graph. The line on the graph had started to level off over the last five years.

"Based on the line, it is as you said — conditions are stabilizing. So ... I think ... that means restoration has a good chance of being successful?"

"Very good. Yes, conditions are optimal. You're a fast learner, Aashi."

A week into our time around Kri, the crew began their first dive programs. They were actively transplanting coral species from the ships. I'd gotten comfortable with putting together the dive equipment but had never actually used it myself or understood what it all did. Mateo volunteered to train me. He laid out a set of equipment for the both of us, explaining each piece.

"Flippers, obviously for your feet, to help you move through the water," Mateo demonstrated using two fingers, one moving up as the other went down in a scissor pattern.

"Mask, so you can see and don't get water up your nose. Wetsuit will help with buoyancy and body temperature. Weight belt to help you sink."

"What's buoyancy?" I asked.

"It's basically whether you float or sink in the water, which brings us to the BCD. When it's hooked up to the regulator and your tank, you can inflate the BCD to float if you're sinking too fast or let air out to go down, using these two buttons." Mateo demonstrated using one of the controls on the regulator.

"Now, the breathing regulators. You have two. One is your main one that you keep in your mouth, breathing in and out, slowly and consistently. The other one is for emergencies, or your buddy, if theirs stops working. You hook it onto the BCD. Good?"

I nodded.

"This is your depth and pressure gauge. It tells you how deep you are and how much air you have left. It is good to check it every few minutes. You never want to get into this red zone on the air gauge. Any questions?"

"No. I think I'm ready."

"Excellent, let's take this equipment and practise in shallow water."

Mateo and I moved a small boat to a place where the water was less than ten metres deep and put our equipment on. He demonstrated all the final checks and procedures before flipping backward off the side of the boat. I inflated my BCD, put my mask on, checked my regulator and put it in my mouth before flipping off the side of the boat like Mateo had just done. I floated at the top of the water, giving the okay signal. Mateo signalled to deflate the BCD and we began our descent.

I raised the control for the BCD and let the air out, slowly descending into the warm, clear water. The first few breaths out of the regulator were strange. With only the use of your mouth, and conscious that humans weren't meant to breathe under water, it was difficult to do the slow controlled breaths.

Mateo was kneeling on the white sand about five metres under water, patiently waiting for me to do the same. I kept checking the gauge of my equipment to make sure the tank was still full, and I could tell my breathing was erratic. I started gasping, sucking in air sharply and bursting it out, causing a spurt and a cloud of bubbles in front of my face. Mateo was moving his hand slowly toward his mouth and then out again to demonstrate controlled breathing.

I reached the sandy bottom with a thud, not properly adjusting my buoyancy, but I'd managed to control my breathing to a slow and steady pace. We practised removing our masks and replacing them, using our noses to clear the water from them. It involved lifting your head to face the surface, pushing down on the top part of the mask, lifting it slightly out from your face at the bottom, and exhaling hard through your nose to get the water out. This was the most difficult and uncomfortable part of diving.

We practised trying to gain neutral buoyancy, to be able to hover in one place, using our breath to control whether we would rise or sink. As our first tank was getting low, we returned to the boat. We were never more than ten metres deep.

"Well done, Aashi. How do you feel?"

"It's a strange feeling at first, but it was wonderful."

"Excellent. We'll take a little break to refresh and then go a little deeper. Does that work?"

"Yes!" I said.

We drank some water and snacked on some fruit.

"We'll go to twenty metres on the next dive and learn some navigation skills. Tomorrow I'll show you what you'll need to know to help with the restoration work. You'll always have a more experienced dive buddy with you, but you're a natural and pick things up quickly."

"Thank you. I'm excited to help in any way I can."

Mateo moved the boat a little farther out. We returned to the water with fresh tanks. With the deeper descent, I remembered to equalize as we went down by plugging my nose and trying to blow out, causing a slight pop in the ears. I'd heard the horror stories of what would happen if I didn't equalize pressure. I was probably overzealous, doing it every breath and descending a metre or two at a time.

We practised the same skills at the deeper depth, then began adding navigation. Mateo had shown me how to use the compass, but that first swim away from him relying on only the compass to return to the same spot got my heart beating.

Staring only at the compass, I swam for thirty seconds due east then rotated the bezel on the compass to return in the opposite direction. Without any defining visual guides, the compass was the only way to know where I was going. I couldn't see Mateo anymore but knew if I kept swimming back the way I came, I would find him. He slowly came into view as I returned to the spot where I'd started. He motioned an applause.

We had enough air in our tank to go a little deeper. So far there had been little in the way of marine life. Just a sandy bottom with a few small silver fish here and there. As we descended, I began to see shapes on the ocean floor. I was expecting the flash of colours and various shapes and textures I'd seen in the videos of coral reefs. Instead, I was greeted by a vast expanse of bones. I knew what I was looking at. It was dead coral. Small fish swam lazily through the eerie waters. I'd grown up in a grey world, but this was different, sadder somehow. We didn't stay long in this place. Mateo motioned for us to slowly return to the surface.

We conducted our rest stop at five metres and I could feel myself tearing up from what I'd just witnessed. We returned to the boat.

"That was so sad," I said, looking at Mateo.

"Yes, no matter how many times I see places like that, it still makes me sad."

"But we're going to fix it all, right?"

Mateo smiled and laughed. "We'll try. There are some healthy reefs nearby as well. You'll see what it's meant to look like soon enough."

Twenty-Four
In the Bunker outside Ontario

I awoke to a knock at my door. It was Nadie. She'd brought me breakfast.

"How are you doing?" she asked.

I was still tired, confused and uncertain of what to do or say next.

"After you've eaten breakfast, meet me on Level A near the gyrocopters. I have a surprise for you."

Though suspicious of what the next surprise they would spring on me would be, I hurriedly ate, got cleaned up and dressed. When I got to Level A, Nadie had a gyrocopter prepared and a bag with supplies for each of us. "I figured you could use some sun and time outdoors," she said.

Nadie got into the gyrocopter and I climbed in as well. We flew over the ruins of a city and more pits that Nadie said used to be mines. It was just the two of us, so I got to sit up front and was given a headset this time.

"This was one of our first projects," she said. "This section of the city was dismantled and reclaimed for nature."

We were flying over ruins, which ended abruptly in a heavily forested area. From there, we hovered over some of the old mine pits.

"The mines were more difficult to reclaim. There were many hazardous chemicals as well as contaminated water and soil. But slowly we're building functional wetlands. One of our goals is to do projects like this on a global scale."

After circling the abandoned mines and cities for some time, we headed west over vast forests. I'd never seen so many trees. There was the occasional road or abandoned little town, but it was green, for the most part, with small lakes here and there. Eventually we reached a larger body of water with several islands. We landed on a rocky outcrop on one of the islands beside a small house made of giant logs. Nadie got out of the gyrocopter, stretching her arms above her head, inhaling deeply. She walked to the edge of the outcrop overlooking a vast expanse of blue water.

"It's beautiful," I said, joining her at the edge of the outcrop. I knew there was a large lake in Zone 1, but I had never seen it up close or stood on its shore. Here the expanse of blue went to the horizon. There was no city in sight, just green rocky islands and calming blue waves. The only noise was the wind in the leaves, the water against the rocks and the occasional bird flapping overhead.

Nadie sat on the rock ledge, closing her eyes and looking up to the sun. I sat beside her, fidgeting and wondering whether I could speak. Time slowed. A couple of small colourful birds chased each other among a large tree beside the house. Glistening green leaves caught in the wind fluttered overhead.

"Kelowna, listen," exclaimed Nadie, without elaborating further.

"Listen to what?"

"To the sounds of the world around you, uninterrupted by the noise of the city. This is peace; this is true freedom."

I sat listening, trying to understand what she expected of me. I heard the rustle of the leaves; I heard the birds and the waves but was no closer to any understanding of what it meant.

While this location was beautiful and peaceful, it made it no easier for me to decide on my next course of action.

"Kelowna, I know you're overwhelmed right now. I can only imagine the questions you might have or the decisions you're agonizing over. My parents died when I was young as well. My mom died of cancer when I was six; my father, I never knew. The One Earth movement raised me."

Nadie seemed to be around my age but was far more knowledgeable. "Our survival depended on uniting as a species and living within the means of this planet we call home. Everything else was irrelevant. But paradigm shifts are difficult. Perspectives, cultures, ideologies, whatever you want to call them, are hard to overcome."

"That's why the Civic Administrators put the system in place," I responded. It was strange to be defending the system that killed my parents.

Nadie tilted her head and smirked at me. "It's true that the Civic Administrators have achieved a level of unparalleled stability. But their stability is selfish. They care only about those within their control. No one else exists. That indifference and ignorance is the same sort of attitude that got humanity into this mess. I don't think they're bad people, just narrow-minded. The people in the cities don't know any better. For them, ignorance truly is bliss. Kelowna, around the world there are people still suffering. This continent fared considerably well out of the wars and climate chaos. Sure, cities were lost, coastlines ravaged, deserts expanded and millions died, but comparatively, we did well. We have only started to regain constant communications with our other cells around the world. Some are openly at war; others lack the resources to realize any effectual change. They're looking to us to lead the charge. But to do that, we need more help."

Nadie stared at me. She was truly beautiful and passionate, in a reserved, not in-your-face way.

"I'm going for a swim. Come on!" she exclaimed.

I followed her over the rocks, down the cliff to a narrow beach. The water was calmer and shallower over here. She stripped down to her underwear and waded out into the water, diving, and effortlessly gliding through the placid waters.

"Kelowna, get in the water. It's quite warm."

I stood nervously. I'd never learned how to swim. I took my clothes off down to my underwear and slowly walked into the water until it was up to my waist. Nadie was off diving below the water, popping up a few metres farther on. She motioned for me to follow her into the deeper water. I stood paralyzed, gazing at the water. A few more steps and it would be over my head.

"I don't know how to swim," I said shyly.

"Pardon?" She swam toward me.

"I never learned how to swim."

"Of course not. Sorry, I should have known." She grabbed my hands, slowly pulling me into the deeper water.

"It's easy. Just kick your legs and move your arms in a back-and-forth motion to keep your head above the water."

She held my waist as I attempted to tread water, bobbing up and down below the water, every so often swallowing enough to cause a coughing fit. Nadie laughed. "Relax. Calm, smooth motions. The more you struggle, the harder it is." I slowed my movements, levelling myself on top of the water. I stared into her eyes and she smiled at me. "Congrats! See, it's not that hard. Now, lie on your back and let's try actually swimming." I did as she asked, her one hand moving to the small of my back. "Now, kick your legs and use your hands as paddles, slowly and calmly."

Soon I was gliding through the water. She released her hand from my back, and I swam for a few seconds before realizing she'd removed it, at which point I instantly started to flounder, dipping below the water in a V shape. She returned to my side. "You'll get there with some practice," she said, pulling me toward the shallows.

She sat at the edge of the water. I sat beside her, staring out across the lake. I reached over and slowly turned her head toward mine, then I kissed her. She pulled back, looking at me — not in disgust, but in surprise. Then, grabbing the back of my head, she kissed me. I laid her down in the sand. My heart was pounding, my stomach swirling with that butterfly feeling. I'd been with women before but had never felt like this. In the city, it had always felt forced, to see if we were compatible. The spontaneity on this occasion, the company, the scenery, it all fit.

As the sun was setting, we returned to the house, hand in hand, without a word. We sat on the edge of the cliff watching the sky turn orange, wrapped in each other's arms. Nadie started a fire as I watched her. We ate dinner and watched as the stars came out. Nadie was in her element. She told me about the stars, about living off what nature could provide, about growing up with the people of One Earth. I listened to it all but couldn't stop staring at her. We stayed up all night talking. Well, she spoke, and I listened. Her life had been so interesting compared to mine. She knew so much, had done and seen so much. By comparison, my life had been a bore. What would I tell her about? School, work, genetic compatibility testing? My only passion was running.

Nadie was out of my league. Yet to her, I was strange and exotic. There weren't very many people from the city in the One Earth movement, and they were scattered across many communes. They were also much older, people that belonged to the movement before and had simply returned. As far as I knew, I was the only one born in the city who'd known nothing about the movement and had now fallen into it. I was as new and exciting to Nadie as she was to me.

I wondered if people genetically matched in the city felt this kind of passion.

Love in the city was calculated, thrust upon people who were genetically matched. Could that even be called love? People who matched seemed to stay together, but did they truly match? Did their hearts pound, stomachs swirl? I would probably never know. The other unknown now was whether Nadie felt the same way about me as I did about her. Would she think I was crazy for feeling this way so soon?

We fell asleep cuddled together. The next day, we awoke with the sun shining through the windows, birds chirping and the gentle sound of waves crashing into the rocks. I stared into Nadie's eyes, wishing we could stay here in this perfect place forever, willing to forget about the rest of the world.

"Nadie, let's stay here, you and I, forget everything else," I blurted out.

She laughed. "What? Are you crazy? Stop being silly and get up; we need to head back," she said, pushing me off the bed. I collected myself off the floor and stood there gazing at her as she collected some things. I felt like a fool. I didn't know what to do or say next. Nadie saw my confusion and came to comfort me.

"Listen, Kelowna. I like you, but I have ambitions and goals beyond just me and one other person. I can't imagine having grown up where you did, where everything is so forced and so phony. You'll see that what you're feeling right now is freedom, a freedom you've never experienced before. You have so much to learn and experience still. You barely know me."

She walked outside to ready the gyrocopter. I felt deflated and broken. I'd put myself out there for the first time in my life and been just as quickly rebuked. I gathered my things and silently sat down in the gyrocopter. The ride back was in silence. Nadie looked at me with pity, which only made things worse.

When we got back to the bunker, Nadie grabbed my hand. "I hope you realize I didn't mean to hurt you and that I still want to get to know you better. It's just, we're going to be conducting a big operation in the city soon and I'll be going in with the incursion team. I hope. I want you to come too. You would be a big help in the city." She squeezed my hands and kissed me. I didn't say anything.

Nadie sighed. "Think about it, please." She walked away.

I returned to my room and went to bed, despite it only being midafternoon. I didn't want to see or speak to anyone.

The next day at breakfast, Nadie came and sat beside me. "There's a meeting this morning that Elizabeth wants you to attend. They've managed to decode more of your mother's work and are preparing an incursion mission that leaves in a week. I want you to be on my team."

"What exactly are you planning to do? Things are good in the city. People are happy and safe. There's no poverty, war or crime. Isn't that a victory in today's world?"

"At the cost of their freedom of choice. You yourself felt constrained there, alone. They murdered your parents! What's the point of peace, safety and order without the freedom to choose what you do and when?"

"Who are you to tell people how to live? Wasn't that what the wars in history were fought over? People telling other people how to live and how to think. Maybe what's been accomplished in Ontario and Michigan is the best humanity can hope for. Maybe that's the only way we can survive as a species."

"I refuse to believe that. Humanity is capable of so much more. Look at what we've done here and in the communes. We don't want a fight with the Civic Administrators. We simply want to show people in the city that other options exist, that they've been lied to. Then they can choose what they want to do."

"You believe there won't be violence. You think you can turn people's entire belief system, their understanding of the world, upside down and they won't lash out. You said they killed my parents. They did it to maintain their order. What do you think they'll do to you?"

"I feel sorry for you, Kelowna. You've spent most of your life trapped, trying to escape, find a purpose, and now when you're presented with one, you want to run away and hide. Your mother said you were her hope. I guess she was wrong."

I threw my dishes off the table and stormed off. I wanted to hit something, go back to Nadie and tell her to fuck off. Who was she to say that to me? Instead, I went to my room and cried uncontrollably into a pillow. I hated my parents, the Civic Administrators, the people here and most of all myself for being so weak. Why had I left the city? My life there wasn't so bad. Meaningless, yes, but easy and comfortable. I'd left seeking adventure only to be confronted by a crude awakening of my past.

I pushed myself up into a sitting position on the bed. I still didn't know if I believed in their cause, but I had to see things through. Not for Nadie or my parents, but for myself. I went to the meeting.

I was late, entering the room as Elizabeth was in midspeech, but she welcomed me warmly anyway. Everyone else just glared. The only empty chair was beside Nadie and she waved me over. I preferred to stand at the back of the room.

"Each insertion team will hack into their respective zone's mainframe and broadcast the message," Elizabeth explained. "The same thing will be done in Michigan. The message will show images of other places in the world and explain the lies they have been told by the Civic Administrators. There's a championship lacrosse game two weeks from now. That's the best time to broadcast the message to get maximum exposure. You'll all be given identity cards that have been inserted into the system."

The screens had a list of names, dates, times and locations.

"Kelowna, you'll be on the Zone 4 team with Nadie," Elizabeth explained, reading from a tablet in her hands.

"Isn't that dangerous? What if I run into someone I know?"

"We're going to alter your appearance. The fact that you know the zone so well is important. Each insertion team has an insider."

I had to ask, "If you succeed and broadcast this message, then what?"

Everyone except Elizabeth was taken aback. She smiled, "That's up to the people that live in the city. It's their choice. We're just showing them what else is out there."

Elizabeth thanked everyone and told them to report to their training captains and be ready to leave at the end of the week. As everyone was getting up to leave, Nadie approached me, but Elizabeth intercepted and asked me to follow her.

Once we were alone in her office, she said, "I heard about your conversation with Nadie this morning. She shouldn't have said that, but she cares about you. I do too. I wasn't sure what use we could make of you when you arrived, but after the question you asked this morning, I'm sure now. You asked the one question no one else here has even thought of. They're so committed to the belief that their values and assumptions are correct. They believe we're saving the people of the city. That type of mindset has always been dangerous for humanity. It has often led to our greatest tragedies. Can I ask you something, Kelowna? Why aren't you angry about the way your parents died?"

"I guess I should be, but they lied to me just as much as the Civic Administrators did. I didn't know my parents the way others did. The way I see it, both sides are guilty."

"Interesting. Please explain further," Elizabeth asked, leaning in closer.

"My parents believed that their cause was just and right, so did the Civic Administrators. Neither side took the time to examine the others side's perspective. To talk. They were both so entrenched in their own beliefs that they created a situation of only seeing the other side as an enemy. You're doing the same thing with this mission."

"Then why help?"

"I don't know. Maybe people do have a right to know the truth. Maybe I owe it to my parents, to myself, to see this through. If all you intend to do is expose the truth, then maybe it will make the world a better place. All I know is I can't just sit on the sidelines."

Elizabeth looked at me as if probing my psyche. I felt uncomfortable, on display for all the world to see. Then she smiled again, nodding her head. "Kelowna, I believe I can trust you. I assure you my motives are pure, but I can't attest to the intentions of everyone in this movement. I hope, like you, that this mission will help to open a dialogue with the Civic Administrators. That we can see past each other's differences and build a better world together." She paused and sighed. "But experience has taught me otherwise. Very few people have insight into a group of people they've never met. You have every reason to hate the Civic Administrators but instead choose to try to understand their motives and recognize what they have accomplished. Many within this movement believe that the Civic Administrators need to be removed from power and that we should set up a council similar to how our communes are run. That won't work. Removing one power and installing another has rarely changed human circumstances. The communes work because they're small scale. There's no real leader and all are equal. These are worthy goals, but at the scale of a city, it's unrealistic. Nothing would get done or decided. Inevitably someone would take control and use that control to define how others exist. Some people are fine with that, as is the case with many of the people in the city. Many people in this movement don't recognize that. They want to destroy the structure that keeps the city functioning. They refuse to see the opposing viewpoint. Unfortunately, I believe that may lead to violence."

She flipped through some items on her tablet before laying it on the desk. "I need your help, Kelowna. After the message is delivered, if violence breaks out, I'll need your help to quell it."

"How can I help?" I asked, not as a serious offer, but rather because I was confused.

"I'll be in Zone 1 when the message is delivered and hope to open a dialogue with the Civic Administrators before anything goes wrong. This is dangerous and I could be captured and removed. I need to operate on optimism, though. I'd considered just letting things be as they are, but once we found you and the rest of your mother's work, things accelerated and most of the council is of the mind that we must do this. We could destroy everything that we've built and everything in the city. The Civic Administrators know we're out here, but they believe they removed the threat embedded within their system. Thousands of people in small communes scattered around don't matter to them. I'm afraid this move may change that. They have the ability to destroy us. We have weapons to fight back if need be, but if that happens, we'll simply be repeating mistakes. We have a chance to get things right this time. To overcome our own prejudices and violent nature. I know you want the same thing, whether you believe it or not. When the time comes, I know you'll do what's necessary." She shook my hand and ushered me out of the office.

Elizabeth was putting a lot of faith and trust in me and I couldn't understand why. She was surrounded by people who grew up in similar circumstances, who believed in this movement. I'd simply refused to be angry and hate those who killed my parents because being angry and hateful was pointless. Living like that would be exhausting. I knew enough about human history to know that hate had never gotten us anywhere. It simply continued a spiral of violence and injustice. Just because I knew these things didn't mean I'd be able to stop them when confronted with them. I was no leader. Leaders believed they could inspire others; I'd always been a recluse. Public speaking made me nervous and uncomfortable. The only courageous thing I'd ever done in my life was cross a river into no man's land. These were not the characteristics of a leader. Elizabeth had mistakenly put her trust in me. Unfortunately, I knew that if the time came, I would fail that trust. I just hoped it didn't cost her or anyone else their life.

Twenty-Five
Heading Back to Bogotá

I met Maria at the open tent first thing the next morning. She handed me black boots and a set of the same dark-green clothes everyone else was wearing. She took me to get a pack and weapons and ammo. That first day of training was spent learning about command structure and rules. I spent the next couple of weeks training in the use of different weapons, learning hand-to-hand combat, urban warfare and tactics. The days were long and tiring. I'd spent the last four years in relative comfort and ease in Paraiso. I'd forgotten what it was like to be sore and tired at the end of each day.

When I wasn't training, I would be asked more questions about the key people around the leader of the gang. I had very little information to give as I'd never learned the soldados' names, and all their faces became a blur. One day they presented me with a picture of a woman they believed to be the girlfriend of one of the gang leaders. It was a grainy photo and I wasn't positive, but it may have been my mother. I lied and said I didn't recognize her.

After three weeks of training, the unit I was assigned to began moving out. I said goodbye to Senora Vasquez, who I'd barely seen in the last three weeks. She hugged me and simply said, "Be careful." I wondered if I would ever see her again.

I was scared to go back to Bogotá. Scared about what I would have to do. What would happen if we were successful? And I was worried about my abuela and Alejandra. Were they alive? If they were, were they still the same people? Would I be able to find them?

As we climbed down the mountains into the valley I had crossed over four years ago, there was little evidence of major change.

My unit commander was a twenty-eight-year-old from Cali who had fought there. He had a scar across his right cheek and a shaved head. He was very strong and tough on his unit. We just called him *Commander*. He explained what happened in the valley.

"The gangs retreated without a fight to the city. The people in the valley welcomed us with open arms and many have joined our cause. Many teams will stay around to secure the valley and prevent the gangs from re-entering."

I wondered about Daniel and Pablo and his family. Were they safe? Were they happy with this change? We were ordered to continue marching to the city. I crossed the same bridge over the same river, this time on top of the bridge.

Units would enter the city from every point. Mine would be approaching the compound in my old neighbourhood. Since the gang members in the valley fled to Bogotá, surprise wasn't on our side, but resources from outside the city were now cut off. Spies had already entered the city and were arming locals and reporting back to command.

The gated communities in the centre of the city were surrounded by the gang. Based on reports, they seemed content to let the gang and the local population fight it out. The core grew some of their own food and had helicopters that could get more supplies, but in the last few days, most of the helicopters had been shot down. It was unclear how long the population in the core could hold out. Meanwhile, things in the west end of the city were falling apart. The gang had increased executions and was burning entire neighbourhoods down. Our spies were doing everything they could to protect the locals but were outnumbered and outgunned until reinforcements arrived. Orders had been distributed to all units to move up the timeline for their objectives. Our commander made us double our speed.

As we approached from the east, it felt like a lifetime ago since I'd left. The hills rose high above the sprawling city below. As we got closer, the hillsides got less and less green. During training, I'd learned more about the city I grew up in, which was now spread before me as we descended in the light of day with no opposition.

The rich core of the city wasn't far to the north of where I grew up, clinging to the same hillsides but in a more ordered way. Trees still lingered on their hillsides. The now fenced-off core represented only 10 percent of the city's population. The remaining areas had slowly crumbled so that most resembled the slums I knew well.

We stopped on a ridge about a half day's walk from my old neighbourhood to wait for darkness. Fires were spreading all over the valley.

Several of our spies were already ahead of us in the slums. Based on their information, most of the fighting was to the north and west. The area around the compound was quiet, with few soldados. Larger units had infiltrated the city from the north and west, where the terrain was easier to manage with large equipment. This forced more of the soldados to leave the siege of the core and their compounds. It was unclear where the gang leader was, but it was expected that he was in the compound, given the scale of assaults from different points.

As it grew dark, we scaled down the ridge. The besieged centre had functioning electricity. Flashes of gunfire and explosions could be seen in the distance. The now massive compound wasn't far below us. It too had electricity and spotlights scanning the surrounding areas. Very few other lights or fires surrounded it. It seemed that no fighting had occurred here yet.

Some of the scouts that were sent ahead returned. "We found some soldados on the ridge," one of them told us. "They've been taken care of. It's clear down to the infiltration point."

"Good," our commander said. "There must not be many soldados left guarding the compound." He turned to us. "Unit, hurry up to the infiltration point."

My unit seemed confident. Many of them had significant training and experience. The gang members, on the other hand, were thugs with guns who didn't understand strategy or tactics. I would soon learn the truth of this. The rest of the night passed without incident as we made our way into my old neighbourhood. It seemed largely empty. We stationed ourselves in buildings at the end of the main road, around eight hundred metres from the new outer compound wall, to wait out the new day.

"Where are all the locals?" I asked one of our spies, who had now joined the rest of the unit.

"We've only come across about a dozen old people in the whole area. We've moved them farther away for medical treatment. We don't know where the rest of the population is," he said.

I asked the commander for permission to go and see if there was anyone there I knew who could help us. He agreed and sent me with two other people from our unit. We were to report back at sunset, which was the time set for the attack on the compound.

We went out the back of the building along a narrow alley, which was littered with more debris than usual. Most of the buildings looked like they would collapse at any moment. This had never been a clean or pretty place, but the change was drastic. Before I left, people would use what little they had to try to grow gardens or make the grey buildings look liveable; children would play in the alleys while older people sat and talked about better times. Now it was a neighbourhood of dirt, grime and ruin.

I went to see the older residents we'd gathered, scanning the room for anyone I knew. There was a woman who'd lived in the building next to ours, who'd occasionally spoken with my abuela. I couldn't remember her name, but I approached her, asking if she remembered me. She looked at me blankly, and I realized how different I must look. I was taller, well fed, clean and well dressed. I told her my name and where I grew up and about my abuela.

She smiled. "Yes, well look at you. You made it after all. Your abuela would be so proud."

"Do you know where she is?"

She looked stricken. I knew what response was coming. "I'm sorry, dear. She was killed shortly after you escaped. When the soldados realized you were missing, they questioned your abuela. They killed her.

She died because of me. I'd known the answer before I'd asked the question, but it still came as a shock. Anger welled up in me. I fought to hold back the tears.

"You'll make them pay, all of them," the old woman said with hate in her voice.

I left her, and we returned to our commander in the forward position. Other members of our unit were hidden throughout the neighbourhood. One of them came running to us. "Commander, gang members are sweeping the roads looking for anyone. The few people they find are being taken to the compound. They'll be here soon."

"Damn. Defensive teams fall back to the medical building. We can't be discovered. Advanced teams break into your four-person units. Alpha team, take the alley. Bravo, the buildings along the cliffs. Charlie, the main road, and Delta, eyes on the compound. Move silently and take out any gang members you come across without raising the alarm. We proceed with our original objective at sunset. Go."

Team leaders issued commands into the radios for other unit members. My team, Alpha, was one of four groups of four that would be assaulting the compound at night. The rest of our unit would take defensive positions along the outer wall to protect our backs. But until sunset, my team had to sweep the alley that ran behind the buildings along the main road.

We moved slowly through what was left of my former home, making no sound. Maria was my team lead. She introduced me to Gael, who would be my partner in the event that we needed to break into twos. He was a couple of years older than me and had grown up in Cali. And our fourth team member was known as Flaco because he was so tall and skinny.

My heart was racing. It all seemed so easy in training. This was the real thing now. We moved one by one, hiding behind corners, listening. The alley was quiet.

From behind one of the dirty and broken shacks in the back of the alley, we saw a small group of soldados come out of one of the buildings around ten metres from our position. They were dragging a boy and two young girls. One of them shouted, "You two take them back to the compound and get them armed. Let the boss decide where they should go. Everyone needs to protect our territory. The rest of you, follow me."

There were only three of them left and they were walking directly toward us. Maria took out her knife and silently ordered the rest of us to do the same. To get behind the soldados, we slipped into the space between a wooden shack and one of the steep cliffs that broke up the slum. The soldados were walking through the alley in a line together without any caution. One of them looked familiar, but I couldn't get a good enough look. I was the last in line on our team.

The soldados passed the shack and we crept out into the alley behind them. My other three team members spread out so that each of them was behind one of the soldados.

It happened so fast.

All three reached out and used their free hand to cover their target's mouth and the other to slit their throat.

But one of the soldados tripped forward and managed to elbow Gael in the face before falling to his knees. The soldado spun around with his gun, but I leaped and kicked it from his hand. Gael was about to lunge at him, but I yelled for him to stop.

The soldado was Javier.

Flaco moved to restrain Javier, pushing him roughly against the cliff edge.

Maria grabbed me. "What do you mean, *stop*? You heard our orders. Take out any gang members we find."

"I know him. I grew up with him. We can't kill him."

"I'm sorry, Miguel. We don't have a choice."

"He could help us. He may know how many soldados are at the compound."

Maria looked at me, then Javier. "You're responsible for him. Let's get these bodies out of the alley and keep moving."

Flaco had tied Javier's hands behind his back. I helped Javier, who was shaking, into one of the buildings, while the rest of the team hid the bodies of the other soldados.

"Javier, it's Miguel. Remember? We were water runners together."

Javier looked at me without any expression. I didn't know whether he thought I was trying to trick him or if he really didn't remember me.

The rest of my team came into the building. "You stay here with him," Maria said. "If he tries to escape or make any noise, kill him. The rest of us will finish clearing the alley and then we'll take him to the commander to decide what to do." She looked angry and left with the others before I could say anything.

"Javier, I won't hurt you. I can help you, get you somewhere safe. You don't need to be a soldado anymore." Javier still didn't react. He didn't speak or scream. "Do you remember me?" I asked.

"Yes."

"I'm sorry about the other soldados. Were they friends?"

Javier shook his head.

"Javier, listen. If you help us, there are places you can go that are better than here. Places that are clean, safe and happy. If you don't, they'll kill you."

"This is your home, too," Javier said. "And now you're going to kill everyone you knew." Javier didn't seem mad. He didn't seem to have any feelings at all.

"Everyone I cared about is already gone. This wasn't a home. I have a home now, far from here. You can too."

"So much death, and for what? The boss won't make it easy."

"We have thousands of troops. They're better trained with better equipment. Javier, where is everyone from the neighbourhood? We only found a bunch of old people, who we are helping."

"Most were forced to move to other neighbourhoods. The boss has plans to turn this whole area into his place. Others are dead. Anyone that can fight is a soldado."

"What about your family?" Javier shrugged and put his head down. "It won't be long before my team is back. Will you help us?"

"How?"

"Anything. How many are guarding the compound? Where is the boss? Any information may limit the amount of killing."

Javier shook his head and snorted. "You've been away too long. The only reason I'm alive is I heard a noise and tripped. Anyone guarding the compound will try to shoot you the second they see you. You'll have to shoot first."

"If we get the boss, maybe everyone else will give up. Is he at the compound?"

"He's always at the compound. Everyone else has to fight and die for him."

"Then help us stop him."

The rest of my team came into the building.

"All clear, let's move," Maria said.

"The boss is at the compound. Javier confirmed it," I told them.

"Let's move." Maria had blood on her hands and shirt. I led Javier out of the building. My team was moving quickly from building to building now. Maria was talking into her radio.

We exited the alley into the main road and crossed to the other side. Several other units were in positions at various points in the road and in the upper levels of the buildings. It was late afternoon, and everyone was in position. The commander had set up in one of the main buildings that was more intact than others. We led Javier in there.

"We have a prisoner with information on the compound, sir," Maria said.

"I didn't order any prisoners." The commander was looking at a bunch of photos and maps on a table, while responding to messages on his radio.

"I know, sir. One of my team members who grew up here recognized the prisoner."

The commander turned around, speaking into the radio before handing it off to another unit member beside him. There were six other fighters in the room, in addition to the commander, Javier and my team.

The commander looked at Javier and walked up very close to him. "Which of your team knows him?"

"Miguel, sir," Maria said, pointing at me.

The commander moved in front of me. "You put your team and this mission at risk."

"The prisoner, Javier, has confirmed the boss is in the compound, sir," I told the commander.

"Has he? And you know he's telling the truth?"

"He never wanted to be a soldado. None of us did," I said, with a little too much anger. Everyone else in the room was tense. The commander just looked at me. "Us? But you're not a soldado. Are you?"

"No, sir. But I would have been if I hadn't escaped years ago. Javier and I were water runners for the compound before he was forced to become a soldado. He can help us. I trust him."

"You don't know him anymore. What he might have done."

"I was given a chance even with the things I've done. The boss is the enemy, not Javier." I forgot to say *sir*.

"I'm sorry, sir," Maria said. "My team has put the mission at risk. We can be part of the defensive team."

The commander looked from me to Javier and back. "No. Your team will stay part of the advanced group. Miguel here has been in that compound before and may know more people." He moved back toward Javier, taking the binding off his mouth. "How many are guarding the compound?" he asked Javier.

"Twenty, maybe thirty. Most are in other parts of the city fighting."

"How do you know the boss is in the compound?"

"He hasn't left the compound in months. He ordered some of us to sweep the neighbourhood this morning. He thought there might be invaders around."

"He was right, except we prefer to think of ourselves as liberators. Why are you selling out your friends so easily? You know most of them are going to die."

"They aren't my friends, and if I don't tell you anything, I'll be dead," Javier responded.

"So, you're saving your own skin?"

"Kill me if you want, but Miguel is one of you, and he said there are better places than here. I want to see those places."

"Commander, the sun is setting," one of the other fighters said.

The commander nodded. "Take Javier to the rear position and keep him tied up and under guard," he said to one of the other fighters, who led Javier out of the building. Then he turned back to me. "Don't make me regret keeping you on one of the advanced teams."

Twenty-Six
In the Bunker outside Ontario

The week of training flew by in a blur. Most of it involved learning to blend into life in the city — learning how to talk, procedures for getting on transit and getting food, as well as mastering our cover stories. This "training" had been the majority of my life, and many members of my insertion team looked to me for guidance and reassurance.

When we weren't learning how to behave in the city, we studied maps, coding and intel on the Civic Guardians' movements. There were safe house locations and procedures if we were caught.

There were five members on my team, Nadie, Ares, myself and an older couple named Tristan and Keila. Tristan and Keila were the tech geeks, Nadie and Ares the surveillance and intelligence operatives. My role was to be the on-the-ground liaison.

The cyber analysts at the bunker had managed to get us all identity cards and put our fingerprint scans into the Zone 4 networks. We were all being "functionally reassigned," as the lingo went in the city, for new duties in Zone 4. We were to each report to the human resource centre in the Hub at different appointment times on the day of our insertion. Reassignments were common in the zones as a means of presenting new opportunities to people and breaking up some of the monotony of routine. I had considered doing it at one point, but never did. It just seemed like another control tactic. Every year, there were two reassignment dates. Some made a career of applying to be reassigned. There were no real rules around it. If someone was interested in something and had the test scores and skills, they'd likely get it.

Based on the information the tech geeks had managed to hack, each zone allowed five thousand applications per cycle. This was a large enough number that five falsified applications from our insertion team would not be obvious. I pictured the individuals reviewing the applications. They'd have very little information. They'd have only the person's identity number and no other information to cross-reference any inconsistencies. Just like when I reviewed food distribution records, it would be nearly impossible to find any falsified information. The Civic Administrators believed they'd built a perfect system. They didn't conceive that someone could hack in and create false identities. I had to hand it to the movement, they'd thought of everything. I didn't know yet if they were all on the same page regarding their end goal, but they'd certainly planned their steps well.

With reassignment came new zone housing. Since people owned only a few possessions, no one would think anything of us moving into new housing with little baggage. All apartments in Zone 4 were furnished almost identically and contained the necessary supplies in kitchens, bedrooms and bathrooms. Only things like clothing, books, decorations and knick-knacks moved with people. The informants in the city had prepared a couple of boxes for each of us with personal items. Up until this point, I'd never considered what might have happened to my things when I disappeared. Likely, they'd tried to cover up my disappearance and say that I was repurposed, and my personal effects were probably sent to stores for resale.

During the week of training, I avoided Nadie as much as possible. She attempted to reach out on numerous occasions, even apologizing for our last conversation. I appreciated her trying but needed to figure out what I wanted to do long term and whom I could trust. My conversation with Elizabeth had made me wary. I was apprehensive about this entire mission. I couldn't afford to be confused and distracted by Nadie.

The day before we were set to leave, Elizabeth asked to see me before I underwent the procedure to change my appearance. "Are you prepared to do what's necessary if the worst happens?" she asked.

"I think so. Do you really think it will come to violence?"

"I hope not, but I want to be prepared for any eventuality. My biggest concern right now is that any violence may come from within this movement. If that happens, the Civic Administrators will have all the reason they need to clamp down on us. What's more, any sympathy we may get from the citizens of the city may be lost."

"I'll only be in Zone 4, though, which is unlikely to be the flashpoint for any outbreaks of violence."

"I know, which is why we'll have gyrocopters on the outskirts of the city standing by. We're also going to try to gain control of the underground transit ways in order to move people from zone to zone if necessary." She handed me a small metal case. "Take this. It's a communication device. Keep it hidden from your other team members. This will allow for two-way communication between you and me. Ares will only have a device for communication between all of us operating on the same frequency across the different zones."

Inside the case was an earpiece. Unless someone were looking into my ear canal, there was no way they would be able to see it.

"Wear it at all times on the day of the message delivery. Good luck, and I'll see you soon."

"Thanks. You too." I still had so many questions and concerns but left Elizabeth to her final preparations and returned to Level F.

The plan was that each team would spend three days doing surveillance on their strike points after insertion. Each zone's servers and communications terminal were in a centralized location in their respective hub, connected to each other through underground cables. The command centre in Zone 1 was the most heavily guarded. Because of the program implanted across their network by my mother, the theory was that a remote link in close enough proximity would infiltrate the command centre. The movement had already tested this several times with some of the informants they had in Zone 1. There were teams in each of the other zones because there were fail-safes that allowed the operators at the communications terminal in each zone to disconnect from the network in the event of a disruption to service. As soon as Zone 1 was hacked, the other zones would override the signal and independently take control. For the plan to work, we needed to simultaneously take over each zone's communications terminal to ensure the message was delivered seamlessly across the city.

I didn't pretend to understand all the technical mumbo-jumbo. That wasn't my role. However, we were all trained in the necessary steps and taught each other's roles in case something happened to any of us. We'd done exercises undertaking various scenarios of what to do if any one of us were compromised. The most important team members were the tech geeks. The rest of us were supposed to compromise ourselves if it meant keeping their cover intact. Each team was capable of operating with a minimum of three. If any team had less than that at zero hour, the mission was to be called off.

Changing my appearance took about an hour. My hair was cut and dyed a dark brown. I was given contact lenses that changed my blue eyes to a hazel colour. Finally, after a minor surgery, the appearance of my nose was altered. I looked completely different.

If I saw someone I knew, I was supposed to ignore them. My new occupation was as a surveillance analyst at the Zone 4 central transit hub. This meant I would be monitoring video screens for unusual behaviour and checking in with Civic Guardians. It also meant I would have access to the train schedules for the underground transit system between zones. Each team had someone assigned to these points. Ares was assigned to be a Civic Guardian. The tech geeks in the bunker had managed to get Civic Guardian identities in a couple of zones. To avoid suspicion, a couple of them had already started their new roles, several weeks apart. Ares had left three days ago.

It was potentially my last night in the bunker. Tomorrow morning we'd head to the city. There were safe houses near the entry point in each zone. The morning after insertion, we would simply emerge as residents of the city.

That last evening, as I was preparing for bed, there was a knock on my door. It was Nadie. I opened the door and waved her in. She sat on the bed as I stood leaning against the wall. I didn't know if she was expecting me to begin the conversation. She looked around the room, examined her hands in her lap and exhaled loudly. "Listen, I know I hurt you and I'm sorry. Under other circumstances, things may have been different. I think I was excited by the prospect of getting to know someone who grew up in such a different situation from me. I had an expectation in my head. I figured you left the city because you felt the same way we do. I was wrong to assume that and to talk about your parents. I can see your point of view even though I don't agree. But we need to be on the same team for this. I need to know you trust me." She looked up at me. "Do you?"

I stared at her, unsure of what to say. I was angry. I'd put myself out there, and while not exactly rejected, was rebuked as if I was an ignorant child. I blurted out the next thought that popped in my head. "That depends on what you'll do if things turn violent."

"What do you mean? We'll defend ourselves if the Civic Administrators go that route."

"I don't mean the Civic Administrators. What if it's your own people that use violence?"

"Why would anyone do that? We believe in peace, freedom and equality. The Civic Administrators have accomplished some of this, but through control of what a person can or can't do. We simply want to show people the alternative."

I knew she believed what she was saying. But to believe that everyone finding out about how they'd been lied to would somehow result in them joining hands in harmony seemed naïve to say the least. "I trust you, Nadie, but I won't help if it comes to violence. The movement will lose all credibility if it comes to that."

"Thank you for your trust. It won't come to that." She stood, reaching for my hands, pulling me to the bed as she sat down again. I sat down beside her, still hand in hand.

"Do you miss it? I mean, the city?" she asked.

"Yes and no. I knew what to expect there. I knew I would be fed, clothed and sheltered. I had a role, if not a true purpose. I'm not sure what use I am here. If that's freedom, I'm not sure how everyone else in the city will react. They've never had to choose their own path."

"They'll have the freedom to choose whether they want to keep that life or try something else, just like you. You aren't a prisoner here … if you want to go back to your old life."

"I'm not sure what I want. In a sense, that feeling is freeing in and of itself. Scary and exciting at the same time."

She reached in to kiss me. I pulled back but then relented, returning the kiss. We spent the night together. If it came to it, I would have Nadie's support. I had to believe she wanted the best outcome. I had to believe that her vision lined up with Elizabeth's. The test would come over the next few days. I went to bed not worrying about the future, secure in her arms.

The next morning, the bunker was a hive of activity. People were running this way and that carrying supplies, consulting lists, hurrying to eat. Nadie had woken up before me and disappeared. There were few people in the cafeteria at the regular breakfast time, so I ate in solitude quickly, worried that I was holding things up. After getting dressed, I headed to the control room for final instructions. Many teams had already left. Others were scheduled to leave later. Elizabeth had already gone, and a younger man that I'd seen frequently in the control room was giving final instructions to Nadie, Tristan and Keila. They'd made contact with Ares, who'd successfully infiltrated the Civic Guardians in Zone 4. It was going well so far in all six zones.

Soon we were all on a gyrocopter heading toward the city. We were flying very low and fast, apparently to avoid detection, but the constant subtle shifts over hills, through trees and around ruined buildings was doing a number on my stomach. After a few hours, we landed. I was nauseous, more so from the gyrocopter ride than the apprehension of the next few days. Nadie was quiet. I couldn't tell if she was anxious or sick as well. With no time for rest, we headed the final twenty kilometres on foot. We were on familiar ground. This route seemed to be the same one I'd journeyed not so long ago in the opposite direction.

By the end of the day, we reached the same underground tunnel I'd used to leave the city. We would hike the last bit underground and wait for complete darkness before crossing the river into Zone 4. When we reached the point of the tunnel with the staircase that I'd so cautiously descended what felt like a lifetime ago, my heart began to race. There were two other people waiting on the platform at the bottom of the staircase, dressed in the civilian garb of Zone 4. One of them was Tyra, my neighbour from Zone 4.

"Hi, Kelowna," she said in a calm voice, nothing like her usual high-pitched greeting.

"Tyra, what are you doing here?"

"About that … um, I've been an informer for quite some time. I was assigned to look out for you. I followed you that first night you crossed the river."

I couldn't help but laugh. I thought I had been so careful and that Tyra was such an annoying moron.

Tyra looked at me apologetically. "I'm sorry for deceiving you. Here." She handed me a bag with Zone 4 clothing. Her partner had handed similar bags to Nadie, Tristan and Keila. "I'm Van. Tyra and I will lead you into the city." We changed clothes and left the underground tunnel with the lights of the city in the distance. It was time to take on our fake personas and become part of the city.

Nadie was still very quiet. I walked beside her. "What's wrong?" I asked.

"I'm nervous. I feel like I've been training for this moment my entire life, but now I don't think I'm ready. Everything in the city is going to be so new. How am I supposed to pretend that it's all routine to me? Tomorrow when we show up for reassignment, they're going to see right through me and the mission will fail." She was tearing up and shaking.

I grabbed her. "You're ready for this. You know what to do and what to say. Everyone around will be preoccupied with their own routine. They won't even know you exist. As far as they're concerned, you're another cog in the machine. Besides, you believe in all this stuff, remember? You won't let it fail." I smirked and gave her a light punch to the arm.

She laughed. "Thank you. How are you feeling?"

"Honestly, if anyone is going to screw this up, it's me. I ran away from that place because I hated being a cog, now I'm voluntarily returning to it. The best part is that I'm going to be one of the people monitoring for suspicious behaviour. The Civic Guardians are going to take one look at me and this will all fall apart. I hope you have a Plan B."

"You're joking, right?"

"Sure. Everything will be cool."

We approached the river near the place I'd crossed it all those nights ago. Soon we were descending the steep hill into the narrow river valley. No one was saying a word. I'd been paired with Keila to go the rest of the way, with Tyra and Nadie crossing the river first. Tristan and Van were behind the rest of us. As we got to the bottom of the hill and saw the river, I could just glimpse Nadie and Tyra on the other side crouching low, headed for the bushes. I motioned to Keila to cross. Soon we were on the other side of the river, headed toward the city. We all headed different directions to end up eventually at the same safe house. Since it was after hours, a group of six would be too difficult to explain if we were caught.

Luckily, we didn't encounter anyone else and soon arrived at the safe house. Nadie and Tyra were already there. Tristan and Van arrived about fifteen minutes after us. Without much in the way of conversation, we had some vegetable soup and went to bed. The safe house was in a perfect spot, on a narrow alley not far from the zone fringe. In the morning, no one would notice that six people suddenly emerged from the same place, especially since we would leave at staggered times. Van lived at the safe house. It was his assigned apartment, and he worked in park maintenance in the Hub. Tyra still lived across from my old place.

"So, do you know what happened to the stuff in my apartment?" I asked Tyra.

"The Civic Guardians came and examined your place a few days after you left. They questioned me and our other neighbours. They told me you hadn't been reporting for work and asked the last time I'd seen you."

"I guess I'll never see that painting again."

"What painting?"

"Just some painting of a farm with horses I spent all my novelty credits on shortly before leaving the city. I guess it doesn't matter now."

The six of us ate breakfast together and went over the details of each person's plan again to make sure everyone knew their part perfectly. Nadie was the first to leave. Her appointment at the reassignment centre was early. I was scared for her but didn't say anything. She put on a brave face and didn't seem to have any of the apprehension from last night. If everything went according to plan, I wouldn't see her again for three days.

Tristan was second to leave and kissed Keila goodbye with a long embrace. They were to be reassigned to the same place but had to pretend not to know each other.

I was next. My past life came back to me vividly. It felt like any other day of my previous life, dressed in the same clothes, walking to the same tram, heading to the same pointless job. It was midmorning already, so the streets were relatively quiet. At the hub station, there seemed to be more than the usual number of Civic Guardians. They stood out in their black-and-silver uniforms. I looked around to see if something had happened, nervous that someone had been exposed already. But the Civic Guardians appeared to be in no hurry and were just strolling along. I guess I'd never really paid attention to them before. Maybe this was the same number that was normally here. I tried to remember some of the training sessions we'd done on their numbers and movements, but I drew a blank. I realized I was acting weird by looking at them, trying to see if Ares was there. They weren't paying attention to me. The average citizen doesn't pay attention to the Civic Guardians. Before I did something even stupider, I left the station and headed for the reassignment centre.

I was ten minutes early and was told to have a seat. A reassignment specialist called my new name at the exact time of my appointment. Actually, she called my new name a few times before I realized that it was me. So far this wasn't going well. I made a terrible infiltrator.

"Sorry, was daydreaming I guess," was all I could think to say. She smiled at me and led me to a small glass-enclosed office.

"So ... moving from data processing to transit surveillance. That's a big change, but your scores are very good." I didn't know if she was expecting a response, but she was looking at me.

"Yes, I haven't taken advantage of reassignment before and feel like surveillance may be a little more exciting for a while."

"Very good. Here are the details of your assignment. You'll start late this afternoon until the closure of the hub station. I see you have your personal belongings. Your new lodgings will be near the Hub, which is very desirable. One of the perks of working closely with the Civic Guardians, they want their personnel close to their places of work. If you'll follow me, we'll finish the necessary retinal scans and ID confirmation so you can see your new place before heading to work."

She handed me an envelope with ID cards, badges, schedules and other information. Everything went well with my ID confirmation, fingerprint and retinal scan. I was worried that this part would cause my old life to reappear, but apparently the tech people had done their jobs well. I was in and out of the reassignment centre in a half hour.

My new apartment was three blocks from the Hub but looked exactly like my old apartment. I arranged my not-so-personal personal effects and headed back to the Hub, since I had no food in the apartment. I grabbed some lunch and had an hour before needing to head into my new job. I sat in the park to kill time, watching the hustle and bustle of the Hub. I was back in the very place I'd left not so long ago. I wondered how Gerald and Victoria were doing and if they'd wondered what had happened to me. I sat wondering about Victoria's friend, whose name I still couldn't remember. I thought about going to the Loon to see if they were there but realized they would still be at work. Anyway, what would that accomplish? My old life, what little of it there was, was gone. There was no point in fixating on the past.

I went to report to my new job. Strangely enough — or I guess not — Ares was the Civic Guardian that gave me the rundown on surveillance procedures and showed me around. His name now was Milton. I couldn't believe how much the movement seemed to have manipulated the city. I had to hand it to Ares, or I guess Milton, for how professional he was. He had the disconnected persona of someone that didn't know me and didn't care, without any of the contempt he'd shown me in the bunker.

The new job seemed just as tedious as my old one in the city. I was to stare at screens for the Hub and the underground transit station to look for suspicious behaviour. No one could get into the underground transit station unless authorized, and there were plenty of security fail-safes and alarms. The hub station, while busy, was filled with the drones of Zone 4. I guess the whole point of my being there, though, was to ensure the alarms didn't go off and the fail-safes didn't trigger the day the message was to go out. There were three other people monitoring the same screens I was but in different rooms. Every other transit station in Zone 4 had similar surveillance personnel.

Day one back in the city finished without any fanfare and I returned to my carbon-copy apartment, dreading the fact that I had to endure two more days of this before the real fireworks happened. It seemed that I was truly a member of the movement, since one day back in the city was enough to make me excited to see the outcome of the mission.

Twenty-Seven
Kyiv

The vote was set to happen at noon.

The sky was cloudy, which made the already dreary square an even duller grey. The only other colours were those on the banners of the various factions. More people, having heard about the vote, had returned. Three booths with numbers were set up in front of the gates of the central building. Posters were being passed around explaining the three options. Option 1 being the centralized democratic government preferred by United Earth. Option 2 being the independently run sections of the surrounding area with potential trade agreements. And Option 3, the free-for-all of go wherever and do whatever.

It was hard to tell which of the various groups was the largest. Many people seemed to come and go. Most of the people seemed to have no particular allegiance and congregated in the middle of the square.

Just before noon, it began to rain. Not a hard rain, but enough to be uncomfortable. A large tent was erected over the voting booths. The intent was to have three lines form. Each voting booth had a box for each option. People started to line up, but the rain wasn't letting up, so it was a slow trickle of people. About an hour after voting had started, many members of United Earth began to line up. Anna dragged me along, but I couldn't help but notice that William remained behind, still clutching his gun. Some people took only a second to make their choice and move on. Others spent minutes agonizing, despite having all that time in line to assess the various options. Anna went ahead of me, and, with no hesitation, picked the first box. She smiled at me as she turned away. I followed, wondering if I was making the right choice.

The rain finally stopped in the late afternoon and the sun began to peek through the clouds. A good sign, I thought. Announcements were made that the voting booths would be closed in the next hour.

William had remained sombre and distant all day. While Anna had joined many of the other United Earth members in debating the details, believing that Option 1 would win, William sat in the corner alone.

I looked at him as he fiddled with the gun, staring at the ground, and finally asked him why he didn't vote.

He shook his head. "What's the point? Do you really think my vote will change the outcome?"

"That depends. We don't know what the outcome will be. Did you used to vote back when elections were held?"

"Yes, like all those other fools that thought it changed anything. We swallowed the promises, believing each candidate that guaranteed change, elicited hope and vowed to do whatever other pointless buzzwords, only to see the system become more corrupt, favouring the established order and continuing our self-destructive spiral. I'm not that naïve anymore. There are good people here, but good people never have the stomach to stand against the bad. They lack the means to do what's necessary to remove that threat."

"Because that would make them no better than the ones we oppose." I knew how foolish my response must have sounded. The truth was, I understood where William was coming from. My mother had been a good person, but she died anyway. Good people had been imprisoned and sent here because they hoped for a better world. History was full of good people doing amazing things but dying all the same, having only reached the base of the mountain they tried to ascend. I didn't believe that those other people were bad per se, just lacking imagination. They were selfish, disconnected or ignorant, products of a broken society.

William just looked at me and smirked. He knew I didn't believe what I was saying. Deep down I was a cynic. Anna kept me going and that was good enough. "Let's hope that thinking doesn't get us killed," he stated, getting up and walking away.

The voting booths had closed and the leaders from the various groups took the ballot boxes to the main building, where it was expected to take all night to tally the results. It was nearly midnight when William returned. He didn't say a word but lay down in the room that the three of us had taken, which used to be somebody's office. The carpet was old and uncomfortable. We had two small blankets and a couch cushion between us. William lay against the wall in the corner, covered by a large winter coat he'd found. He'd slept in worse conditions. Anna had the couch cushion propped against the wall to use as a pillow. We shared the two blankets.

Anna was positive that Option 1 would carry the vote. I wasn't so sure. Even if Option 1 did win, there would be so many things to figure out. Rebuilding a functioning society would take time.

It was a sleepless night for Anna. William was sound asleep in the corner, his gun propped against the wall. I stared at Anna, wondering what she was thinking. She was chewing on her fingernails. She didn't speak, but I could tell she was preoccupied with a thousand thoughts.

As the sun began to rise, the sounds of gunfire erupted. William was up in a flash with gun in hand, staring out the window.

"What is it?" I asked.

"There are guards at the gate, a crowd forming, running toward the gate. Some of the guards are forming barricades across the broken gate; others are running into the building. Let's go."

Anna looked on the verge of tears. Outside near the United Earth tent was chaos. Most of the leadership was still inside the building. No one seemed to know what was going on. The occasional gunshot rang out in the cool morning air.

Representatives of other groups were demanding answers at the newly raised barricade. They only got scowls. The guards were dressed in all black with white arm bands.

"What faction is that?" I asked William.

He shook his head. On the far side of the courtyard at the corner of the building, I could see bodies. Their uniforms and arm bands indicated they were members of one of the communist groups.

People were demanding to know the results of the vote and started rattling the gate. One of the guards fired warning shots into the air. People cowered and backed away. William grabbed us and hurried toward the alley at the side of the building we were staying in.

"It seems one group didn't like the results of the vote and took over."

"You don't know that," Anna said, looking back over her shoulder at the crowd around the gate still demanding answers.

"Please, stop being so naïve," William said. "Dead soldiers from one militant group, and the only people present at the gate are members of another militant group. They decided to strike first. We have to get out of here, head west."

"What?" screamed Anna. "We have to find out what happened. We can't let them get away with this."

"What are you going to do, walk up there and demand answers? Good luck with that." William was agitated. He was glaring at me. I could tell he wanted me to say something, to talk sense into Anna. He didn't know her the way I did. There would be no convincing her. She would walk right up to one of those guards and begin to lecture them, unarmed, about the importance of democracy and human rights.

"There has to be another way to get in there to see what's going on," I finally said.

Anna smiled. William looked at me like I was nuts and then laughed. "The three of us are going to storm that place and then what, politely ask what's going on?" William shook his head and began to walk away.

It began to rain again. Dark clouds were rolling in. More gunfire erupted. William turned back around. The crowd at the gate was dispersing. Bodies were lying near the barricade. The guards inside were exchanging gunfire with armed people outside. Innocent bystanders were being caught in the crossfire.

"Come on, now's our chance." William urged us to follow. He ran down the alley, turning right at the next alley. We were running along a dark, deserted building that ran along the side of the wall around the main building. William broke his way through a door of a large building, which led to a derelict staircase. He climbed to the fourth floor. We headed toward the wall around the main building. Most of the windows were boarded up. William began to pry open some of the boards to get a look. We were about level with the wall, but it was lined with razor-sharp wire.

Outside was a full-blown thunderstorm. It was dark with periodic flashes of lightning followed by deep rumbling thunder. There were no visible guards on this part of the wall. We couldn't see the courtyard, the front of the building or the barricade, but saw the occasional flash of gunfire.

William pried all the boards off one of the windows. It wouldn't open far enough, so he began to slowly shatter the glass. With all the noise outside, it was unlikely anyone heard it. We were so close to the wall, less than a metre. If only we could jump over the wire.

Soon there was a space in the window large enough to get through. William started to look around. It was hard to see since it was so dark outside. William went to one of the adjoining rooms and yelled for me to come help. He was using the end of his gun to break the hinges off the door and needed me to hold it steady.

Once he'd freed it of its hinges, William carried the door back to the adjoining room. He looked outside again along the length of the wall. The door just fit through the window. William used it as a platform to cover the razor wire. He went first, then Anna and last me. We were on the wall with no one else in sight. He pushed the door back, causing it to tumble down between the building and the wall. We ran off along the wall in the opposite direction of the front courtyard. William moved cautiously, crouching, looking anxiously at the windows in the building we needed to get into. They were dark, for the most part, except for some of the lower levels. We still hadn't seen a single person.

There was a faint light coming from the guardhouse at the corner of the wall. William motioned for us to stay back, keep low and be quiet. William moved off toward the guardhouse and crept inside. He wasn't gone long before he came back and motioned for us to follow.

On the floor was a young man dressed in all black with a white arm band. William reached out, handing Anna and me each a gun. Anna looked stunned and held hers awkwardly.

"Is he dead?" I asked.

"What do you think?" William responded, picking up his gun from a desk and looking around the small room for any other weapons. "I didn't have a choice."

"You killed him? Was that really necessary?" I asked.

"What do you think would have happened if he caught us here? We don't have time for moral questions. Whoever this group is, it has no problem killing rivals." He pointed at the guns Anna and I were holding. "Do either of you know how to use those things?"

We both shook our heads.

"Safety on, safety off," he said, demonstrating on the gun in my hand. "Trigger, point and shoot." He looked at as both, slowly nodding for reassurance that we understood. "Just follow me and try not to get yourselves killed."

I looked at Anna. She was breathing heavily and staring at the weapon in her hand.

"It'll be okay," I said. She nodded, taking another deep breath. I couldn't tell which one of us was more scared.

William found some keys, a knife and extra ammo on the guard. We discovered a trap door in the floor of the guardhouse, which opened up to reveal a ladder underneath. William took the lead, with Anna and me climbing down after him.

There was a small door at the back of the building. The wall was only two metres from the building at the back. The door was unlocked. William raised his gun and slowly went inside. A long hallway led to the front of the building. There were many rooms on each side. The first room on the left was empty. William shuffled through some of the cabinets.

"What are you looking for?" I asked.

"Would one of you watch the door? I'm seeing if there are any blueprints or floor plans." Anna watched the door.

"Okay, listen. We're going to have to clear each room one by one. There are no silencers on these guns, so try to avoid firing them. Let me go first and watch my back. There's probably a security room near the front entrance that would have the layout of this place. Let's hope the cameras aren't functioning. Anna, you follow me. Elliott, take the rear and watch for anything behind us."

My heart was racing, but Anna seemed to have calmed down and quickly fell in line behind William, mimicking his moves. Each room along the hallway was as empty as the last one, which only increased my anxiety. It was quiet. We could still hear the rain outside and the occasional thunder. One thing was missing — gunfire. As we got closer to the front of the building, William slowed down, keeping close to the left wall and kneeling to listen after each step.

We could hear talking and doors opening and closing. Hurried footsteps were running up stairs. It soon quieted down. William motioned for us to stay put and darted across the hall to a room on the right in the corner of the building. He pulled out his knife and bolted into the room. The door opened and he motioned for us to hurry. The room was empty. The front of the building was a large foyer. The main doors were in the centre, about fifteen metres away. There was a large staircase directly across from the entrance. On the opposite side of the foyer was a large room with dark plate glass.

"That must be the security office," William said. "If there's anyone in there, they must not be looking this way; otherwise, we would've been found out. We'll have to be quick. This area is too exposed. There could be guards at the top of the stairs. Or anyone could come through those front doors. I'll go first and clear the stairway; you both follow close behind and watch the front doors. If anyone exits the room across the foyer, be ready."

We both nodded. Before I could second-guess this plan, we were in the front foyer. The stairway was clear, and William was already moving toward the door on the far side. My gun was pointing at the front doors as I followed, moving quickly backward. Anna was covering the stairway. She seemed to be a natural. There was another long hallway running down the other side of the stairway. There was nowhere to seek cover, so we lined up along the wall beside William, who was right beside the door to the security office. He had the gun in his right hand and the knife in his left. He slowly pushed the door open and crept in. I followed close behind. There were two guards with their backs to us monitoring a radio and a couple of computer screens. William handed me the knife and pointed to the one on the left. His eyes were insistent with a don't-fuck-this-up look. We moved quietly toward them. William had his arms around the neck of the guard on the right before I could think. The guard on the left reached for his gun. I thrust the knife into the back of his neck. He lurched forward, still reaching for his gun. I pulled the knife out, grabbing his head, and pulled him back, stabbing him in the chest. His eyes looked at me, pained, before glossing over expressionless. My hands were covered in blood. William nodded at me. I dropped the knife, stumbling backward. Anna reached out to me, but I motioned her away.

"Elliott, you had no choice," William said. "Next time, slit their throat or stab them in the chest first." He surveyed the room and fumbled with the computers.

I wanted to punch him in the face. *Next time.* I just killed someone and watched as they died. Anna was looking at me with pity.

"Anna, watch the door. And Elliott, snap out of it before you get us all killed."

Anna reacted swiftly, positioning herself beside the door.

"Elliott, come here. Look at this. There's power to some of the building. Here, on the second level, they have prisoners."

The security cameras were active on the second and third levels of the building. Some of the rooms had more bodies, but it seemed like most of the leadership from civilian or pacifist groups were being held prisoner. The outside courtyard cameras were active, too. There were many bodies, but also many guards moving around dressed in black with white arm bands. Inside, the building was quieter. Whatever group this was, they didn't seem to be large. Based on the camera sweeps of the second and third levels, there didn't seem to be more than two dozen guards inside the building and probably another thirty outside.

"There are still too many for us to do anything," I said. "We should leave."

"It's too late for that; besides, there are at least fifty prisoners. If we can free them, we'll have the advantage," William responded.

There was a weapons and ammo cache on the far side of the room. William found a silencer for a handgun and took a matching gun off one of the dead guards. He replaced his old rifle with a modern military weapon. Then he pulled some other items from one of the lockers and turned to Anna and me. "This is a smoke grenade, and this is a flashbang," he said, giving us one of each. "Use them only if I tell you to." Then he handed Anna a knife and kept one for himself. Next, he walked over to the guard I'd killed and pulled the knife from his chest, wiping the blood off on the guard's uniform. He handed it back to me. I held it lightly, my hand shaking.

Anna was watching the monitor with the courtyard camera. Two guards were entering the front door. William noticed too. He told us to get down along the wall. There was no time to do anything about the dead guards or blood. Through the dark plate glass window, we could see out to the foyer, but no one could see in. The guards were heading toward our room. William pointed the gun with the silencer. The door opened with laughter. The first guard was down with one shot. William leaped toward the door, firing another shot before the other guard could so much as scream. He went outside the room. The first guard was lying face down, his body holding the door open. William dragged the second one into the room by the feet. Anna had moved to get the first guard out of the way before I could react, pulling him by reaching under his arms. William grabbed a shirt from one of the lockers and wiped the blood outside the room.

"There's nothing we can do to hide the bodies, but it's time to move," he said. "The prisoners are being held on the second level in a large conference room at the back-left side of the building. There are a series of rooms and checkpoints to get there. There are at least eight more guards on the way there and five in the room. As soon as any one of them gets a shot off, more will come. Any ideas?"

"We need to cut the power," said Anna.

William went back to the security screens, looking for where the generators may be. It was likely the guards would just think the power went out. The city had been without reliable power for a while.

"Damn it. The generators must be on one of the other levels. We don't have time to look for them. I have another idea. Elliott, you aren't going to like it."

William's idea was to dress like the guards. The guard whose neck he broke had an intact, clean uniform and so did the first guard that fell face first through the door. We found handcuffs to put on Anna. The problem was we didn't know what language this group spoke. William said we would know the first time we got asked a question and would just have to hope one of us spoke enough of it. Anna and William began stripping the dead guards before I could protest. And I didn't have a better idea. Before I knew it, I was dressed in a dead man's clothes with Anna as my prisoner.

"This is stupid," I said as we climbed the stairs. "The second they see us they'll know we aren't part of their group. There aren't many of them."

William motioned for me to shut up and kept climbing the stairs. He had the military-style rifle slung on his back and the handgun with the silencer tightly gripped at his side. As we got to the top of the stairs, we headed left toward the hallway that went to the back of the building. As we turned the corner, there were two guards at the end of the short hall before a large door.

They called to us in a language none of us understood. It sounded like it might be Polish. William tensed. The smirks on the guards faces quickly turned to confusion. Before they could raise their guns, William shot them both in the head with two silent, perfectly aimed shots. They collapsed to the floor with a thud. William ran forward to the door. William operated like a man possessed. I didn't know whether I was more scared of him or this situation.

"Okay, new plan. We only have a couple seconds before each guard realizes we aren't part of their group. We'll have to move quick and shoot first. I only have six more bullets for the handgun. After that, the rifle, which will be loud. Elliott, grab those guns," he said, pointing at the weapons on the floor. "And once we reach the prisoners, we can get some backup. Cover my back."

His tone indicated he would not tolerate any arguments. We moved the dead guards away from the door. Anna opened the door slowly and William darted through, firing two more shots. Two more guards went down in the next hall, but the rooms along this hall were open, with glass walls. Gunfire rang out, shattering the glass. William rolled across the floor, swinging his rifle around and returning fire. Anna moved in after him, firing across the room.

I was frozen. Anna had fired her weapon. She was mimicking William's moves. Where had this come from?

"Elliott! Check behind," William yelled.

I spun around and looked at the stairs behind us. No guards. Yet.

William cried out to keep moving. I closed the door behind me, but there was no way to lock it. I surveyed the hall and saw at least two more bodies in one of the adjoining rooms. William and Anna were already in the next hall where more gunfire erupted. Everything was happening so fast.

We moved through corridors that zigzagged toward the rear of the building. Small rooms, large rooms and lots of doors. I kept walking backward, covering the rear. I stumbled over a couple more bodies as we moved closer to the back of the building.

Suddenly, another young man dressed in all black with white arm bands came running around a corner from behind us. I fired blindly in that direction, hitting the wall and the young man, who crumpled to the floor.

William ran back in the direction we'd just come, looking around the corner before darting back to my side.

"Do you speak any Polish?"

"What? No."

"The next room is where the prisoners are, but it's large and there are too many guards. If one of you spoke any Polish, we might have been able to convince them that everything is okay now. Shit."

William was erratic, running multiple scenarios through his head, when two more guards came around the corner. William took the first down with a series of shots. The other one darted into an adjoining room, returning fire. We all hit the floor, William crawling along the wall. Anna returned fire. The walls in this part of the building were concrete, so bullets couldn't penetrate. There was no door on the room the guard had retreated to. I kept my eye on the other corner, waiting for more guards. Anna was covering our backs. William spun around through the door. I could hear groans, punches and the sounds of metal hitting the ground. I ran to assist, Anna now covering both directions. William had the man in a chokehold on the floor, asking him if he spoke English or German. He said he spoke some English.

"Here's how this is going to go," William said. "I'll spare your life if you get us into that next room and tell your friends there that the intruders are dead except for one prisoner."

The guard looked confused. William placed a blade against his neck and jerked his head back roughly. "Understand?" The guard nodded. William pulled him up and we moved toward the room with the prisoners. "Don't try anything funny," William said. Then he instructed Anna to walk toward the room with her hands up. She handed over her guns and knife. "As soon as I say *now*, hit the floor. Elliott, watch our backs."

With a knife in his left hand against the back of the guard and the rifle in his right, we proceeded to the door.

We knocked. From inside came angry shouts. Our prisoner guard shouted something back. William twisted the knife against his back. "What's going on?" he whispered to him.

"They asked who is and what happen. I say name and enemy dead. Have new woman for prison." He turned back to the door and shouted something else. A response came. "They say enter."

We slowly moved into the room. The prisoners were lined up, two rows deep, along the walls at the back. Two guards were standing in the middle of the room with their guns pointed at us.

William shouted, "Now!" He knocked our prisoner to the ground as Anna dove down. The rifle in his right hand flung up and fired at the two in the middle of the room. I fired at one in the corner to our right. William threw his knife at one to the left, hitting him in the chest. He fired his gun wildly into the ceiling. Two of the prisoners jumped at another guard in the back corner, beating him down. Anna got up, retrieving a gun. She tried to calm down the prisoners. William handed a couple more guns to other prisoners that stepped forward.

No one was watching the guard we'd taken prisoner. He'd slunk off to his dead compatriot to the left. Out of the corner of my eye, I saw him grab the gun and point it at William. Before I knew what I was doing, I darted for William, pushing him to the ground as loud pops echoed through the room and a searing hot pain hit me in the side. I hit the floor as more shots echoed.

Anna fell to my side, cradling my head as William stood over me dumbstruck, shouting for a doctor or medic. I could feel blood oozing from my left side. A woman was applying pressure to my side. She said something about multiple bullets and too much blood. Anna was crying and begging. William had fallen to his knees and was holding my hand.

I began to lose feeling across my body, until I felt nothing but cold. Anna kissed my lips and the world went dark.

Twenty-Eight
The Pacific Ocean

The ship was still anchored in the calm turquoise waters interspersed with verdant islands. The breezes were warm and salty. Mateo and I spent another day with three training dives. He showed me how to prepare the restoration patches and we practised emergency situations. I even got quite good at maintaining neutral buoyancy.

Later, back on the ship, Mateo and I ate the evening meal together.

"Tomorrow, you'll help me with one of the restoration patches. It's a good spot with enough healthy reef left."

"Looking forward to it." I was eating yellow curried potatoes with a fresh green salad. We had a table to ourselves. The meal room had a few other scientists eating quietly and going over data on their electronic pads.

What made you decide to be a marine biologist?" I asked.

"I grew up by the ocean. My father was a fisherman, so I was always on the water. As I got older, the fish became fewer and fewer and the garbage more prevalent. It made me angry. I wanted to stop it."

"It must have been so difficult to witness everything fall apart."

"Yes. It still makes me sad. We knew what we were doing, but…" Mateo fiddled with the food on his plate.

"But what?"

"It doesn't matter. Things are changing now. That's good."

We ate the rest of the meal in silence. Mateo wished me good night and told me to be up on deck with the equipment at 0700 hours.

The next morning, we took a boat northwest of the ship to a set of islands that had noticeably darker water all around them. We could look down through the clear water and see they were reefs. Four other researchers were on the boat with Mateo and me. Each pair would work on a different part of the reef.

On that first descent, I could already see more life than on any of the previous dives. Small and large fish swam around hard and soft corals — live ones. And there was colour! So much colour. The fish, the corals. Yellows, reds, purples, blues. Mateo had to tap me on the shoulder to remind me what we were doing. I was too distracted. There was so much to see. Schools of fish swam lazily around the reef. Other fish chased each other between corals. There were patches of dead coral, too, but more that was living.

Mateo and I started removing a section of dead coral heads and replaced them with artificial structures for some of the specimens from the tanks on the ship to cling to and propagate from. Every day for three weeks, teams from each of the four ships would carry out meticulous transplants throughout the waters of this area.

Toward the end of the three weeks, we began installing monitoring equipment that would link to satellites providing real-time and continual data on the marine conditions. We also installed devices that involved low-voltage electrical energy to alter the water chemistry around coral structures, allowing the corals to devote more time and energy to reproduction and growth rather than forming skeletal structure. Some members of the crew would be staying on the islands to continue to monitor the reefs directly and repair equipment as needed.

The last few days before departing from Kri would be spent transplanting the fish species from the tanks. It was believed there was enough living coral now to provide sufficient habitat and food and that, in time, other larger species could be incorporated to redevelop the food chain completely.

After departing from Kri, our ship headed east, alone. We moved along the vast island of New Guinea. Our first destination was a city on the north coast, where we were planning to resupply and meet another vessel before heading to join more coral restoration programs.

Mateo told me that once this expedition was over, I should request to be part of New Guinea projects. He explained that the island was still a beautiful verdant oasis where the diversity of life was astonishing.

The crew was much more relaxed and jovial on this stretch of the journey, since there was little work to be done until the lab was resupplied. Most evenings were spent in the common room with music, dancing and games. The crew consisted of people from around the world, and, despite the differences in language, cultures and experiences, everyone had a common purpose.

Mateo and I had become good friends and I loved listening to his stories. I saw Shani now and then, but never for long. No one from my research team was close to my age, but they'd all warmed up to me and were more willing to teach me new things and answer questions. They never asked me about myself, which was just as well, as I had nothing good to tell and there were some things I didn't care to revisit.

One night, Mateo and I were up on the aft deck watching the stars when I began to tell him about my life. I don't know why I started; neither of us had said anything, we were simply absorbing the cool, clear night air around us. I told him about my childhood, Jahi, Randhir, Amar, Visshaly, even about the night Jahi and Randhir were killed. Mateo never interrupted, never asked a question, just stared at me as all these emotions I'd caged up came pouring out. I didn't even realize I was crying until he hugged me.

"You're very brave and strong, don't ever forget that," he said.

"I don't know about that. I couldn't save Jahi, Randhir or Amar. And I don't have the strength or bravery to be like Visshaly."

"They loved you and protected you. It's not your fault what happened to them. You survived, so keep their memory alive and do something with it. You could have given up; you could have retreated. You could have decided to use your trauma as an excuse to do worse things or be hateful, vengeful or violent. You didn't do any of those things. No, you've chosen to be a part of something meaningful and good, in spite of everything. To me, that's brave and strong."

I hugged him tighter, thanking him.

After resupplying, we continued down the coast of New Guinea to a series of islands off the southeastern tip of New Guinea. It was here that I saw my first dolphins and turtles. The waters were still teeming with life. The dives among colourful schools of fish of all shapes and sizes, soft and hard corals, gliding rays and mesmerizing turtles were, up to this point, the greatest experience of my life. We made our way slowly through the archipelago, collecting samples and specimens to restock in less vibrant areas. The people that lived among these islands were friendly and familiar with the ships and their mission. It was evident that they'd been communicating for some time. It gave me hope to know that Sri Lanka wasn't the only place where people were good and kind.

We then journeyed to the Solomon Islands, where we stayed a couple of months. While not completely devoid of life, those islands lacked the diversity and larger species of New Guinea. We then spent a month slowly travelling to Vanuatu. Again, the waters, reefs and islands were in various states of ecological health. We were each given time to explore and relax off ship. Shani decided to join me for a week-long excursion on the heavily forested island of Maewo. We spent the time hiking through the lush woodland, along creeks and rivers that led to deep cool pools of fresh water fed by majestic waterfalls.

"I'm impressed, Aashi, with all that you've learned and done. I'm sorry I haven't had more time to see you."

"I understand. Besides, it's important that I learn to be more independent."

"Well, you seem to have adjusted quite well. I'm glad for you."

Shani was right. I'd found a home and purpose. I often slept comfortably through the nights. And I rarely cried during the days.

"I owe all I've done and learned to you, Shani. I hope we can be good friends."

"That sounds like a good deal."

After that wonderful week on land, it was back on the ship. We were slowly making our way south from island to island. It had been over six months since we left Sri Lanka. Every day was a new lesson and experience and, for the first time in my life, I wasn't fearful of the future. Mateo was training me to take on more significant research responsibilities.

After reaching the southernmost tip of the Vanuatu chain, we headed east toward Fiji. The water there was the clearest blue I'd seen yet. The shores of the large and smaller surrounding islands glistened with white sands as green hills rose behind them. The reefs were pristine and abundant, and it was here that I saw my first shark. I'd learned a great deal about sharks from Mateo so knew not to fear them. Instead, I felt awe to be in the presence of a creature that had survived for hundreds of millions of years. It had endured extensive human persecution and abuse yet remained the top of the food chain in the ocean. The grace and ease with which this magnificent creature glided through the waters kept me transfixed. As cliché as it sounds, Fiji truly was paradise.

One morning, Shani ran into my cabin, bursting through the door and brimming with excitement. "Put your swimsuit on and come up on deck. You have to see this." Just as quickly, she ran off again. I stumbled from my bunk, reaching for my swimsuit hanging on the wall. I was groggy with sleep but did my best to hurry.

On deck, Shani and most of the crew were on the port side of the ship. We'd dropped anchor, and everyone was giddy with excitement. The sun was shining brightly off the placid ocean surface. The green mountainous islands were off the starboard side. Some people were climbing down the ladder off the side of the ship, with fins and goggles in hand.

As I reached the side of the deck, a greyish behemoth breached the surface of the ocean, twisting as it rose from the depths. Its belly was white, and two fins, larger than the tallest human, protruded from its sides.

"Humpback whales!" Shani said, clasping her hands in front of her with the biggest smile on her face. Another member of the crew was explaining that they came here to breed, as the waters were calm, shallow and warm. Bursts of water shot up into the air as the backs of the great beasts grazed the surface. People were swimming with snorkels toward the whales. Shani had run off, returning with two sets of goggles and fins, grabbing my hand.

"Shani, is it safe? They're massive creatures."

"More than safe. They're gentle giants, hardly concerned with our presence."

The whales lazily and playfully moved about, seemingly unaware of the small bipedal mammals swimming around them. I knew that many of the great whale species had been decimated through hunting and the degradation of the oceans. The largest species, the blue whale, had gone extinct. I knew I was witnessing the profound resiliency of nature. What these people were doing was right.

I breathed in the salty air, surveying the shimmering turquoise waters. The sun was bright, rising higher in a clear blue sky. Amidst this idyllic scene, swam these majestic creatures that had survived all odds. Tears of joy slid down my cheeks. Life was a miracle.

Shani stood by my side, embracing me with one arm. She grabbed my hand and together we headed to the ladder and climbed down to a floating platform at the side of the ship. With fins on, she leaped into the water. I stood still, enthralled by the scene before me. Putting my fins on, I jumped into the warm and clear water and swam to catch Shani.

Twenty-Nine
Kyiv

Elliott died later that night. As his wife, it was up to me to finish his story. I hadn't even known about the journal until William gave it to me. Now it was all I had left of my husband.

I remembered every detail of his last day. And I did my best to record it for him. I saw the look on his face as he followed us. He thought I was so brave. The truth was, I was probably even more terrified than him. As difficult as it was, finishing his story was how I could ensure others would know about the man I loved.

Elliott believed there were only four types of people in the world and they couldn't move from one group to the other. He'd placed himself among the Reconciled. Yet, he stood by me through everything, risked his own life to find me, and in the end, saved William. He may not have believed a better world was possible, but he believed in those he loved. We all fail to live up to our potential now and then, but Elliott came through in those most extreme moments. That places him among the Valiant.

William and I left Kyiv and headed west a few days after Elliott's death. Outside of the city, we burned Elliott's body and collected the ashes. Returning to our farm outside of Budapest, I spread his ashes on a hill overlooking the Danube. Elliott's dad had not returned.

With time, I may have faith again and champion those things I still believe in. For now, it is good to be back in a place with so many happy memories and people I care about. To give up and do nothing would be the ultimate betrayal. In time, I would honour Elliott, his parents and all the others lost in a struggle for a better future.

Anna and Elliott Campbell
2076

Thirty
Bogotá

The sun had set. Our commander issued final orders. The advanced teams split into their four groups of four and headed toward the compound, which was lightly defended, according to our scouts. Another twenty-eight of us would take defensive positions along the outer wall once it was taken.

It was dark, but the outer wall had many spotlights, which shone into the empty dirt roads outside of it. There were many lights along the top of the wall as well. From our hidden positions, we could see ten guards along its length. Most of the soldados stood near the lights, thinking they could see the roads better.

We stuck to the shadows where they couldn't see us and avoided the spotlights, which didn't cover enough of the area. Snipers took out all the soldados along the wall at once. No alarm yet.

Hooks and ropes were flung over the wall and each team member climbed up. I followed my team closely as we moved along the top. The outer wall was taken in no time. The defensive teams moved in.

The main compound had fewer lights, so the approach was easy as well. We took our time clearing all the buildings between the main compound and the outer wall. All the buildings in our section were empty. We moved toward the wall of the main compound.

There were no guards visible. The main compound was surrounded by a wall on three sides and a steep cliff on the fourth.

The compound wall that ran along the main road had the only gate. Beside the heavy metal gates were larger towers with powerful guns.

My team and another unit of four scaled up the closest side while the other two units circled around to the far side of the compound. The goal was to clear the wall of any soldados and secure the gate before continuing on.

My unit was the first to scale the wall. Flaco flung a hook and secured it on the first try with minimal noise. I followed my team members up the rope. By the time I reached the top, it had already been cleared and my team was moving toward the gate. I saw at least two bodies on the floor in the tower room at the end.

We were all armed with pistols equipped with silencers, powerful machine guns, a deadly hunting knife, a couple of smoke and explosive grenades and one flashbang. So far only the pistols and knives had been used. Within minutes, the gate was captured, and the two highest-ranking fighters were talking quietly in a corner. The compound courtyard below was dark and quiet. There were lights on in some of the buildings but no guards visible at any of the doors.

There were more buildings than I remembered and the main one had been expanded. I wasn't sure where the command centre would be. We were ordered to work our way around the outlying buildings before converging on the main building, clearing each room and floor and splitting up into four-person units if necessary. We needed to move quickly, as eventually someone would notice that the guards on both walls were no longer responding to radio calls.

We went down the tower stairs, heading for the first small building. We stayed close together in single file. Gael was behind me, Flaco in front. Maria opened the door and Flaco and I burst in. It was full of weapons and ammunition, nothing else. We headed to the next building. Maria was crouched below its window and slowly stood up to peek inside. She gave the signal for all-clear, and we kept moving. As I passed the window, I saw storage for food, drinks and other supplies. The next building had two floors, and its lights were on. We were huddled by the door and could hear voices inside.

Everyone in the two units stood along the wall. Maria pushed the door open and spun into the building. All I heard was the crash of a chair falling over. The first room was a small kitchen and common area with a few tables. Three soldados lay dead around one of the tables. We split up again into teams. My team took the first floor. The next room we entered had empty bunks and a shower room and bathrooms. The final room on the main level was another bunk room with two sleeping soldados. Maria and Flaco had already slit their throats by the time I entered the room. We were moving back toward the main door as the other team was coming down the stairs.

The other eight had also finished clearing their outlying buildings and all sixteen of us were heading toward the main building. It was the largest building and had at least four floors above ground. There were three entrances, the main doors in the centre and two smaller doors at each end. Our unit of four would be entering from the small door closest to us, while one of the other units would use the other far door. The remaining eight would infiltrate from the main door. Orders came down that there was no need to maintain silence anymore and that use of the machine guns was acceptable. We were all ordered to maintain radio contact and find the command centre. The main objective was to capture the gang leader, alive if possible.

We entered the main building. I was trying to control my shaking hands. We were in a narrow hall running along the edge of the building. There were numerous doors leading to other halls and stairs. Maria ordered Gael and me to head toward the rear of the building. She and Flaco were going to proceed along the front.

"We should head to the top floor and work our way down," I suggested to Gael, who nodded and let me lead the way while he covered our rear.

We headed to the top floor, which was well lit and had fancy-looking furniture and rugs, nicer than anything I'd ever seen. I was scanning each corner with a heightened sense of awareness. We heard the faint sound of gunfire from somewhere nearby.

At the next hall, a half-dressed soldado stepped out of one of the rooms. He fell with a bullet in his head, shot by Gael. A scream came from the room.

The next minute happened in a flurry. Gael and I quickly moved toward the room and entered in a crouch. Gael fired his gun again and I followed him in. There was another body on the floor. Another gun fired and I heard the blast hit the wall just behind me. I turned to the other corner of the room, firing at another soldado. Gael had spun to shoot at the opposite corner. There were several young naked girls behind overturned chairs. Gael aimed at them.

"Stop!" I yelled. "Secure the room."

I pulled the body out of the threshold and closed the door. Then I moved a heavy shelf to block it. Gael moved toward the other two doors at the far side, just as one flew open. Gael hit the ground firing. One of the girls moved toward the body in the far corner to grab a gun. I fired mine in front of her to scare her and ran to grab the gun.

I tied the three girls up with bindings we'd brought and found tape to cover their mouths. Gael kept his eye on the two other doors. The girl that had gone for the gun put up a fight, but the other two just looked scared.

"Don't worry, we won't hurt you. I grew up in this area. You'll be safe soon," I told them. I didn't recognize any of them.

Gael went to the door he'd fired through. It led to a large bedroom in which a dead man and woman were now lying side by side.

We went to the other door, which opened into a long hall. There were four doors along the left and three on the right. At the end, it opened onto a big empty and dark space. We slowly moved from one door to the next. They were all closets or empty rooms, but there was a light coming from under the last door on the left.

As we opened the door to another large sitting room, shots rang out. The bullets hit the wall on the other side of the hall. Gael threw his flashbang through the opening, and a moment later, we rushed in.

Two blinded soldados were behind flipped chairs in the middle of the room. We fired at them before they could react. We quickly looked around the rest of the room. There were small beds along both sides. They were empty on my side. As I turned back into the middle of the room, I saw Gael kneeling on the floor, and a woman next to him, pointing a gun at his head.

"Drop it or he dies!" she yelled.

I stood frozen with my gun pointed at the woman. I knew her.

"Don't shoot," I said. "Don't you know who I am?"

She was digging the end of the gun into his head.

"I'm your son, Miguel." She looked at me and sneered. My gun was still pointed at her. "Where is Alejandra?" I asked.

"Alejandra, your brother is here. What should we do with him?"

A thin young woman with too much makeup, fancy jewellery and very little clothing came out from behind one of the small beds. She had a gun in her hand. She looked at me with a dead expression and went over to stand a few feet from our mother.

"Alejandra, please, come with me. I can take you away from here."

"She's not going anywhere, and neither are you. You should have learned your place. When it came time for you to become a man, you ran away like a coward. Why should she trust you?"

I looked at her with disgust.

"You knew I was a runner set to become a soldado?"

"Of course I knew. Once you were both old enough, you would be given esteemed positions here, but you threw that away."

I turned to face my sister. "Alejandra, there are better places out there. I've been there, beautiful and peaceful communities. Alejandra, the soldados killed abuela."

"They killed her because of you!" my mother screamed.

Alejandra looked at her, stunned, but my mother was still staring at me.

Alejandra's hand was shaking, a tear rolling down her cheek.

"Alejandra, be a good girl and shoot your idiot brother. Mommy and Boss Daddy will reward you."

"He's not our father, and he won't be leaving this place as the boss. Alejandra, remember what they did to you that day, the last time I saw you. I'm sorry I couldn't help you. I'm sorry ... I was too weak. Forgive me."

Tears filled my eyes, but my mother just laughed again.

"See how weak and pathetic he is? You're no son of mine. Alejandra, kill him. Now!"

Alejandra pointed her gun at me. I kept mine fixed on my mother, my eyes darting between the two of them. I didn't know what to do. The tears were clouding my vision.

And suddenly, *bang!*

I stood frozen. Was I hit? My mother slowly dropped to the ground, her eyes rolling into the back of her head. Alejandra stood with the gun pointed where my mother had stood. Gael bent down, retrieving his own gun, spinning to point it at Alejandra.

"No!" I yelled at him. Then I turned back to my sister. "Alejandra, it's okay. Drop the gun."

I walked toward her, reaching for the gun and helping her to lower it. I grabbed her, hugging her tight as she broke down in tears. She put her arms around me, grabbing as tight as possible. We stood there hugging for what seemed like hours. And then our radios started going off and Gael reported in. The command centre had been stormed and the boss was dead. The rest of the compound was secure. The soldados in the command centre had tried to call for reinforcements, but no one had responded. Three of our fighters were dead.

More and more of our fighters had entered the compound. What was left of the gang in the rest of the city had either been picked off as they ran or had surrendered. The private army of the elites in the core had also surrendered, offering their former bosses as prisoners. The city was taken. Casualties on all sides were high, but the innocent civilians had suffered the most. It would take days, possibly weeks, to truly know how many had died.

I was ordered to report to my commanding officer. Alejandra had hardly left my side. Gael, who had witnessed everything, offered to stay with her.

My commander already seemed to know much of what had happened.

"Why didn't you tell us you might have family in the compound?" he said.

"I didn't know they would be there, sir."

"Still, you saved your partner's life. What do you intend to do now? We could use help rebuilding the city and earning the trust of the people left here. That might be easier with more people like you, who grew up here."

"Thank you, sir. I'd like to take my sister and Javier to Paraiso."

He shook my hand. "Turn in your weapons before you leave."

Two days later, Alejandra, Javier and I left Bogotá. The journey this time was safe. No one would be hunting us, and no gangs patrolled the roads or villages. We visited Pablo and his family and spent a few days with them. Pablo said they were happy with how things had changed so far. They could move freely around the valley and share what they produced, instead of being forced to give it away. I promised to return to see them again soon.

We took our time reaching Paraiso. Alejandra and Javier said very little, but both smiled often. Neither of them had ever been outside the city. Alejandra had never left our slum. They would stop to look at flowers or birds flying from tree to tree. I taught them the names of many of the things we saw.

As we entered Paraiso, I saw Senora Vasquez in her garden. I called out to her. She looked up and smiled and waved, walking toward us.

Without a word, Senora Vasquez hugged Javier and then Alejandra, welcoming them to Paraiso.

Thirty-One
Ontario

Judgment Day. The test would come at 7:00 p.m. This was the time that most residents of the city would be near a public broadcasting screen, whether at their homes or recreational venues in the Hub, watching the big championship lacrosse game. It was a day off for me. The streets would largely be empty, since most people would be watching the game. The Civic Guardians would be where most of the people were, making sure things stayed calm, even though they always did during these games.

I did my check-in at midday and everything was still a go. All teams were ready, and no one had been compromised. I went for a run in a park near my apartment to clear my head. It felt like forever since I'd gone for a proper run. Mostly, I was just trying to kill time, to prevent my brain from second-guessing what was about to happen.

6:00 p.m.

I was to go into work and explain to the other surveillance operatives at the transit hub that they'd been given the time off to watch the game. Ares was there to give the orders as the Civic Guardian on duty. The others left without question, excited for the big game. There wasn't much in the way of movement anymore. The Hub's bars, restaurants and squares were packed with people glued to screens as the game started.

6:30 p.m.

Ares and I put the lockdown program in play on the surveillance network. It would run a continuous loop of the feed from the last hour. It would be too late before anyone noticed. Locking the surveillance offices behind us, we left to rendezvous with the others. Any other Civic Guardians on duty at the transit hub would be distracted by the game, and since Ares was assigned to the surveillance offices, they wouldn't think to check if anything was wrong.

6:45 p.m.

Ares and I rendezvoused with Nadie, Tristan and Keila in an alley behind the building that housed the Zone 4 communications terminal. Ares used his communication device to confirm mission status with teams in other zones. I could hear Elizabeth's voice both over the device and in my ear, giving me the green light. All teams were synchronized.

6:50 p.m.

Nadie and I were on the lookout as Tristan, Keila and Ares entered the building through the back door. Nadie was noticeably tense and anxious. I tried to comfort her, but she was focused on the job. The alley we were in was narrow. At the one end was the Hub's central square, which was full of people. Time passed slowly.

6:59 p.m.

I could hear the one-minute countdown in my ear. Nadie had a communication device linked only to Ares, who confirmed everything was good to go. I told Nadie, "Let's go watch." We moved out of the alley and joined the crowd in the square watching the game on a giant screen.

7:00 p.m.

The screen went black. Suddenly images of the Earth were displayed. The crowd became unsettled. A quiet murmur rose up as a voice began telling them that they'd been lied to. Ontario and Michigan weren't all that was left of humanity. There were pockets of people around the world. There were thousands just outside the city. Images flashed of daily life in one of the communes. The message was that the Civic Administrators sought to control what they did and when, but *we* would give them the freedom to choose their own path. Our mission was to unite the Earth, repair the damage we'd done and ensure humanity survived. The video closed with the words, "The choice is yours." After that, the screen went blank.

Ares, Tristan and Keila blended into the crowd with us. Many of the Civic Guardians were spellbound, staring at the black screen like most of the crowd. Others were running for the communications terminal. People in the crowd were murmuring; some were shouting and shoving in confusion.

"Now what?" I asked Nadie.

There was no buzzing in my ear anymore. I couldn't hear Elizabeth's voice. Some of the Civic Guardians were on the stage near the big screen. They were trying to set up a speaker system. I couldn't see Ares, Tristan or Keila anymore. Nadie was looking nervous and scanning the crowd.

"Stay close," I told her.

The Civic Guardians on the stage managed to get the sound and projection equipment set up. None of the trams were moving. People were spilling out of the bars and restaurants. Some were shouting at the Civic Guardians, demanding answers.

The screens behind began to buzz, and a hush went over the crowd. The symbol of the Civic Administrators was displayed. A voice began telling everyone that a group of rebels and anarchists seeking to disrupt their peace and tranquility had managed to infiltrate the city and that it was the duty of all good citizens to seek them out. The voice also told everyone to calmly go home; the game would be rescheduled and those responsible for this disruption would be brought to justice. Hundreds began to move toward the trams, others still loitered, looking confused and angry. More Civic Guardians were filing into the Hub. Isolated scuffles broke out. The Civic Guardians now carried weapons, causing the crowd to get more agitated. A cry began rising from the crowd, "We want answers. We want answers. We want answers."

I saw Ares among the Civic Guardians on the stage, but a large group was pushing its way toward the stage. Some of the Civic Guardians were trying to keep them back. Shots rang out. I had no idea where they came from. The Civic Guardians reacted. Now people were panicking, running every which way. I grabbed Nadie and ran for the stage along a treed segment of the square, approaching it from behind. Ares was issuing orders to the other Civic Guardians and then to the crowd via a microphone: "If you don't disperse and return to your homes, you'll be arrested and punished as rioters."

I ran up the stage, grabbing him from behind. "What are you doing?" I asked.

He shoved me off. "What's necessary," he said, then he turned and continued to issue orders. More of the crowd rushed the stage. Ares pulled out his weapon and fired at the first person to leap onto the stage. The body fell lifeless to the ground. I got up, darting at Ares. He flung me off again, turning his gun at me as Nadie knocked him to the ground from behind. I could hear Elizabeth in my ear again, telling me to get to Zone 1 immediately. Ares and most of the other Civic Guardians were being subdued by the crowd at this point. I grabbed Nadie and a weapon from the ground.

"We have to go!" I shouted.

We ran to the transit hub, which was jammed with people. The trams were still not moving. I used my card to enter the surveillance offices, which led to a special passageway to get to the underground transit line.

"I'm in the underground transit tunnel with Nadie, but I don't know how to operate it or when the trains run," I shouted to my earpiece. Nadie was following me, but she seemed dazed.

"A train will be there soon," the voice in my ear explained.

There were four Civic Guardians on the platform where the train would come. Because they were focused on the main access point that civilians would use on the other side, they didn't spot us. I walked slowly out toward the tracks, holding Nadie's hand and hiding the weapon. Two of the Civic Guardians turned. It was Tyra and Van.

"Don't worry, we control all the underground line access points now," Van said.

"Of course *we* do," I said, shaking my head.

The train arrived empty and we got on. When we got to Zone 1, more Civic Guardians there escorted us to the street. Things were quieter in Zone 1. The main square was lined with incredibly tall and beautiful buildings. At the end of the square, the tallest building was all silver glass piercing the sky in a point that radiated light. Our escort told us to take cover behind some trees. We could hear gunshots. As I looked into the square, I saw several bodies.

Our escorts motioned for us to move. At the entrance to the silver building, there were more bodies, mainly Civic Guardians. As we entered, an explosion shattered some glass at the far side, and I saw Civic Guardians on an opposite street in a gun battle with more Civic Guardians.

We got on an elevator and headed for the top floor. Elizabeth was waiting in a room overlooking the city. Beside her stood an old man; his head was down, and his hands were bound behind his back.

"Kelowna, Nadie, this is Alexander Green, the man in charge of the Civic Administrators," Elizabeth said.

"What the hell is going on?" I screamed. "People are dying. You promised me this wouldn't happen."

"I'm sorry, Kelowna. I hoped this wouldn't happen, but Mr. Green refuses to go on screen to calm things. I'd considered doing it myself, but I think you would have more of an effect."

"Me? Why?"

"You're from here and part of the movement. You can calm both sides before more people are hurt. Please, Kelowna."

Nadie grabbed my hand. "You were right, Kelowna. Now help us stop this." She was crying. This wasn't what either of them had wanted.

"Kelowna, Mr. Green here is the man that gave the order to kill your parents," Elizabeth said.

I looked at him. "Why?" I asked him.

He slowly lifted his head. "To prevent this."

"Bullshit."

"People can't be trusted to choose the right course; history has proven that. We established control and order, which led to peace and stability. Your parents and these people here are trying to destroy that, and look at the result. You witnessed it as you came in. I did what was necessary."

"I heard that not that long ago from someone on the other side. The ends don't justify the means. You don't have the right to dictate how others live. If they choose wrong, so be it." I was furious at both sides and, turning to Elizabeth, stated, "I'll do it."

She nodded and a young woman came in with a camera. "This will be broadcast across the city," Elizabeth told me.

I turned to the camera. I nodded. A green light came on. "Good evening. My name is Kelowna. I grew up in this city. My parents were killed by the Civic Administrators because they believed that all the wars, all the diseases, the history of humanity had led us to the point where we could finally build a better society. They believed that better society depended on the freedom to choose your own path. The Civic Administrators disagreed. They believed peace and order were more important. The movement is global. The images they showed you earlier are true. I didn't believe it at first myself. I spent my life in Zone 4. Bored with life here, I ventured to the no-go zone and encountered members of the movement. I've been to their communes, seen what life is like. It's a good life. But it's a good life here too. We're not enemies, so please, everyone, end the violence. I know you want answers, and you'll get them. No one is trying to destroy anything. Those that have instigated violence will be punished. But stop now. There's no going back; there's only forward."

I moved to stand between Mr. Green and Elizabeth, astounded at the clarity and vigour with which I spoke. The camera panned to face all three of us. "This is Alexander Green, the face of the Civic Administrators. A prisoner right now of Elizabeth, one of the council members of the movement. What happens next doesn't depend on them. It's your choice. Lay down your weapons and let's figure this out together. Let's try to build a better world."

I left the room as Elizabeth continued to talk. Down the hall, Nadie and I held each other. Hours later, Elizabeth joined us.

"Things are calm in all zones now. Thank you, Kelowna."

"At what cost?"

"I'm not sure yet. Mr. Green has agreed to set up a transitional government. People that showed leadership in each zone are being brought to Zone 1 to set up a council to decide what happens next. Things will return to normal shortly. I'm sure you're both hungry and tired."

Nadie and I spent the next few weeks in the city together, and things slowly returned to normal. Over six thousand people were dead. Things went about the same in Michigan, which was slower to regain the peace, but both cities were in constant communication now. Trials were being set up for those accused of crimes on both sides. Ares had been killed in the ensuing chaos in Zone 4. A provisional ruling council, with representatives from each zone had been established. Mr. Green was to stand trial as well. Many of the other Civic Administrators had handed over information showing that Mr. Green ruled with an iron fist. Most were willing to move toward a more egalitarian governance structure. People were given the choice of whether to stay in the city or establish communes. Those who stayed would get to vote on major changes. Most decided to stay and help establish a new system. People were genuinely excited to see what was going to happen next.

Elizabeth asked Nadie and me to stay as part of the provisional government. We both declined. A week later, we returned to the bunker. A week after that, we headed to the small house on the island where we'd first kissed.

Epilogue

Katherine has a soothing yet authoritative voice. "Stories are powerful tools. They can unite us or divide us. They can make us cry, laugh or smile. Human history is full of stories. Told the proper way, they have the power to change the world. Each one of you has a story to tell." Katherine pauses, scanning the room, lovingly pointing at people, with a wide smile. "I've spent the last decade documenting the stories of people from around the world. As our movement grows in every corner of this world, more stories will be chronicled."

The room erupts in applause and cheers. "As I look around this room, I can't help but feel immense pride. This room is a representation of the diversity of our own species. Every day, newcomers around the world join the movement. Some are more organized than others, mind you. Some living in vibrant, sustainable cities, others in small villages. There are even groups researching, developing and using new technologies to restore, reclaim and bring balance back to the natural world. The movement goes by many different names, but the one thing we have in common is a desire to prevent the mistakes of the past from ever happening again."

Katherine is dignified in her speech, raising only a finger in emphasis for the one thing we have in common, as she continues pensively. "These last years have been the best of my life, knowing that a new ethos is emerging. Nature is our shrine, temple and cathedral. Remember that! Science and traditional knowledge, our foundation of thought and understanding. Embrace and nurture rational thought."

She gives the room a moment to ponder her last statement as she slowly nods her head and continues. "When humanity climbed out of the trees and stood on two legs, our only advantage was our cranial capacity. We weren't the fastest, strongest, biggest or most agile. Our skin offers little in the way of protection. Our brains are what sets us apart. All species exist to better themselves, to evolve. An intelligent species is no different. We forgot that somewhere along the road of our evolution. We forgot to better ourselves and leave behind a better world for those that come after us."

Katherine is less animated and dramatic than the boss, but she's more engaging. She speaks with a restrained eloquence. The room gazes, enthralled. "No one is ever remembered by the things they owned in life. When you're staring down your own mortality, it's experiences that matter. The deeds and intangible accomplishments of a life are memorable. Too many spend their last days, when they know they're near the end, focusing on regrets. An individual that lives each day to the fullest, on their own terms, has no regrets."

Katherine pauses, once again scanning the room and smiling. She moves her hands out in front of her and swings them slowly outward, gesturing at everyone in the room. "So, live an inspired life, live for the moment, live to bring joy and happiness to others, live to leave the world a little better."

She takes a sip of water, still scanning the room. "My home is on the shores of Lake Victoria, where I spend the evenings listening to the symphony nature provides. I listen to the leaves rustling in the wind, waves gently caressing the shores, birds singing their songs, and the insects buzzing about their days. All of this under the tapestry of innumerable stars that remind me of my singular luck. To be born a human on planet Earth — now that's luck. One planet, orbiting one star that happens to contain a plethora of life in a galaxy made up of millions of possibilities. You could have been an ant or an eagle, a blade of grass or a large tree, but you were born a human. Think about that."

She gives everyone a moment. The only sounds are the occasional creak of a rickety bench and the whir of the ceiling fans. "Our imaginations created stories to give us purpose. Our curiosity sought to answer the mysteries of the universe and the point of our existence. The point of life is simple. It's a symbiotic circle. We grace this Earth for a short span to give and return. Why does there need to be a higher purpose? Why does there need to be an afterlife?"

Katherine pauses, but no one answers her questions. "We're here to learn from the wonders around us, to see the beauty in every detail of nature, to impart that wisdom to those who come after and leave the world in a better state than what we found. Share your stories, write them down, pass them on. The Chronicles must be a tool with which we impart knowledge to future generations and remind them of our past mistakes. As I collect the stories of individuals like each of you from around the world, I'm amazed at how singular the human experience truly is."

Katherine points to a stack of paper behind the chair she is sitting in. She is louder now, almost giddy. "Those stories are the human experience. Individuals that overcame great odds, witnessed terrible things. Individuals that sought answers, hoped for a better life. Individuals that tested their own limits, changed their beliefs. We're all unique, yet the same. That isn't a contradiction. That makes me proud. It's up to each of you to add your own part to the Chronicles. As I look around this room, I believe we may have finally moved beyond what separates us."

Acknowledgements

I'd like to thank the team at Iguana Books for publishing my first novel. Greg, Meghan and Lee for the support and help through this process. Paula, my editor, for your patience and valuable input to improve the final product. Holly for reviewing the first manuscript and the final one. Finally, Ruth for the cover design.

Thank you to my good friend Laura for being one of the first people to read earlier versions and all the helpful advice you provided along the way.

I'd also like to thank all my family and friends that contributed to making this novel a reality: Meghan, Mom, Melissa, Ben, Keelen, Justin, Kent, Carly, Charlotte, Ned, Emily, Ryan, Lindsay, Andre, Vanessa, Tim, Angela, the Jacobs family, Darren and Ariel. I couldn't have done it without you!

While this novel is a work of fiction, the stories are entirely plausible based on current societal trajectories. So, I'd like to also acknowledge the countless scientists, conservationists, environmentalists, social justice activists and others around the world striving to build a more equitable and sustainable world.

www.ingramcontent.com/pod-product-compliance
Lightning Source LLC
Chambersburg PA
CBHW030649020726
47493CB00006B/1943